Eugene Lemoine Didier

The Life and Letters of Madame Bonaparte

Eugene Lemoine Didier

The Life and Letters of Madame Bonaparte

ISBN/EAN: 9783337016050

Printed in Europe, USA, Canada, Australia, Japan

Cover: Foto ©Raphael Reischuk / pixelio.de

More available books at **www.hansebooks.com**

THE LIFE AND LETTERS

OF

MADAME BONAPARTE.

BY

EUGENE L. DIDIER.

SECOND EDITION.

London :

SAMPSON LOW, MARSTON, SEARLE, & RIVINGTON.

CROWN BUILDINGS, 188, FLEET STREET.

1879.

PREFACE.

THE long, eventful, and romantic career of Madame Bonaparte made her one of the most famous women of the country. Her remarkable history covers a period of ninety-four years. Born four years before the organization of the United States government by the original Thirteen States, she lived to see the Union composed of thirty-eight States, with a population of nearly fifty millions. At the time of her birth, Baltimore was a small town of little more than four thousand inhabitants; she lived to see it a large city of little less than four hundred thousand. Born the daughter of a Baltimore merchant, Elizabeth Patterson became, by her marriage with Jerome Bonaparte, the sister-in-law of the Emperor Napoleon and the half-dozen kings and queens whom the French Cæsar placed upon the thrones of Europe. In all respects the equal, and in some the superior of those thus favoured, Napoleon nevertheless excluded her from the imperial court ; yet, after the Emperor's final downfall, there remained for her a social career in Europe, the brilliancy of which has hitherto been but vaguely described. The recent discovery of her letters, written to her father during this period of her social success—when beauties envied her beauty and wits dreaded her wit, when kings sought her acquaintance and princes claimed her friendship—will enable us to give to the world the true story of the most brilliant years of this remarkable woman's life. Her letters display an amazing knowledge of the world, a keen analysis of men's motives, and an eager pursuit of worldly honours. This Baltimore girl, married at eighteen and deserted at twenty, seems to have possessed the *savoir-vivre* of Chesterfield, the cold cynicism of Rochefoucauld, and the practical economy of Franklin.

EUGENE L. DIDIER.

CONTENTS.

CHAPTER IV.

CHAPTER V.

CHAPTER VI.

CHAPTER VII.

CHAPTER VIII.

CHAPTER IX.

CHAPTER X.

CHAPTER XI.

CHAPTER XII.

THE LIFE AND LETTERS

OF

MADAME BONAPARTE.

———•———

CHAPTER I.

The Patterson Family.—William Patterson, the Father of Mme. Bonaparte.
—Childhood and Youth of Elizabeth Patterson.—Jerome Bonaparte visits
the United States.—His First Meeting with Miss Patterson.—Their Engagement and Marriage.—Opposition of Napoleon.—Jerome ordered
back to France without his Wife.—His Hesitation.

WILLIAM PATTERSON, the founder of the Patterson
family of Baltimore and the father of Madame Bonaparte, was born in the county of Donegal, Ireland, on
the 1st of November, 1752.   His father was a small
farmer with a large family; his mother was Elizabeth
Peoples; and they were both descended from a mixture
of English and Scotch families that had settled in Ireland after the conquest of that country.   After a plain
education, William was sent by his parents to Philadelphia when but fourteen years old.   He arrived in that
city in the month of April, 1766, and entered the count-

ing-house of an Irish shipping merchant. The industry
of the young clerk was remarkable ; early and late he
was at his post, acquiring those methodical habits of
business and that spirit of commercial enterprise which
distinguished him through life. This penniless and
homeless boy was to become one of the merchant
princes of America, and the friend of Washington, La
Fayette, Carroll, and Jefferson.

By the time he reached his majority he was established in business for himself, and in a few years was
recognized as one of the rising young merchants of the
country. At the beginning of the American Revolution
he was actively engaged in the shipping business in
Philadelphia, with an extensive European and West
India trade. With that keen business tact and enter-
prising spirit which never failed him, he put all his fortune into two vessels, which he loaded with suitable
cargoes and despatched to France, investing the proceeds in arms and ammunition, which he saw would be
required for carrying on the war of Independence. He
embarked on one of the vessels himself, and on his return stopped at the island of St. Eustatius in the month
of February, 1776. He was persuaded to remain there
for the purpose of collecting war material to be shipped
to America, and sent his vessel forward to Philadelphia,
where it arrived in March. The valuable cargo of pow-
der was just in time, for Washington's army was before Boston and had hardly sufficient ammunition to fire
even a salute. This was the first of a number of similar
successful ventures, and the name of William Patterson

soon became a familiar one both in the American army and in Congress.

After remaining at St. Eustatius eighteen months, he found that the Dutch government, however willing, was not able to protect the American trade against the British, and he removed to Martinique in the autumn of 1777. Here he continued for a few months the business so successfully begun at St. Eustatius; but in the summer of 1778 he prepared to return home. He sailed about the last of June with a small fleet, and arrived in Baltimore in July, bringing with him, as the result of two years' commercial speculation, one hundred thousand dollars in gold and merchandise. One-half of this sum was invested in real estate in the rising town where he was now permanently established. This property, together with all subsequent purchases of real estate in the city of Baltimore and in the State of Mary-land, Mr. Patterson retained until his death; for he made it an invariable rule never to speculate in land, but to buy only for safe investment. The other half of the amount brought from the West Indies—fifty thou-sand dollars—he put into the shipping business, and soon became the leading merchant of the place, and, in a few years, the wealthiest citizen of the State—perhaps of the United States—except Charles Carroll of Carroll-ton.[1] As soon as he made money he invested it in real estate, and at the time of his death, in 1835, he was one of the largest real estate owners in Maryland.

---

[1] So stated in a letter from Jefferson to Livingston, 1804.

Soon after establishing himself in Baltimore, Mr. Patterson married Dorcas Spear, a lady of high social position, and a fair representative of the Maryland women of her day ; and from this time he rarely left his home and business.

"I always considered it a duty to my family," he said, toward the close of his long life, "to keep them as much as possible under my own eye, so that I have seldom in my life left Baltimore, either on pleasure or business. Ever since I had a house it has been my invariable rule to be the last up at night, and to see that the fires and light were secured before I retired myself, from which I found little risk from fires, and managed to have my family keep regular hours. What I possess is solely the product of my own labour. I inherited nothing of my forefathers, nor have I benefited anything from public favours or appointments."

In the same reminiscences he referred also to the fact that he had rarely undertaken public duties : "I have never sought for offices of honour or profit, and when I have in any way acted in a public capacity, it was from the consideration that every citizen should contribute more or less to the good of society when he can do it without too much loss or inconvenience to himself." The few such offices he held were generally of a character fitted to his peculiar talents. When the Bank of Maryland was established at Baltimore, in 1790—the first bank ever chartered south of Philadelphia—William Patterson was chosen its first president. When, during the war of 1812, a committee of supplies was formed for the protection of Baltimore, then threatened by British invasion, he was appointed a member of it, and worked zealously and effectively. Finally, when the Baltimore and Ohio Railroad was chartered, William Patterson was appointed one of its first directors, and although then in his eightieth year, he took an active part in the affairs of the company which did so much in developing Baltimore's commercial prosperity.

This outline of her father's life shows us in what position and under what influences Elizabeth Patterson passed her childhood. She was born on the 6th of February, 1785. Even as a young girl she displayed that extraordinary beauty, wit, and fascination of manner which was destined to make her life so strange, interesting, and romantic. She was educated chiefly by her mother, and from the beginning showed great natural gifts, especially an unusually retentive memory. When only ten years old she was familiar with the best English poetry, and could repeat by heart her favourite books, Young's "Night Thoughts" and Rochefoucauld's "Maxims." Mr. Patterson's position made his daughter sure of success as soon as she appeared in general society, even without her growing reputation for wit and beauty ; and by the time she was eighteen, Elizabeth Patterson was a recognized belle of Baltimore— the most beautiful woman in a city always famous for its beautiful women. But, beautiful as she was and great as was her local celebrity, who could have imagined the astonishing career that was before her ? It was hardly possible to conceive that this young girl, who had never

left her father's home, was destined by her suddenly de-
veloped ambition to disturb the plans of the greatest
conqueror of modern times, to produce a rupture between a pope and an emperor—destined, though a
deserted wife, to become a brilliant leader at foreign
courts, to eclipse the most renowned beauties, and to
excel the greatest wits. Yet this destiny, impossible as
it seemed, was already opening before her.

In the summer of 1803, Jerome Bonaparte landed at
New York, where honours of every kind were lavished upon
the young brother of the First Consul of France. Upon
hearing of Jerome's arrival in the United States, Commodore Joshua Barney, who had a year or two before
been in the French navy and served with Captain Bonaparte in the West Indies, invited him to visit Baltimore.
The invitation was accepted, and in September the
young officer arrived there with his suite. The commodore not only entertained his visitor at his own house,
but made him the lion of the day in general society.
The leading people of the city made him their guest,
and he was present at every form of entertainment.

It was at the fall races that Jerome saw, for the first
time, Miss Elizabeth Patterson, then in all the early
bloom of her wonderful beauty. The impulsive young
Frenchman was fired at once. He declared, enthusiastically, that he had never beheld so lovely a being before. A few days afterwards he was introduced to her
at the house of the Honourable Samuel Chase, one of the
Maryland signers of the Declaration of Independence,
and Commodore Barney's father-in-law.

Jerome soon became madly in love with the fascinating girl, and, forgetting France, Napoleon, future prospects and all else, determined to marry her. The young lady, dazzled by so brilliant an alliance, was equally eager for the match, and in a few weeks after their first acquaintance Captain Bonaparte and Elizabeth Patterson were engaged. Mr. Patterson, who knew the young Bonaparte was a minor, entirely dependent upon his brother, the First Consul, saw the great risk his daughter would run by marrying a Frenchman under the legal age, without the consent of his legal guardians. Therefore, in order to break off the engagement quietly and without violence, he sent his daughter to Virginia, hoping that absence would conquer the sudden affection of the young lovers. But the experiment was useless. After a short visit Elizabeth returned to Baltimore, the acquaintance was immediately renewed, and on the 29th of October, 1803, a licence was obtained from the Baltimore County Court for the young couple's marriage.

In less than a week after the issuing of the licence, a warning letter was sent to Mr. Patterson, informing him that Captain Bonaparte only wanted to secure a home for himself until he could return to France, when he will be the first "to turn your daughter off, and laugh at her credulity."

This had its effect, and he once more used his authority to break off the engagement—but this time again without success. In spite of the warning of friends, in spite of the remonstrance of her father, Miss Patterson had determined to marry, declaring that " she would rather be the wife of Jerome Bonaparte for an hour, than the wife of any other man for life."

Finding her so resolute in the matter, Mr. Patterson at length gave a reluctant consent. He took all the necessary precautions to give the union both a religious and official sanction. The ceremony took place on Christmas eve, 1803, and was performed by the Right Reverend John Carroll, Bishop of Baltimore, afterwards Archbishop, and the first Primate of the Catholic Church in America. The marriage contract[2] was drawn np by Alexander J. Dallas, who was afterwards Secretary of the Treasury, and the wedding was witnessed by M Sotin, the French Consul at Baltimore, by Alexander Le Camus, Jerome's secretary and afterwards Minister of Foreign Affairs of the kingdom of Westphalia, by the Mayor of Baltimore and other leading citizens. A gentleman who was present on the occasion said, " All the clothes worn by the bride might have been put in my pocket. Her dress was of muslin, richly embroidered, of extremely fine texture. Beneath her dress she wore but a single garment."

---

[2] The following extracts from the marriage contract establish the fact that the Patterson family looked for possible trouble from the union :—

" ARTICLE I.—In case of any difficulty being raised relative to the validity of the said marriage either in the State of Maryland or the French Republic, the said Jerome Bonaparte engages, at the request of the said Elizabeth Patterson and the said William Patterson, or either of them, to execute any deed necessary to remove the difficulty, and to confer on the said union all the character of a valid and perfect marriage according to the respective laws of the State of Maryland and of the French Republic.

" ART. IV.—That if the marriage should be annulled either on demand of the said Jerome Bonaparte or that of any member of his family, the said Elizabeth Patterson shall have a right in any case to one-third of the real, personal, and mixed property of her future husband "

Shortly after his marriage, Jerome and his wife visited Washington, where they were entertained by General Turreau, the French Minister, and enjoyed for several weeks the gaiety of the national capital ; later they made a long tour to the Northern and Eastern States, and in Philadelphia, New York, Boston, Albany, and, elsewhere, met with one continual round of hospitality and brilliant entertainment.

On the 10th of February, 1804, Mr. Patterson addressed a letter to the Honourable Robert R. Livingston, American Minister to France, upon the subject of the marriage ; from the following extract it will be seen what view he took of it :—

. . . . " I can assure you with truth, that I never, directly or indirectly, countenanced or gave Mr. Bonaparte the smallest encouragement to address my daughter ; but, on the contrary, resisted his pretensions by every means in my power consistent with discretion. Finding, however, that the mutual attachment they had formed for each other was such that nothing short of force and violence could prevent their union, I with much reluctance consented to their wishes."

He goes on to say that, the marriage having taken place, it was his duty, as well as his inclination, to protect the interests of his daughter, and to endeavour to reconcile the Bonaparte family to the match. With this view, he asks Mr. Livingston to furnish the First Consul with copies of letters on the subject written to Mr. Livingston, by the President of the United States and the Secretary of State at Washington. He begs the minister to advise him of the result of his communi-

cations with the Bonaparte family, and whether the
marriage will meet with their approbation or not.

Nor were letters the only means which he employed.
To watch over his daughter's interests, Mr. Patterson
soon after despatched his son, Robert, to France. The
trouble anticipated by the anxious father was not long
in coming. Even during the bridal tour alarming news
arrived. Robert Patterson reached Paris on the 11th of
March, 1804. On the next day, he informed his father
that immediately upon his arrival he had waited upon
the American Minister, who was using every exertion to
reconcile the First Consul to Jerome's marriage, but that
Napoleon was highly incensed with his brother. Robert
went on to say that for the present it would be much
better for Jerome to remain in America ; but that, if he
should decide to return to France, his wife should by all
means accompany him. The result of the interview
with Mr. Livingston was, he said, " of an alarming and
desponding nature."

In passing through London, on his way to Paris,
Robert had obtained letters of introduction from Miss
Monroe, the daughter of James Monroe, who was at that
time American Minister to England, to Madame Louis
Bonaparte, who had been Miss Monroe's school-mate at
Madame Campan's Academy, at Paris. The latter was
a sister of M. Jenet, who had been Minister of the French
Republic to the United States during the administration
of Washington, and married the daughter of De Witt
Clinton. Madame Campan was on very intimate terms
with the family of the First Consul, and it was expected

that her influence would be useful in favour of Madame Jerome Bonaparte.

Among the friends of the Patterson family at that time in Paris was Captain Paul Bentalou, of Baltimore, who had served with distinction in Count Pulaski's legion of cavalry during the American Revolution. This gentleman acted as interpreter in the interview between Robert Patterson and Lucien Bonaparte, which took place on the 14th of March, 1804.

" Tell Mr. Patterson," said Lucien, " and let his father know, that our mother, myself, and the whole family, with one voice and as heartily as I do, highly approve of the match. The Consul, it is true, does not for the present concur with us, but he is to be considered as isolated from the family. Placed on the lofty ground on which he stands as the first magistrate of a great and powerful nation, all his actions and ideas are directed by a policy with which we have nothing to do. We still remain plain citizens, and as such, from all we have learned of the young lady's character and the respectability of her friends, we feel highly gratified with the connexion. They should not in the least be hurt by the displeasure of the Consul. I myself, although of an age to be my own master, and occupying distinguished places under the Government, I have also, by my late marriage, incurred his displeasure, so that Jerome is not alone. But as, when we marry, we are to consult our own happiness and not that of another, it matters not who else is or is not to be displeased. Our present earnest wish is that Jerome may remain where he now is, and take the proper steps to become, as soon as possible, a citizen of the United States." Here Captain Bentalou informed Lucien that Jerome would have to swear fidelity to the United States and renounce all titles of nobility.

"Very well," Lucien retorted, "Jerome must do all that ; he must go through that novitiate. The dignified attainment of the citizenship of the United States is well worth it. His situation is much preferable to ours. We are yet on a tempestuous sea, and he is safely moored in a safer and incomparably happier harbour. He must positively change his mode of living, and must not, as he has hitherto done, act the part of a prince of royal blood ; must not think himself anything more than he really is, and to strive as soon as possible to assimilate himself to the plain and uncorrupted manners of your incomparable nation, of which we shall all rejoice to see him a worthy member. We are now making arrangements to provide genteelly for him. We wish him to live on equal footing with your most respectable citizens, but never beyond any of them."

With the view of establishing Jerome in the United States, an income of twenty thousand dollars a year was mentioned as a suitable allowance, while a town and country residence were contemplated.

In a letter written subsequent to this interview, Robert Patterson spoke of Lucien as a man of firm and decided character, who thought and acted independently, and gave as his (Robert's) opinion that the "consular recognition or disavowal of the marriage would be deter-

mined by future occurrences—that much would depend
on Jerome, and if he acted the part of an honourable
man, all would go right." In conclusion he says, "It
is the duty of my sister, as a wife, to retain and increase
the affection of her husband ; and her exertions ought,
if possible, to be doubled from the peculiarity of her
situation."

During all this time Napoleon had remained silent.
At length he spoke, and to the purpose. On the 20th
of April, 1804, M. Dacres, French Minister of Marine,
by order of the First Consul, directed M. Pichon, the
Consul-General of France in New York, that no money
should be advanced on the order of the Citizen Jerome.
The letter said :—

"Jerome has received orders, in his capacity of lieutenant of the
fleet, to come back to France by the first French frigate returning
thither ; and the execution of this order, on which the First Consul
insists in the most positive manner, can alone regain him his
affection. But what the First Consul has prescribed for me, above
everything, is to order you to prohibit all captains of French vessels
from receiving on board *the young person to whom the Citizen
Jerome has connected himself, it being his intention that she shall
by no means come into France, and his will that, should she arrive,
she be suffered not to land, but be sent immediately back to the
United States.*"

Jerome should be urged, the letter continued, not to
lose the opportunity of pursuing a glorious career, by
acting in opposition to the wishes of the hero to whom
he had the honour to be related ; that while Napoleon
exalted and honoured those of his family who partici-
pated in his own elevated sentiments, he treated with

cold indifference those who dared to act independently
of him.

M. Dacres goes on to say that the First Consul was
indignant at the effeminate conduct of his brothers and
the obstacles they threw in his way. He then alludes
to Lucien's recent marriage : " Citizen Lucien, with the
reputation of past conduct and a fortune perfectly independent, has formed connexions repugnant to the
views of the First Consul ; and the consequence is that
he has just quitted France, and that, obliged to abandon the theatre of the glory of his own family, he has
exiled himself to Rome, where he becomes the simple
spectator of the destinies of his august brother and of
the empire." . . . .

" Jerome is wrong," said Napoleon to Dacres, " to fancy
that he will find in me affections that will yield to his
weakness. *Sole fabricator of my destiny, I owe nothing
to my brothers.* In what I have done for glory, they have
found means to reap for themselves an abundant harvest ;
but they must not on that account abandon the field
when there is something still to be reaped. *They must
not leave me isolated and deprived of the aid and services
which I have a right to expect from them.* If I completely
abandon him who in maturer years has thought proper
to withdraw himself from my direction, what has Jerome
to expect ? So young as yet, and only known by his
forgetfulness of his duties, assuredly if he does nothing
for me, I see in it the decree of fate which has determined
that I ought to do nothing for him."

M. Pichon was instructed to warn Jerome not to

bring back with him "the young person to whom he had attached himself." If he loved her, as he protested he did, he must learn, for her sake, to leave her and share the fortunes of his brother. "Be her accomplishments what they may, they would produce no effect upon the fixed determination of the First Consul not to receive her. The order has been issued to prevent her from landing, and it will not be revoked."

On the same day M. Dacres addressed a letter to Jerome himself, in which he urged him to return to France without delay. He appealed to him in the name of their early military association—of the dangers and the glory they had once shared together. He endeavoured to enkindle again in the heart of the young man the love of military glory with which the genius of Napoleon had covered the name of Bonaparte. "War is going on," said the letter, "and you are quiet and in peace at a distance of twelve hundred leagues from the stage on which you ought to be acting a great part. . . . . How will men recognize in you the brother of the Regulator of Europe? In what temper of mind will you find that brother, who, eager after glory, will see you destitute even of that of having encountered dangers —and who, convinced that all France would shed its blood for him, would only see in you a man without energy, yielding to effeminate passions, and having not a single leaf to add to the heaps of laurels with which he invests his name and our standards?"

On one condition only would Napoleon forgive him. "I will receive Jerome," said the First Consul, "if *leav-*

ing in America the young person in question, he shall come hither to associate himself with my fortunes. Should he bring her along with him, she shall not put a foot on the territory of France. If he comes alone, I shall forgive the error of a moment, and the fault of youth. Faithful services, and the conduct which he owes to himself and to his name, will regain him all my kindness."

Following these letters came this enactment of the French Senate :—

" By an act of the 11th Ventose, all the civil officers of the empire are prohibited from receiving on their registers the transcription of the act of celebration of a pretended marriage that Jerome Bonaparte has contracted in a foreign country, during the age of minority, without the consent of his mother, and without previous publication in the place of his nativity."

These documents reached Jerome in New York early in the summer of 1804, while he and his wife were enjoying their brilliant social life. He was frightened by the determined action of Napoleon. At first he hesitated to return, fearing to meet him in his anger. That which caused him the most terror in all these communications, and filled him with the most serious apprehensions for the future, was the paragraph informing him that Napoleon had quarrelled with his brother Lucien, for presuming to enter into a matrimonial alliance beneath the present brilliant fortunes of the Bonapartes. Lucien was sacrificed on the altar of ambition—Lucien, who had saved Napoleon at the crisis of his life—who had bravely stood between him and political ruin, degra-

dation, and perhaps death.   If Napoleon had not hesitated to abandon the brother who had opened for him .
the way to the consulate and empire, what clemency
could Jerome expect, who had done nothing for the glory
of his family, and whose first act was a disobedience ?

At len th he screwed his courage up to the necessity
of the case, and prepared to sail.   On the 14th of June,
1804, it was published in the New York papers "that
M. Jerome Bonaparte, his lady, and Mr. Patterson, of
Baltimore, her father, arrived in this city on Tues-
day.   Report says that the young couple are about to
depart for France, but the correctness of the rumour is
considered questionable."   Two days later we read that
" two pilot boats, sent out each with a French officer on
board, to ascertain whether British vessels of war are off
the harbour, returned yesterday afternoon with information that the coast is clear.   M. Jerome Bonaparte
went down to the French frigates at the watering-places
yesterday morning.   It is understood that he is to take
his departure in the commodore's ship, the ' Didon,' of
fourteen guns, reputed the best appointed and fastest
sailing frigate in the French or English navy.   It was in
this vessel, according to report, that Napoleon escaped
from Egypt."   On the 19th it was announced that
" Jerome Bonaparte and lady were rowed up yesterday
from on board the ' Didon,' and were safely landed oppo-
site their lodgings in Washington street, at twelve
o'clock.   The Frenchmen say they would not mind the
' Cambrian ' frigate and ' Driver ' sloop of war, but the
heavier ships they say are in the offing, they wish to

avoid." On the 20th follows still another item : " The reports to which the arrival of the British vessels of war have given rise are numerous and contradictory. At one time it is said the Frenchmen are determined to sail at all hazards—at another, that they have no such intentions. It is now reported that Jerome has magnanimously resolved to take his passage in the ' Didon,' and share with his countrymen the dangers of a rencounter with the enemy ; now, that he has prudently laid aside the idea, until the concurrence of more favourable circumstances." Jerome, it will be remembered, after an incomplete education at Madame Campan's school in Paris, had been placed in the French navy, the First Consul hoping that he would develope a genius for naval affairs, which should enable him to cope successfully with Lord Nelson, whose brilliant achievements had made England the mistress of the seas.

On the 21st the report was that " M. Jerome and lady had taken their departure in a sloop to overtake the ' Silenus,' which sailed a few days ago for Amsterdam —a previous arrangement having been made." But the newspapers added : " We are now informed that they are still in the city, and it is expected they have abandoned their contemplated departure for the present. The number of the British frigates, &c., on the coasts, and the sharp look-out that will be kept for them in different parts of their voyage by vessels of superior force, would render their safe arrival in France extremely improbable."

Following these newspaper reports, we find the following statement made on July 9th : "Jerome Bonaparte, it is understood, has abandoned all intentions of immediately returning to France, and contemplates commencing in a few days a pretty extensive tour ; in the course of which, after passing through the Eastern States, he will visit the Springs of Lebanon and Ballston, and pursue the customary route to visit the grand Falls of Niagara. His lady will be of the party."

On August 20th, this "tour" had evidently been accomplished, for we read : "Jerome Bonaparte, having returned to this city from the Eastern States, partook of an elegant entertainment on board the French frigate 'Didon' on last Friday. We are informed that the French officers addressed him by the title of His Imperial Highness, and that a late number of the *Moniteur* invites this style of address."

About this time General Armstrong had been appointed Minister to France in place of Mr. Livingston. General Armstrong at first agreed to take Madame Bonaparte to France with him while her husband sailed in one of the French frigates. In a letter dated New York, Sept. 5, 1804, written to her father, Madame Bonaparte says that General Armstrong, after promising to act as her escort, had suddenly changed his mind and gone off without her. Reports about Jerome Bonaparte and his wife continued to be published in the New York papers during the early part of the autumn of 1804, but, notwithstanding the repeated rumours of their intention to sail, they remained in America.

Jerome was, however, not without allies. On the 19th

of October he received a kind and even affectionate
letter from his brother Joseph, who had recently been
made by Napoleon a Senator of France and Grand
Officer of the Legion of Honour. An extract shows that
Joseph by no means shared the feelings of Napoleon.

"I do not know your resources in the country where you are.
Do not forget that everything I have is at your disposition, and that
I shall share with you everything I *could* have, with great pleasure.
Since your affections have led you far from your family and from
your friends, I feel, for my part, that you cannot renounce them.
Tell Mrs. Jerome from me, that as soon as she arrives, and is
acknowledged by the chief of the family, she will not find a more
affectionate brother than I. I have every reason to believe, after
what I have heard of her, that her qualities and character will
promote your happiness, and inspire us with an esteem and friendship that I shall be very much pleased to express to her."

On the 12th of October, a scandalous paragraph appeared in the Parisian journals, to the effect that Jerome
Bonaparte might have a mistress in America, but he
could not have a wife, as he was a minor and could not
marry without the consent of his parents. Upon this,
Robert Patterson wrote,—

"The Consul's determination is now but too plain. It is fortunate Jerome is still in America. He ought to remain there for
the present, until his friends have recognized his marriage. If his
family are determined on proceeding to extremities, they will possibly, to oblige him to return, curtail his supplies—perhaps withhold
them altogether. I can scarcely, however, think such a plan would
be persevered in. Our dependence is now entirely on Jerome's
honour. With firmness on his part, the affair may yet terminate
favourably. There is much to be apprehended : when the emperor
has made up his mind on any subject, he seldom gives way or
recedes from his opinions."

Yet, in a letter dated Amsterdam, Nov. 7th, Robert writes again that "Capt. Bentalou does not by any means think the prospect so gloomy as appearances would seem to indicate."

In all he did, Robert Patterson appears to have been most wise and prudent, carrying out his part in this interesting drama with great discretion: and had success been possible, he would have obtained it. He constantly recommended quiet and caution in the conduct of the affair—that it was absolutely necessary to avoid every measure which would have the effect of irritating the emperor—that Jerome should by all means remain in the United States, if he could do so without direct opposition to his brother's wishes; but, if he should decide to return to France, that he must bring his wife with him, be the consequences what they might.

Jerome determined to follow this last advice; and about the middle of autumn, 1804, Captain Bonaparte and his wife returned to Baltimore, finding it impossible to secure a safe passage from New York. Toward the end of October, accompanied by Miss Spear, an aunt of Madame Bonaparte, they at length embarked at Philadelphia in the ship " Philadelphia," for Cadiz. In passing down the Delaware the vessel was driven ashore off Lewes by a gale. They were obliged to abandon the vessel, and narrowly escaped with their lives; after being in the water for some moments, they managed to get into a boat, Madame Bonaparte being one of the first who was rescued. They were hospitably entertained by a gentleman in the neighbourhood, at whose

C

table Madame Bonaparte enjoyed a hearty meal of roast goose and apple sauce, much to the horror of her staid old aunt, who thought she should have been upon her knees, thanking God for sparing her life. A daughter of the gentleman at whose house they were was long in the habit of relating how the young *madame* ran backward and forward from the house to the yard, watching her handsome clothes which were drying upon the line after the shipwreck.

This was their last attempt to sail for Europe that year.

The two French frigates which had been lying at the port of New York during the summer and autumn arrived at L'Orient, France, on the 15th of December. Napoleon was angry with Jerome for not sailing with them ; and at the same time, speaking of the marriage, said he could only regard it in the light of a "*camp*" one—the laws of France not acknowledging any marriage contract as valid when entered into by a minor. Madame Mère informed a friend of the Patterson family that orders had been sent to all the ports of France to arrest Jerome in case he brought his wife with him, and to send her back to America. She recommended his going to France alone, and sending his wife to Holland ; and said that if he adopted this advice, a reconciliation might still be effected.

CHAPTER II.

IN the meantime, great and unexpected events had happened in France. On the 18th of May, 1804, Napoleon
declared himself Emperor. The position of the First
Consul of the French Republic did not satisfy his ambition. Sprung from the people, he wished to re-establish
the empire of Charlemagne after the lapse of a thousand
years ; the son of a Corsican lawyer, he proudly called
himself the successor of St. Louis. As Charlemagne
had been crowned by Pope Leo III. in the 9th century,
so Napoleon wished to be crowned by Pope Pius VII.
in the 19th century.

The Pontiff complied with this request, and on the
2nd of December, 1804, in the midst of one of the most
magnificent scenes ever witnessed in modern times,

Napoleon and Josephine were crowned, in Notre Dame, Emperor and Empress of France.

An imperial court was next created : Joseph and Louis Bonaparte were declared princes of the empire, with the right of succession should Napoleon fail of issue.

These were only preludes to still higher honours. Joseph was soon made King of Naples, and Louis King of Holland. Lucien and Jerome were excluded from the imperial dynasty. Murat, the son of an innkeeper, who had married Caroline Bonaparte, was made a prince of the empire, and Grand Duke of Berg. Eugene Beauharnais, the adopted son of Napoleon, was also made a prince and arch-chancellor of the empire, while lesser honours were conferred upon marshals and generals.

While these extraordinary events were taking place in France, Jerome and his wife had returned to Baltimore, where they were enjoying to the full the brilliant social life they led there. In the midst of it, still more alarming news than before came from France ; the emperor expressed his determination to throw Jerome into prison as soon as he arrived, there to remain till he consented to repudiate his wife, and marry some one whom Napoleon should select. Before these threats had reached the United States, however, Jerome and his wife, having failed to secure passage on other vessels, had arranged to sail in one of Mr. Patterson's own ships, the " Erin."

Madame Bonaparte was confident that even the cold heart of Napoleon would melt before the enchantment of her beauty—that even his inflexible will would bend before her eloquence and yield to her tears. Therefore she determined to go with her husband, that they might together throw themselves at his feet and ask his forgiveness and recognition.

After a quick and prosperous voyage, the "Erin" arrived at Lisbon on the 2nd of April. Here they had at once a proof of Napoleon's despotic power. A French guard was placed around their vessel, and Madame Jerome was not allowed to land. An ambassador from Napoleon waited upon her, and asked her what he could do for *Miss Patterson.*

To whom she replied, "Tell your master that *Madame Bonaparte* is ambitious, and demands her rights as a member of the imperial family."

Soon after arriving at Lisbon, Jerome hastened to Paris, hoping, by a personal interview, to win Napoleon over to a recognition of the marriage. On his way through Spain he met Junot, who had just been appointed Minister to Portugal. Junot endeavoured to dissuade him from resisting the wishes of Napoleon. Jerome declared that he never would abandon his beautiful young wife. "Strong in the justice of my cause," he said solemnly, "I am resolved not to yield this point." He then showed Junot a miniature of Madame Jerome, which represented a young lady of extraordinary beauty. "To a person so exquisitely beautiful," said Jerome, "are united all the qualities that can render a woman enchanting."

When Jerome reached Paris, he requested an interview with Napoleon, which was refused. He was told to address the emperor by letter, which he did, and received the following answer, which put an end to all his hopes :—

"I have received your letter of this morning. There are no faults that you have committed which may not be effaced in my eyes by a sincere repentance. Your marriage is null, both in a religious and legal point of view. *I will never acknowledge it.* Write to Miss Patterson to return to the United States, and tell her it is not possible to give things another turn. On condition of her return to America, I will allow her a pension during her life of sixty thousand francs per year, provided she does not take the name of my family, to which she has no right, her marriage having no existence."

When Napoleon declared that Jerome's marriage was " null, both in a religious and legal point of view," he was expressing his own wishes rather than stating the facts. At the time of Jerome's marriage to Miss Patterson, Napoleon was only the First Consul of France, and could have no control over the members of his family. Jerome's mother, and eldest brother, Joseph, were the only persons whose consent was necessary, and they concurred in approving the marriage. The marriage had been celebrated according to the prescribed rites of the Catholic Church, of which Jerome professed to be a member, and the ceremony had been performed by the highest dignitary of that Church in America.

When Jerome was at length admitted to the presence of his brother, Napoleon thus addressed him : "So, sir, you are the first of the family who has shamefully abandoned his post. It will require many splendid actions to wipe off that stain from your reputation. *As to your love affair with your little girl, I pay no regard to it.*"

In the meantime, what had become of the "beautiful young wife," left by her husband a stranger in a foreign land, surrounded by open enemies and false friends? About the middle of April, Madame Jerome Bonaparte, finding that she would not be allowed to land at Lisbon, or any port from which Napoleon had power to exclude her, sailed for Amsterdam.

There she arrived on the 1st of May. But her troubles were not over. Napoleon, who was now the absolute master of the continent of Europe, in anticipation of her arrival in Holland, had ordered Schimmelpenninck, the Grand Pensionary of the Batavian Republic, to prevent Madame Jerome Bonaparte, "or any person assuming that name," from landing in any port of that country. In compliance with this command, when the ship "Erin" arrived in the Texel Roads, she was ordered off immediately, and all persons were forbidden to hold any communication with her, under severe penalty.

The "Erin" was in the Texel eight days, during which time she was strictly guarded, being placed between a sixty-four gun-ship and a frigate. There were even difficulties about visiting her. Sylvanus Bourne, who was United States Consul to Amsterdam at that time, addressed a letter to the Grand Pensionary, in which he referred to the rigorous orders, forbidding any communication between the ship and shore, and requested that permission should be granted for supplying the vessel with fresh provisions. Whatever may have been Schim-

melpenninck's good intentions, he was powerless to act in
the matter, for he was absolutely under the control of
Napoleon.

Excluded from all the ports of Continental Europe,
and fearing that an attempt would be made upon her
life if she remained in the Texel, Madame Bonaparte
sailed for England. She arrived at Dover on the 19th
of May, and so great was the desire of the crowd to see
this now celebrated woman, that Mr. Pitt, the Prime
Minister of England, sent a military escort to keep off
the multitude that had assembled to watch her disem-
bark. Her first and only child was born at Camberwell,
near London, on the 7th of July, 1805, and named Jerome Napoleon Bonaparte, after the husband from whom
she believed herself only temporarily parted. Five
weeks after the boy's birth Madame Bonaparte wrote to
her father a letter, in which she gives all the information
she could obtain concerning that husband's whereabouts
and intentions.

MADAME BONAPARTE TO WILLIAM PATTERSON.

ENGLAND, August 14, 1805.

DEAR SIR,—Mrs. Anderson[3] is extremely anxious to return to
America, and, as she will be no material loss, she takes her departure in the " Robert."

We have at length concluded on remaining here the winter, but
not in London, as my going into public or showing myself would
be highly improper. I have received no letters from Bonaparte
since he has seen the emperor. He wrote to me from Madrid and
Mount Cenis, which is near Milan, where the emperor then was ;
but, on his arrival, his brother refused to see him, and he is now

---

[3] Madame Bonaparte's companion.

cruising before Genoa. He sent Le Camus from Milan to Amsterdam to meet me, and upon finding I was neither at Amsterdam or
Embden, Le Camus refused to leave his letter for me with Robert.[4]
I, however, have just received a message from Bonaparte as late as
29th of June, that he was as much attached to me as ever. He sent
this to me through the medium of some English friends of the
Marchioness of Donegal, who resides at Genoa. I suppose he finds
it impossible to have a letter conveyed. I request you will not
mention a word of my affairs to Mr. O'Donnell;[5] for, although
he would not willingly injure me by telling, yet he is incapable of
keeping a secret, and everything that is said the French Minister,
Turreau, will certainly write to France. They have had poor Bentalou[6] in the Temple, but he is liberated; they took from him a
letter from you to Bonaparte, and I have never been able to get a
single letter sent to him. I am sure, likewise, that Turreau has
orders to try and sound you with respect to my consenting to a
separation from Bonaparte on certain conditions; but, as we have
no reason to suppose that he will ever consent to give me up, we
must certainly act as if we supposed him possessed of some principle and honour. Turreau will likewise try to find from you what
were his intentions on leaving the United States in case the emperor would not receive me; but a perfect silence, if he sees you
or talks of me, would be the safest.

We imagine that Bonaparte is in some measure a prisoner, and
we must wait patiently to know how he will act; in the meantime,
it would be extremely imprudent for me to go out or see any one,
and I must avoid getting into any scrapes which I might be led
into from thinking that he would desert me. No matter what I
think, it is unjust to condemn until we have some certainty greater
than at present, and my conduct shall be such as if I had a perfect
reliance on him. I think that by returning to the United States
it would seem as if I had yielded the point, and by next spring
everything will be decided.

---

[4] Brother of Madame Bonaparte.

[5] John O'Donnell, Esq., a wealthy East India merchant in Baltimore,
at the beginning of this century.

[6] A French officer who served in the American Revolution.

Mr. Monroe[7] and family are in London, and have shown us the greatest civility and kindness. It is of the greatest importance for you to be very guarded with respect to Turreau; for I have every reason to know that they will try to prevail on me to consent to a separation, and if they can get anything from either you or myself like encouragement, they will persuade Bonaparte that we have no objection, provided, &c., &c., &c.

Do not speak of my connexion with the Marchioness of Donnegal, as, if it were known that she conveyed a message from Bonaparte to me, or from me to him, which she has promised, she might be brought into trouble, and no one would venture to oblige us again. We received last evening a letter from Garnier[8] at Genoa; he says that Bonaparte desires me to return to the United States, that he will be absent from me a year or eighteen months, and that he strongly objects to my staying in England. But we think it is a trick of Garnier's, and that Bonaparte knows nothing about the letter—especially as we know Garnier to be a villain. The emperor has offered to give me twelve thousand dollars a year during my life, on condition that I would return to America and give up his name. I request you will not mention this proposal; I have never taken the smallest notice of it. I never talk before any one of the emperor or any of his family, and one advantage of my staying the winter in this country is that I escape observation more than in Baltimore, where you know people are always on the watch, and where many stories would be written to France. We received yesterday letters from Mama and Miss Spear,[9] of the 29th of May; they express surprise at me not saying anything about the decree the emperor had passed to annul my marriage, in our letters from Lisbon. But not one of us knew it until Bonaparte had departed, and he was ignorant of it when he left us. You must place no confidence in what the English papers say, as they often publish that I will appear in public, when I am sitting quietly in my room.

I remain, dear sir, yours,   E.

---

[7] James Monroe, afterwards President of the United States.

[8] Dr. Garnier, Jerome's physician in America.

[9] Cousin of Madame Bonaparte.

Three months after this letter was written the young mother and her child embarked for the United States, and, after a prosperous voyage of four weeks, arrived in Baltimore.

On the 24th of May, 1805, the Emperor Napoleon addressed a formal letter to Pope Pius VII., requesting him to publish a bull annulling Jerome's marriage with Miss Patterson. In this letter occurs the following paragraph :—

"I have frequently spoken to your Holiness of a young brother, nineteen years of age, whom I sent in a frigate to America, and who, after a sojourn of a month, although a minor, married a Protestant, a daughter of a merchant of the United States. He has just returned. He is fully conscious of his faults. I have sent back to America Miss Patterson, who calls herself his wife. By our laws the marriage is null. A Spanish priest so far forgot his duties as to pronounce the benediction. I desire from your Holiness a bull annulling the marriage. I sent your Holiness several papers, from one of which, by Cardinal Casselli, your Holiness will receive much light. I could easily have this marriage broken in Paris, since the Gallican Church pronounces such matrimonies null. But it appears to me better to have it done in Rome, on account of the example to sovereign families marrying Protestants. I beg your Holiness to do this quietly, and as soon as I know that you are willing to do it, I will have the marriage broken here by civil process. It is important for France that there should not be a Protestant young woman so near my person. It is dangerous that a minor and a young man of high rank should be exposed to such seduction against the civil laws and every rule of propriety."

Accompanying this letter Napoleon sent a magnificent gold tiara to the pontiff, hoping thereby to gain a favourable answer.

The emperor's letter contained several important mis-representations : Jerome had been in the United States *four* months instead of *one*, before the marriage took place ; the ceremony was performed, not by a Spanish priest, but by the Right Reverend John Carroll, Bishop of Baltimore, and the highest dignitary of the Catholic Church in the United States.

Pius VII. gave the matter the consideration which its importance demanded.   The secret archives of the Pro-paganda were examined ; the treasures of the Vatican Library were ransacked to see whether there existed in the whole history of the Church a precedent for such an act.   There was none to be found.   The Catholic Church has always held the marriage tie inviolate. Knowing that he had not the power to dissolve a mar-riage celebrated with all the formalities required by the Church, Pius VII., indifferent to the frowns of Napoleon, and careless alike of his threats and of his power of exe-cuting them, unhesitatingly declared that he neither could nor would annul the marriage between Jerome Bonaparte and Elizabeth Patterson.   The course adopted by Napoleon in this affair was the beginning of a series of cruel measures, which culminated in the divorce of his own lawful wife and the imprisonment of the inflexible Pius VII. in the chateau of Fontaine-bleau, where a few years later the emperor himself was compelled to sign his abdication of the throne of France.

The following passages from the Pope's letter to Napoleon show that, while he was conciliatory, he was

firm in his determination. The position of the Holy
Father should have been respected by a ruler who
proudly proclaimed himself the " eldest son of the
Church : "—

FROM THE VATICAN, June 26, 1805.

EMPEROR AND ROYAL MAJESTY,—We beg your Majesty not to
attribute the delay in the return of the courier to any other cause
than a desire to employ all the means in our power to comply
with the requests of your Majesty, communicated to us by your
letter, which, together with its accompanying documents, was
handed to us by the courier in person.

In everything which depended upon us, namely, inviolable
secrecy, we have felt honoured in yielding to the solicitations of
your Majesty with the most scrupulous exactness ; hence, we have
confined entirely to ourself the investigation of the petition concerning the judgment on the marriage in question.

In the crowd of affairs which overwhelm us, we have taken all
the care and given ourself all the trouble to derive personally from
all sources the means of making the most careful researches to
ascertain if our Apostolic authority could furnish any method of
satisfying the wishes of your Majesty ; which, considering their end,
it would have been very agreeable to us to second. But, in whatever light we have considered it, the result of our examination has
been that of all the motives that have been proposed or which we
can imagine, there is not one which allows us to gratify your
Majesty, as we should be glad to do, by declaring the nullity of the
marriage. The three documents which your Majesty has sent us,
being based on principles contrary to each other, are reciprocally
destroyed. The first, setting aside all other absolute impediments,
assumes that there are only two which can apply to the case ; difference of the religion of the contracting parties, and the absence
of the curate at the celebration of the marriage. The second,
rejecting these two impediments, deduces two others : from the want
of the consent of the mother and the relations of the young man. a
minor, and from the offence known under the name of seduction.
The third disagrees with the second, and proposes as the motive

of nullity the want of consent of the curate of the husband, which it assumes is necessary, since he has not changed his residence, because, according to the disposition of the Council of Trent, the permission of the curate of the parish is absolutely necessary in marriages. But, from an analysis of these conflicting opinions, it results that the proposed impediments are four in number. On examining them separately, however, it has not been possible to find one which, in the present case and according to the principles of the Church, can authorize us to declare the nullity of the marriage contracted and already consummated. The difference of religion considered by the Church as an absolute impediment does not obtain between the persons who have been baptized, even when one of them is not in the Catholic communion. This impediment obtains only in marriage contracted between a Christian and an infidel. These marriages between Protestants and Catholics, although disapproved of by the Church, are nevertheless acknowledged as valid. We earnestly hope that your Majesty will be satisfied that the desire which animates us of seconding your wishes is in this case rendered ineffectual by want of power, and that you will accept this very declaration as a sincere testimony of our paternal affection."

Napoleon found his own council of state more complaisant than the Pope ; and on the specious plea that the marriage was not binding, because it was contracted when Jerome was under age and without the consent of his guardian, it was declared by the civil tribunal null and void.

The weak and fickle Jerome soon forgot his "dear little wife," as he once was fond of calling her. After leaving her at Lisbon, in April, 1805, Jerome addressed her frequent and tender letters, declaring repeatedly that his "dear little wife" was the sole object of all his love, for whom he would be willing to give up his life. As late as October, 1805, he wrote to her from Paris :—

"Ma chère et bien-aimée femme, la vie n'est rien pour moi sans toi et mon fils. Sois tranquille, ton mari ne t'abandonnera jamais."[1]

On the 16th of the same month he wrote to her again :

"Te quitter, ma bonne femme, je n'en eus jamais la fatale pensée ; mais je me conduis en homme d'honneur, en brave et loyal militaire. J'aime mon pays, j'aime la gloire ; mais je les aime en homme qui, accoutumé à ne rien craindre, n'oubliera jamais qu'il est le père de Jérome Napoléon et mari d'Élise. Je t'embrasse comme je t'aime, et je t'aime autant que ma vie."[2]

In another letter Jerome assures her that he prefers her to a crown. Again he writes :—

"Crois, mon Élise, que ma première pensée en me levant, comme la dernière quand je m'endors, est toujours pour toi, et que si je n'étais pas certain d'avoir le bonheur de rejoindre ma bien-aimée femme, je cesserais de vivre."[3]

His often-repeated determination "never to abandon his beautiful young wife" melted away before the frowns

---

[1] "My dear and well-beloved wife, life is nothing to me without thee and my son. Be tranquil ; thy husband will never abandon thee."

[2] "My good wife, I have never had the fatal thought of leaving thee ; I act as a man of honour, as a brave and loyal soldier. I love my country, I love glory ; but I love them as a man who, accustomed to fear nothing, never forgets that he is the father of Jerome Napoleon and the husband of Elise. I embrace thee as I love thee, and I love thee as my life."

[3] "Believe, my Elise, that my first thought on waking, as my last in falling asleep, is always of thee ; and if I were not sure of the happiness of rejoining my well-beloved wife, I should cease to live."

and brilliant promises of Napoleon. In a few months
after separating from her in Lisbon, he consented to a
divorce. As a reward of his pusillanimity, Jerome was
created a prince of the empire, and raised to the rank
of Admiral of the French Navy.

CHAPTER III.

Madame Bonaparte's disappointed Ambition.—Jerome's perfidy confirmed by the Marriage with the Princess of Würtemberg.—Madame Bonaparte's Residence in Baltimore. —The Stuart Portrait.—The course of Events in France.—Madame Bonaparte again visits Europe.—Her letters from England and France, 1806—1816.

WHEN Madame Bonaparte returned to her father's house in Baltimore, after her unsuccessful trip to Europe, there was around her a glamour of romance, poetry, and suffering. Those who had envied her as the beautiful and brilliant bride of Jerome Bonaparte could well afford to sympathize with the disappointed and deserted young wife. Her ambition had led her to contract what seemed to her the most splendid matrimonial alliance ever made by an American woman. But this ambitious marriage, which she had fondly hoped would open for her a dazzling career at the court of Napoleon, whose genius she enthusiastically admired, was destined to be the source of all her future troubles.

She herself soon accepted the result as inevitable. She was too thorough a woman of the world to be deceived by the honeyed words which Jerome addressed to her after their separation at Lisbon. Rochefoucauld had made her cynical. Still she had long retained some of that tender confidence in the man she had once trusted,

D

which is so characteristic of a woman. She had hoped
against hope; but when she found that he was actually
a puppet to his brother's threat, her love and admiration
changed to complete contempt. The bright and joyous
girl whose loveliness had captivated Jerome Bonaparte became a brilliant, cynical woman, with wit like lightning,
which soon made itself feared. It was by no means safe
for people who felt no sympathy for her misfortune, but
on the contrary rejoiced at her disappointment, to show
their joy in her presence.

At the conclusion of the peace of Tilsit, July, 1807,
Napoleon informed Jerome that the members of the
imperial family were required to form alliances which
would support his throne. It was not enough that he
had repudiated his lawful wife; his previous obedience
had indeed gained him the throne of Westphalia, which
was formed out of the territories of the Grand Duke of
Hesse; but to support his new dignity he must now
go even farther. On the 12th of August, 1807, he was
married to the Princess Frederica Catharina, daughter
of the King of Würtemberg; but not until he had previously made two unsuccessful attempts to form a matrimonial alliance with other princesses. The marriage
was celebrated with all the pomp and ceremony with
which Napoleon knew so well how to dazzle the French
people. After the festivities the new king and queen
left Paris to take possession of their dominions; and in
his miniature kingdom Jerome soon banished any
memories which may have haunted him, in a boyish
imitation of the taste and splendour of his brother.

Madame Bonaparte remained in the United States. Her time was spent between her father's residence in Baltimore and his various country-seats in Maryland. She was much sought after in society, where her extraordinary beauty, fascinating manner, and romantic history made her an object of interest ; but, except this, her life was for a while uneventful. About this time we find her corresponding with an old friend of her father's in Baltimore, Mr. Robert Gilmor, relative to the unfinished portrait of herself, commenced by Gilbert Stuart in 1804. This picture, consisting of three positions of the face, was intended as a study, and for years has hung in the gallery of the Maryland Historical Society, Baltimore. From this study Stuart intended to paint a handsome portrait, but, owing to his habit of accepting more orders than he could execute, the picture has remained unfinished. It was considered by Madame Bonaparte the best likeness of her ever taken. " It looked," she said, " like *herself ;* the others looked like any other woman."

Robert Gilmor was a wealthy Baltimore merchant, possessing a love of art. He induced Gilbert Stuart to come to Baltimore, and through his influence obtained many sittings for him. As seen by the following letter, it was through his interference that Madame Bonaparte, after a long delay, finally succeeded in getting her portrait into her possession, though in its incomplete state.

MADAME BONAPARTE TO ROBERT GILMOR.

SPRINGFIELD, CARROLL CO., MD., Sept. 30, 1807.

SIR,—I entreat you to accept my acknowledgments for your successful application to Stuart for the portrait—an act as flattering to me as it is pleasing, and which augments, if possible, the sentiments of regard by which I have ever been actuated towards you. Stuart has hitherto remained inexorable to all our solicitations, and his prompt acquiescence in your demand affords a proof of the estimation in which you are held by this distinguished artist. You will, I flatter myself, have the goodness to retain the picture in your possession until my arrival in town, where I shall have the honour of personally offering you my thanks.

I have the honour to remain your obliged, humble servant,

ELIZABETH BONAPARTE.

It may be imagined with what profound interest Madame Bonaparte watched the course of events in France during the crowded years that intervened between her return and the end of Napoleon's empire. When she heard of the divorce of Josephine, and knew that Napoleon could thus sever his own tenderest ties, she must have understood, if never before, with what little compunction he had wrecked her happiness.

She saw the Corsican adventurer marry a daughter of the Hapsburgs, imprison the Pope, and laugh at his excommunication. From this moment she followed the varying course of the emperor's downfall, until his final overthrow at Waterloo.

This was the event which again set at liberty her restless ambition. Two months after it we find Madame Bonaparte in Europe, this time at Cheltenham, England.

Her son she had left at school at Mount St. Mary's College, Emmettsburg, Maryland. How and why she had gone abroad is explained sufficiently in extracts from her correspondence.

MADAME BONAPARTE TO WILLIAM PATTERSON.

CHELTENHAM, August 22, 1815.

DEAR SIR,—I have been obliged to remain here owing to indisposition, but shall proceed to Paris when my health will permit me to travel. I have been agreeably surprised at the kind and flattering reception which I have received from the most fashionable and elevated ranks in society in this country—nor is there anything left for me to desire except the presence of my American friends to witness the estimation in which I have the happiness to be held. The political state of Europe is still fluctuating.   France is a volcano, from which occasionally are emitted sparks of fire which threaten alike all parties. Louis XVIII. remains at Paris, protected by the combined forces of Europe. Napoleon is gone to St. Helena, but has left behind him a reputation which adversity has not subverted.

.   .   .   .

Every one wishes me to educate my child in England, and they are good enough to flatter him by saying that Bonaparte talents ought to have English education. He would indeed be much more highly considered in Europe than in America, where unfortunately he possesses no rank ; and could I combine with the interest he excites here, the solid advantage of a large fortune, I should be too happy ! As a last resort, he must be a professional character, and the talent with which nature has so lavishly endowed him might lead him to the highest eminence in Europe. America and its institutions are yet in a state of infancy—nor is there, from the commercial complexion of all its pursuits, the same field for successful exertion of the kind of mental superiority which your grandson, happily or unhappily, possesses. Splendid intellectual endowments may be a misery or a blessing to their possessor, and everything depends on the method of directing them in early age.[1] My conduct in leaving America was the result of much previous reflection, nor do I see any reason yet to regret it ; on the contrary, my most sanguine expectations have been exceeded.

With love to the family, I remain, sir, respectfully and affectionately,

Yours,

E. PATTERSON.

In this year, by a special act of the legislature of Maryland, Madame Bonaparte was divorced from her husband, in order to prevent him, after the downfall of Napoleon, from claiming any share of her fortune. In this measure she showed her usual prudence and foresight, for, believing that the King of Westphalia was ruined, and having but a low opinion of his sense of honour, she determined to forestall him in any attempt he might make to enrich himself at the expense of one whom he had so basely deserted.

On the 2nd of September, Madame Bonaparte again wrote to her father from Cheltenham as follows :—

MADAME BONAPARTE TO WILLIAM PATTERSON.

CHELTENHAM, September 2, 1815.

DEAR SIR,—I perceive with much regret, by your letters respecting me to persons of this country, that you announced to them that I *conceived* myself ill, and had embarked contrary to the wishes of my friends. I shall answer categorically these two accusations, and answer them without temper. The physicians of England are willing to give a certificate of their opinion that there is an accumulation of bile on my liver, which would have killed me,

---

[1] At this time her son was ten years old.

or produced the last stage of hypochondria in three months, had I not gone to sea and tried change of climate. They will likewise state that if the disease does not yield to a course of mercury, or the waters of this place, it will fall on the lungs and terminate my life.

As to leaving America without the consent of my friends, it appears to me that, if indeed I have friends there, they would have wished me to come to a country where I am cherished, visited, respected, and admired. It appears to me that, if I have friends in America, their friendship might have been shown in some more agreeable mode than finding fault with me for being miserable in a country where I never was appreciated, and where I never can be contented. It appears to me natural too, that, if I have friends in America—which I have, I reluctantly confess, sometimes doubted—that their pride might be gratified in hearing that I am in the first society in Europe, and that, too, for my personal merits; for, without vanity I may say so, since I have neither rank, fortune, nor friends of my own, willing to assist or protect me. I acknowledge that the standing I possess in this country is highly flattering, and that it is not surprising I should prefer people of rank and distinction who are willing to notice me. Their attentions are very gratuitous, for I am a very poor stranger, and a very unfortunate one on many accounts.

My misfortune and the declining state of my health have excited more interest here than in my own country, and have been a passport to the favour of the great. My talents and manners are likely to preserve their good opinion. What you have written of me to Europe will have very bad effects. Either people will wonder you should not wish my health restored, and that you should not be pleased at knowing me in the first society, or they will consider me to be a hypocrite and disobedient child, who has bribed medical men to say my life is in danger. There is likewise another effect likely to result from your writing such things of me, which is this : every one who knows me has heard that your wealth is enormous, and consequently they think I shall have a large fortune from you. In Europe a handsome woman who is likely to have a fortune may marry well ; but if it gets about that her parents are dissatisfied with her, they will think she will get nothing by them, and if she had the beauty of Venus and the talents of Minerva, no one will marry her. People here are not such fools as to marry poor beauties, however much they may admire them. The reputation of your fortune would be a great advantage to me abroad, and I am sure you cannot object to my having the honour of it, provided you keep the substance. I beg that, whatever you may *think*, you will *say* nothing and especially *write* nothing about me, unless it be something likely to advance me. The power of riches here is great, and your money, I assure you, would, if you say nothing more about me or your not liking my absence, be of great use to me. I mean *only* the *reputation* of it, for alas! the substance is not mine. I get on extremely well, and I assure you that although you have always taken me for a fool, it is not my character here. In America I appeared more simple than I am, because I was completely out of my element. It was my misfortune, not my fault, that I was born in a country which was not congenial to my desires. Here I am completely in my sphere (money excepted), and in contact with modes of life for which nature intended me. The ambition of my character made me wretched amidst scenes where it could only be disappointed ; here it might be satisfied. I have taken a house beside and under the protection of my amiable friends, Sir Arthur and Lady Brooke Falkener. The family with whom I came over remain at a boarding-house. My friends advised me to move, as people of fashion never live in boarding-houses. Everything you write to McElhiney he will tell, to give himself a consequence in being connected with us. In this country distinctions in society are so much attended to, that connexions with people who are not known, however honest and respectable they may be, are not tolerated. He is a well-meaning man, but entirely unfit for your confidence, only proper to be written to on business, since there is no danger of bragging of that. I feel convinced that your own good judgment will properly appreciate my motives in writing this letter, and that it is not a motive of vanity which dictates what I tell you.

Your own pride must be interested in having me the object of public esteem, and your interest is to have me placed in an elevated situation. As to the opinions of old Mr. Gilmor and other very respectable and worthy persons, that I ought to be in Baltimore, they only tell you so because they know that their daughters might come here and never be known. Besides, they are envious of your fortune and my situation. Look how they run after the poorest sprigs of nobility, and then you will know what they think of my standing in Europe. I am surprised you do not see the advantages of my position, compared with that of the daughters of the other people in Baltimore, and that you permit the chattering of envious people to influence you. You well know that the wealth of our family, and the consequence which from many circumstances we possess, must be very disagreeable to others, and small towns are always worse than others in every respect. If people do not approbate my conduct in America, what is the reason they paid me so much attention? Ask George [2] what I was in New York. What other American woman was ever attended to as I have been there? Who ever had better offers? I never would marry without rank, or God knows I might have got money enough by marriage. They are afraid of your supporting me in a rank, and of your sending my child where he will be in one which all their government stock, insurance stock, and real property could never put them. Let them come and try which is of most consequence, they or me! I confess that it would have been perhaps a blessing if I could have vegetated as the wife of some respectable man in business; but you know that nature never intended me for obscurity, and that, with my disposition and character, I am better as I am.

Adieu, my dear sir. I am going to dress for a ball at Lady Condague's, and am then obliged to go to one at General Trivin's. I expect the Americans in Europe who cannot go out will write lies about those who can. I beg this letter may not be shown to Robert, as he never keeps anything to himself, and that you will consider the impropriety of writing anything except what will produce a good effect in this country.

All my conduct is calculated, but you will undo the effects of my prudence if you write to certain people, who show your letters. Let people think you are proud of me, which indeed you have good reason to be, as I am very prudent and wise.

E. P.

---

[2] George Patterson, a younger brother of Madame Bonaparte.

Mr. Patterson's answer to this letter showed that he was by no means carried away by the social honours which so flattered and delighted his daughter.

WILLIAM PATTERSON TO MADAME BONAPARTE.

BALTO., 16 Nov., 1815.

MY DEAR BETSY,—Your letter of 2nd Sept. came to hand this day, commencing as follows :

" I perceive with much regret by your letters respecting me to persons of this country that you announce to them that I *conceived* myself ill, and had embarked contrary to the wishes of my friends."

In answer I say that the only time I have ever mentioned your name since your departure, was in a postscript to a letter to Mr. McE——, when writing to him on business, wherein I expressed the above sentiments, and it was very improper in him to have communicated those sentiments to any person whatever, as my intentions were merely to let him know that you had embarked for Europe that he might have rendered you any services in his power, should his services be necessary.

It was generally understood by those who ought to have known, that your illness was more from conceit than reality, owing to the unsettled state of your mind—rather with a view to form an excuse for going to Europe, so long the object of your wishes. You certainly embarked contrary to the advice and wishes of your best friends, for you cannot suppose your situation and conduct can be a matter of indifference to them who have very much disapproved of the mode you took to revisit Europe a second time.

I cannot say I am satisfied with the attentions you seem to receive from great people in England ; they cannot be lasting ; they must arise chiefly from curiosity and compassion. Your regret and disappointment hereafter will be in proportion to the elevated notions you may entertain at present from those attentions.

You say you are prudent and wise ; God grant it may be so, for surely nothing would give me more pleasure. I must, however, say that your ideas of wisdom do not accord with mine. People must look at home for real substantial happiness, for it is impossible to find it for any length of time elsewhere. Edward [3] writes you respecting your son, and I hope you will soon be tired and satisfied with Europe, so as to induce you to return, convinced like myself that this is the most proper place for you to reside. I shall therefore be uneasy and unhappy until you return.

I am, dear Betsy,

Yours very sincerely,
WILLIAM PATTERSON.

How much her father's excellent sense impressed her may be seen from her next letter, which, however, contains the only patriotic expressions found in her whole correspondence.

MADAME BONAPARTE TO WILLIAM PATTERSON.

CHELTENHAM, September 23, 1815.

DEAR SIR,—I every day find new reasons to think we succeed best in strange places, since human infirmity seldom stands the test of close and perpetual communion. Europe more than meets the brilliant and vivid colours in which my imagination had portrayed it. Its resources are infinite, much beyond those which can be offered us in a new country. The reception I am happy to meet in England makes me regret the loss of health which sometimes obliges me to decline brilliant parties. The Portuguese ambassador, Count Tonsall, sent me, through Viscount Lord Strangford, late ambassador at the Portuguese court, an invitation to a grand ball given to the nobility of Cheltenham. I left my bed at ten o'clock to go, as my attendance was expected, and at one in the morning I found myself so ill as to be unable to go to the supper-table, and to be obliged to return. The Count La Chatre, ambassador from France, has just sent me my passport for Paris; but that beautiful country is still torn by faction. The necessary presence of the allied armies renders Paris an expensive residence to strangers, as every house is filled and the indispensable wants of

---

[3] Madame Bonaparte's favourite brother.

life are consequently much more exorbitant than in times of tranquillity.

My fervent desire of European pleasures was not the vision of a
distempered fancy, it was only a prophetic spirit of the fascinations
which here surround existence. The purposes of life are all fulfilled
—activity and repose without monotony. Beauty commands homage,
talents secure admiration, misfortune meets with respect.

In this country, the term *old*, which is so often repeated in
America, is completely banished from the polite vocabulary.
Women of forty, even fifty, are more cherished and as advantageously married as chits of sixteen. They are not here cheated
out of their youth, as with us, but retain the glorious privilege of
charming until at least sixty. Another advantage too they possess
—of generally marrying men as young or younger than themselves.
Since I am so happy as to be in the best society, I much deplore
the absence of American friends to witness the estimation in which
I am held. I have taken a house for myself, as the customs of this
country do not authorize any person of fashion in remaining at a
boarding-house ; Lady Falkener has been kind enough to chaperone
me, and my house communicates with hers. There is no danger
of my committing a single imprudent action—circumspect conduct
can alone preserve those distinctions for which I sighed during ten
years.

Experience has not been lost, and time, in destroying many
personal charms, has substituted discretion and self-command.
Youth and beauty were not the season for great prudence. The
intoxication of flattery required indulgence, for where exists the
nature so inflexible as to remain unsubdued by it ?

The laurelled hero, the sceptred monarch, the subtle statesman,
the profound politician, have all been betrayed by the *ignis fatuus*
of admiration into ruin and degradation. The situation of a young
and beautiful woman has ever been one of peril. Detraction
accompanies praise, and the advantages of loveliness are dearly
purchased by the pains which envy inflicts.

I have experienced the perfect truth of the observation that in
mediocrity alone can be found happiness.

The favourites of nature are indeed seldom those of fortune. But
since we possess not the power of organizing ourselves, wisdom

consists in pursuing the course our talents and ambition point out to us. Our errors bring with them their penalties, and in the course of time we are corrected. The noblest natures have sometimes been those which have committed the greatest faults; as the sun has shone with more brilliancy after being obscured by clouds.

The Americans begin to excite respect and interest. Their war, so calamitous in its existence, has produced beneficial results. My compatriots enjoy a degree of consideration abroad which was long denied them. They are admitted by their proud enemy into the scale of nations. American institutions, government, manners, climate, &c., &c., have become the subject of inquiry and concern. I feel some little complacency in pronouncing myself an individual of a country which every one seems to think will one day be great. I contribute my mite of applause to the valour of its defenders and the wisdom of its councils. *Vive la patrie!* I exaggerate when I descant on its amusements, since whatever may be the great destinies which Baltimore may develope, its pleasures have not yet dawned. Patriotism induces me to draw a veil over the defects of my country, and policy as well as fashion dictate patriotic feelings. The British are, as they modestly confess, the greatest nation in the world. We must acknowledge that their monstrous vanity is excusable when we know that their gold, their armies, and their councils have successfully directed the efforts of combined Europe against the man whose talents menaced their existence. He was the object of their admiration and dread, and they have in him subverted the glory, the existence of France as a nation. They do not in England pretend to revile Napoleon, as some persons in America have done. His stupendous abilities are admitted—his misfortunes almost respected by his enemies. I listen silently to any discussion in which he bears a part. I easily perceive that he has more justice done him here than with us.

Mr. Beasley has written several times to me, offering his services. Mr. Rubel writes me from Stockholm Mr. de Caramon is made chargé-d'affaires at the Hague, and has written me in the most friendly manner. Mrs. Glennie, too, has written. All the Americans in Europe, except Mrs. Mansfield, have been very civil. Mr. and Mrs. Mansfield have said that their letters from America all say that I came away without even informing my family, and that my poor child is in great distress. *Her* mother advised me to come constantly; she never ceased telling me I was a fool to stay in America, and she has written her *dear Molly* that it was improper for me to come. *Aunt* ever was an old hypocrite, and her conduct on this occasion proves that deceit and wickedness will go with her to the other world. She was never easy until she got me married, and ever since she has been advising me to leave America. As to Mansfield, he is only afraid that I will write to Baltimore a true account of his entire insignificance in London. I know no one who has ever seen him, and they are in *no* society. I heard what they said of me through a *secondary sort* of person, but in fact their company and mine are *very* different, which is the reason they do not like to hear of my arrival. I shall certainly let their friends in Baltimore know what *great personages* they are in this country. They may rest assured I will; since they chatter about me, I must tell the truth about their consequence here. Aunt is too bad in first advising me to come and then writing stories.

Adieu, dear sir, yours affectionately,

E. B.

Mr. Patterson's reply to this is interesting :—

WILLIAM PATTERSON TO MADAME BONAPARTE.

13th December, 1815.

DEAR BETSY,—Since I wrote you on the 16th ult., in answer to yours of 2nd of September . . . . I have received your two letters of 22nd August and 23rd September, with all the notes and tickets accompanying the last. They have been seen or heard of by no person but myself, and, to be candid with you, I would have been ashamed to expose them to any one else. From those letters, as well as the former, I am persuaded you are pursuing a wrong course for happiness; but I hope and pray you may soon perceive your mistake, and that you will look to your mother-country as the only place where you can be really respected, for what will the world think of a woman who had recently followed her mother and her last sister to the grave, had quit her father's house, where duty and necessity called for her attentions as the only female of the family left, and thought proper to abandon all to seek for admiration in foreign countries; surely the most charitable construction that can be given to such conduct is to suppose that it must proceed in some degree from a state of insanity, for it cannot be supposed that any rational being could act a part so very inconsistent and improper.

I am, dear Betsy,

Yours very sincerely,

W. P.

In the winter of 1815-16, Madame Bonaparte visited Paris, whose pleasures she had so long anticipated. The empire had fallen; but Paris was gayer and more brilliant now than ever during the empire. The giddy Parisians, who had clamoured for the blood of the best of the Bourbons, hailed with joy the restoration of the weakest of the family, and it was in the midst of the festivities attending this Madame Bonaparte arrived in Paris, and entered immediately upon the life most to her taste. Her success was greater than that ever before enjoyed there by any American woman. Her sufferings had made her a heroine, and her grace and beauty now made her a social queen.

Louis XVIII. expressed a wish to see her at court, but she declined to be presented, saying that, as she had received a pension from the emperor, she would not appear at the court of his successor, ingratitude not being one of her vices. The Duke of Wellington was among her admirers, Talleyrand praised her wit, Madame de Staël extolled her beauty, and the leading men of her time sought her acquaintance. She met Chateaubriand, who had returned from his sentimental pilgrimage to the East, Sismondi, Humboldt, Canova, the Duchess de Duras, and other celebrated men and women, who hastened to Paris after the restoration. The gay life she was then leading did not allow her much time for correspondence, and we find only one brief letter from her during this period.

MADAME BONAPARTE TO WILLIAM PATTERSON.

Paris, 22 February, 1816.

Dear Sir,—I have received your letters by Triplicate. As all mine are liable to be opened and published, I wish you would have the goodness to avoid mentioning such things as you have done. I am really pained at your sentiments respecting the course I have pursued. It is the only one which can make me happy, and was adopted after the experience and reflection of my whole life. I am not half as foolish as you imagine, or I should, perhaps, have been more contented. There is but one single chance of securing tranquillity for the future years which I may have to live, that is, to remain in Europe. I can never be satisfied in America. It was always my misfortune to be unfitted for the modes of existence there, nor can I return to them without a sacrifice of all I value on earth. I have everything necessary to my complete success, except money. I possess the means of commanding everything else. I preserve amidst the corruption, the pleasures, the liberty of Paris, the most irreproachable conduct. I have the courage to submit to every privation when a departure from the strictest propriety is required. I form no plans, I try to hope that some unexpected happiness may continue me where alone I attach value to existence. The ex-King of Westphalia is now living at the court of Würtemberg. He has a large fortune, and is too mean to support his own son. He ought to pay you your money.

I remain, sir, affectionately yours,

E. &c., &c.

CHAPTER IV.

Madame Bonaparte returns to America.—Her third visit to Europe.—
Pauline Bonaparte.—John Jacob Astor.—An invitation by the Princess
Borghese to visit Italy.—1819-20.

NOTWITHSTANDING Madame Bonaparte's repeated de-
clarations that she could not be happy in America, she
returned to her native city of Baltimore in the summer
of 1816, where she remained until the 1st of May,
1819. Then, with her son, she again sailed for Europe,
and, after a tedious voyage of seven weeks, arrived at
Amsterdam on the 25th of June, whence they started in
a private conveyance for Geneva, where Jerome was to
continue his education. The expenses of the journey,
amounting to seventy-five guineas, were duly reported
by Jerome to his grandfather, Mr. Patterson. Immediately upon their arrival in Geneva, Madame Bonaparte became the recipient of attentions from the most
distinguished people who were residing at the time in
that city. Among others, were the stepson of the
Duke of Kent (father of Queen Victoria) ; the Princess
Potempkin, of one of the oldest families in Russia ;
Princess Galitzin ; and Prince Demidoff, then the wealthiest noble in Europe) whose ancestor was originally a
Russian serf, who fled from his native village to avoid

E

conscription, and laid the foundation of his immense fortune by the manufacture of arms during the reign of Peter the Great.

The young Jerome Bonaparte kept up a frequent correspondence with his grandfather Patterson during this visit.   In his first letter after arriving at Geneva he says the Princess Potempkin had sent another princess to his mother, inviting her to her country-seat near the city ; and that, after placing him at a boarding-school, she was to take up her residence one mile from the town for two months.

The first letter that we have from Madame Bonaparte after her return to Europe, is dated Geneva, April 10, 1820.   In it she informs her father that the Princess Borghese (Pauline Bonaparte, Jerome's sister) had signified, through Mr. John Jacob Astor, her desire to see herself and Jerome in Rome.   She gives also a description of the Bonaparte family then residing in Italy.

MADAME BONAPARTE TO WILLIAM PATTERSON.

10 April, 1820.

DEAR SIR : . . Two weeks ago I received a letter from Mr. Astor, of New York, who spent a month last summer in the same boarding-house with me in this country, which he left for Italy in the autumn.   His letter, dated Rome, 15th of March, contains : " Last evening we had the honour of an introduction to the Princess B——, who immediately inquired after you and your son. When I informed her that I had left you at Geneva, she expressed much regret at your not having made the journey with us.   She then said : ' I am very happy to find an opportunity of speaking frankly to you.   I wish very much to see Madame P. and her son here. I have spoken to Mr. Russell and Commodore Stewart; both promised me to speak and write to Mrs. P——, but as yet I have no account of them or her. My object is to make some provision for the son of my brother, who is poor and can give him nothing. I am rich and have no child, and find in myself every disposition to do everything for him.' She requested me to write to you without delay in her name, to invite you to make her a visit, and to bring your son."

Having never heard either from Russell or Stewart—your letter of February 26th not having reached me, nor that to which you allude as having sent some days previously, directed to the care of Vanbaggan, Parker and Dixon (the latter not now arrived)—I wrote the letter to the princess, copy of which I enclose to you. I made every inquiry concerning her circumstances, disposition, and mode of life. She has, perhaps, some fortune of her own. Her husband has been compelled to make her an allowance (which, I presume, is only for her life). They are separated, but not divorced. She is about thirty-seven years of age, the handsomest woman in Europe of her age, excessively luxurious, consequently expensive in her habits, said to be extremely capricious in her attachments. They are a sort of state prisoners, who can move only with the permission of the sovereigns of Europe, and the wife of Joseph was refused permission to inhabit her chateau in Switzerland last summer. My opinion is that I should go to the princess myself in the autumn for three months, that Cricket should be left at his present boarding-school, as his education is the only certain fortune which I can calculate on for him, that he should remain ignorant of the expectations which are held out to him, and on which I think there is no reliance to be placed, until he has acquired sufficient instruction to enable him to pursue some useful and honourable occupation in life. She is perhaps sincere in her present intentions, but the fortune of a pretty woman of thirty-seven is a bad object of calculation for nephews, and nothing but an irrevocable deed would make me found any hopes sufficient to authorize a change in my mode of education. If I were to take the child to a palace, he would naturally prefer pleasure to study; the habits of the Italians are delightful, but do not lead to personal distinction. Once there I might not be permitted to take him out of the country, the present favourable dispositions of the princess might vary, the means of education are very inferior to those I find here, admitting that my present authority should remain entire, which is not very probable. Suppose that she should secure the half of her property to him, he could not expect to possess it during her life, and in all human probability he will be sixty before he inherits. In the meantime, he must live, and without an education he would find himself condemned to dependence on the caprice of others.

My wish is, then, to educate him with the idea that he has his fortune to acquire by his own exertions, but at the same time to profit by all the good intentions of his relations in a way that will not interfere with his attainment of personal distinction, which, after all, is better than money, and which will always command it. The uncertainty of events in this century confirms me in the opinion that the only certain fortune parents can give their posterity is some lucrative and respectable profession, such as the law, which renders them at the same time proper for foreign embassies or the situation of statesmen at home.

My present plan is a good one, and has obtained the approbation of the most enlightened men here : it is to give him a tincture of Greek, considerable knowledge of Latin and mathematics, perfect acquaintance with the French and English languages, after which he will pursue a course of chemistry, physics, &c., before commencing his study of jurisprudence. History, mythology, geography, of course, form part of his studies at present, with drawing, equitation, fencing, and dancing. Politeness, &c., usage du monde, are not neglected. He goes to a ball on Saturday evenings, where he meets some of the first persons in Europe. Sunday is devoted to exercise and visits. I am not sparing of advice respecting the necessity of application to his studies, and I inquire constantly of his preceptors into the mode of tuition. In short, if he should prove ignorant and insignificant, the fault will not be mine. I spare neither money nor personal exertions to procure for him every possible advantage and to conscientiously fulfil my maternal duties.

I hope he will reward by his success all my cares, and I rejoice that I have no more children to toil after, never having envied any one the honour of being a mother of a family, which is generally a thankless position.

The desire of the princess for my residence with her offers many advantages and disadvantages. Rome is a delightful place; she occupies a superb palace, receives the homage of all strangers of distinction : pleasure is the sole pursuit in Italy. Her modes of existence are magnificent, although capricious and spoiled by adulation, which in a beautiful woman and a princess is very natural. They say she is good *au fond*. I should prefer Rome to Geneva, a palace to my apartment, strangers of distinction to my present resources, pleasure to work, elegance to economy, my liberty to all these attractions, and the interests of my child to every other consideration. I expect her answer to my letter, which will decide my departure. I shall remain three months near her; my object is to judge by my own eyes and ears, to engage a continuation of her present friendship for the child, and to convince her of the necessity of letting him pursue his education here for three or four years. It appears to me that this project is more reasonable than taking him from his studies upon a promise which will most probably never be performed, and exposing him to the danger of contracting habits of expense entirely unsuitable to my means of expenditure, at the same time losing the most valuable part of his life in idleness ; the consequence would be that, after having spoiled him, he would be left to me to support. I cannot say that I have the least reliance upon that family, although I am disposed to reciprocate their kind words and receive their offers of friendship without allowing myself to be deceived by either. They are less wealthy than is supposed ; they are all extravagant and disposed to promise more than they give ; at least, if I may judge of the future by my past knowledge of their generosity, the child has nothing to expect from them. This conviction does not prevent my acceptance of the invitation, which, if it does me no good, can produce no evil result to me ; but I cannot consistently with my ideas of propriety expose my son to the danger of losing his time in a country where amusement is the sole pursuit. Three years will produce great changes. It is not prudent for him to change his place of residence at the present moment ; if he joins them, he will be obliged to share their captivity ; at present he is considered as entirely separated from their destinies, which are very fluctuating and completely under the dominion of others. My resolution is uninfluenced by personal feelings, never having felt the least resentment toward any individual of that family, who certainly injured me, but not from motives which could offend me : I was sacrificed to political considerations, not to the gratification of bad feelings, and under the pressure of insupportable disappointment became not unjust.

I believe some of them are amiable ; but when there is question of parting with money, good-will is generally exposed to a great trial, and it is most discreet for persons to rely on their own exertions when they possess sufficient capacity to exist independently. I have observed nothing positive in the offers held out to me ; it is politic to appear to confide in them, and wise to act as if they had not been made. I have not communicated a syllable to the child, desirous of saving him the pain of disappointment, and anxious to preserve in him assiduity to his studies, and to impress him with the useful knowledge of economy.

Adieu, sir,

Yours affectionately,

E.

The letter addressed to the Princess Borghese by Madame Bonaparte, alluded to in the foregoing, was as follows :—

MADAME BONAPARTE TO THE PRINCESS BORGHESE.

GENÈVE, 25 Mars, 1820.

MADAME,—Monsieur Astor m'a écrit qu'après avoir eu l'honneur d'être présenté à votre altesse, vous avez eu la bonté de vous informer de mon fils et de moi, et que vous avez en même temps exprimé le désir de nous voir. Sans être ainsi assurée de l'intérêt que vous daignez témoigner à nous, je ne me serais pas permise de vous écrire maintenant.

Les intentions généreuses dont Mr. Astor m'a fait part m'ont pénétrée de reconnaissance, et augmentent le regret que je ressens de ne pas avoir l'avantage de vous connaître personnellement. Mon but en venant à Genève est de procurer à mon fils les moyens d'une éducation distinguée qui ne se trouve point en Amérique, et de trouver le genre de vie simple qui convient à la destinée que je puis lui offrir. Je l'ai élevé à savoir que j'ai peu de fortune à lui donner, et que son rang dans le monde ne dépendra que de ses propres efforts. Convaincue que c'est un des plus grand malheurs d'avoir des prétensions sans espérances, j'ai taché d'éloigner de lui de fausses idées d'ambition, et de diriger celles qu'il possède à la culture de ses moyens intellectuels. Sans peut-être posséder une grande capacité, il en a cependant assez pour parvenir par le travail à un rang honorable dans la société. Jusqu'à présent je n'ai pas eu à me plaindre de son zèle. Mon premier désir, comme mon premier devoir, est de lui donner une éducation distinguée ; j'en trouve tous les moyens à Genève, j'y suis venue pour cela, et j'y reste pour y veiller. Cela ne m'empêchera pas de faire le voyage d'Italie dans quelques mois d'ici, pour vous dire, madame, combien je suis touchée de l'intérêt que vous voulez bien prendre à mon fils, et vous témoigner ma reconnaissance. Je vous aurais même presenté mon fils, si j'étais moins décidé à ne jamais interrompre son éducation. Le mérite personnel est la seule chose digne de son nom que je puis lui laisser : voilà pourquoi une bonne éducation est le premier soin de mon cœur. Ni Mr. Russell, ni le Capn. Stuard (*sic*), ne m'ont écrit. J'imagine qu'ils ignoraient mon départ des États Unis.

Agréez, madame, l'homage des sentimens distingués, et la vive reconnaissance avec laquelle j'ai l'honneur d'être de votre altesse, la très-humble et très-obéissante servante.

ELIZABETH PATTERSON.

TRANSLATION.

GENEVA, 25th March, 1820.

MADAME,—Mr. Astor wrote to me that, after having had the honour of being presented to your Highness, you had the goodness to ask about my son and about myself, and that you had at the same time expressed your desire to see us : without being thus assured of the interest you have condescended to express about us, I would not have taken the liberty of writing to you at present. The generous intentions which Mr. Astor made me acquainted with have filled me with gratitude, and have increased my regret that I have not had the advantage of your personal acquaintance.

My object in coming to Geneva is to procure for my son the means of education suitable to his rank, which I could not find in America, and to find simple kind of life which would accord with the destiny I have to offer him. I have taught him to know that I have very little fortune to give him, and that his rank will depend upon his own efforts. Convinced that it is one of the greatest misfortunes to have pretensions without hopes, I have tried to remove from him false ideas of ambition, and to direct him to the cultivation of intellectual pursuits. Without perhaps possessing great talents, he is capable of arriving by his own efforts at an honourable station in society. So far I have nothing to complain of as to his application. My first desire, as it is my first duty, is to give him an especially excellent education suitable to his rank. I have found means of doing so at Geneva. I came for that purpose, and shall stay here to accomplish it. This will not prevent me from making a voyage to Italy a few months hence, for the purpose of telling you, madame, how I am touched by the interest you have taken in my son, and of expressing to you my gratitude.

I would at the same time present my son, if I had not decided not to interrupt his education. Personal merit is the only thing worthy of his name that I can leave him. This is the reason why a good education is the first desire of my heart.

Neither Mr. Russell nor Captain Stewart has written to me. I imagine that they do not know that I have left America.

Accept, madame, the respectful assurance and lively recognitions with which I have the honour to be your Highness's most humble and most obedient servant,

ELIZABETH PATTERSON.

On the 23rd of April, Mr. Astor wrote to Madame Bonaparte from Florence, as follows :—

Your letter to the Princess I received at Rome, and gave it to her myself ; the day after she sent a friend to me to inquire about your circumstances. I told her what I thought was the case : that your father is very wealthy, but that his property consisted chiefly

in houses and lands, which at present did not produce much ; that
he has a large family, say seven besides yourself; and that I
believed you had to economize to educate your son. I was then
asked whether you did not receive anything from the King of
Westphalia. I said I was pretty sure you never received a dollar
from him. Then the emperor was mentioned. I said I knew that
he once made some provision, but that it had long been withdrawn.
The result was that the person did not know what the princess
would do ; and you know I had no right to inquire farther. My
own opinion is that she feels an interest in your son, and I suppose
that under certain circumstances would do something for him. I
presume she would wish to have him, but I give it as my opinion
that at present you would not give him up to any one.

She has your letter. I think you will do well to depend on yourself and keep your son steady to his education. She was quite
unwell when I left Rome, so much so that I could not see her to
take leave. Your son will have sense enough not to be flattered
with prospects which may prove vain.

.   .   .   .

JOHN JACOB ASTOR.

In her next letter to her father, Madame Bonaparte
again alludes to the Princess Borghese's invitation, and
at the same time expresses her want of confidence in
her promises to do anything for her son. She also gives
a very flattering account of " Bo," and fears there is
no pecuniary advantage to be derived from his father ;
but at the same time she thinks it is better to remain on
good terms with all the family.

With her economical ideas, she dwells with regret
upon the fact that education is very dear in Geneva
but she is determined to spare no expense, believing this
to be the best gift she can bestow upon her son.

GENEVA, 25th of April, 1820.

DEAR SIR,—Your letter of 29th of February, enclosing one from Miss Spear, and a copy of Mr. Harper's communication, has reached me to-day. I received a duplicate of the same in your letter of the 26th February, to which I replied two weeks ago, enclosing you a copy of my letter to the Princess B——, which I had written immediately after the reception of Mr. Astor's letter from Rome, in which he invited me in her name to go to Italy. There was no mention in her conversation with him of any intention of making a deed, or securing in any form a part of her property. Had I received Mr. Harper's information before writing to her, I should have taken it for the text of my letter, and written exactly as if I believed it. I shall wait now a few days to give her time to write to me, and if I do not hear from her, I shall write another letter saying I have heard from Col. Raoul in America, and that I accept most gratefully her offers, that I shall go to her in the autumn, and consult her whether it is not better to continue the child where he is.

The fact is that these offers are not at all to be relied on, and I almost regret they have been made, as they place me in a very perplexing situation. If the child were five years older, and his education finished, I should set out with him immediately. He is now making a progress in everything ; he thinks he has nothing to depend on but his own industry. I have taken an apartment for two years and bought all my furniture, and, as I have effected a sort of popularity in the best society, I can maintain a more agreeable position here than any other stranger has ever done at so small an expense. Travelling is a great expense. The princess is said to be very capricious ; if I take him there, I shall not find the same means of instruction, and very probably he will, like all other young persons, have his head turned by the splendour of his great connexions, and fancy he will be rich enough to dispense with study ; he will be spoiled for any *common* pursuits, and perhaps be left to live on my scanty means, as I fear there is little reliance to be placed on their promises. It is very unfortunate for him and me that they have so *unseasonably* recollected us ; it agitates me uselessly.

I am desirous to profit by every remote chance of wealth for him, and at the same time conscious that a good education is the only certain advantage I can command for him. I wish to make him acquainted with the old lady, of whom, by the way, I have heard nothing ; and if I take him there it will not be in my power perhaps to bring him here again, as none of that family are allowed to come here, and once received by them, he will be considered as one of them. The French Chargé at Amsterdam refused me a passport for him to travel through France, which would have been a shorter route to this place : he said his resemblance to the emperor was so striking that it would expose me to great inconvenience in that country, and that he could not accord him a passport without first stating this fact to the government, and obtaining their decision.

In this country the higher class are opposed to that dynasty, as they prefer being a republic ; the lower have lost their commerce, and the exportation of watches, jewellery, &c., to France, for which reason they regret their independence. The higher classes here are very aristocratic, and it is more difficult to obtain access to their society than in any other country. For whatever cause it may be, I have been better received than any other stranger of greater rank or infinitely greater wealth has ever been. They say they never did as much for any one before, and I have been obliged to entreat them not to invite my son every evening. . . . .

The fact is my task is no easy one ; this child has more conversation and better manners, a more graceful presentation, than other children of his age, consequently he excites more attention, and I am constantly tormented with the fear of seeing him spoiled by the compliments paid him in society, of which, if I compel him to abandon, he will lose the ease and habits of politeness so difficult to acquire at a later period. He has grown taller, and much better looking ; he is thought very handsome, but I do not myself think him by any means a beauty, and regret that others tell him so, as it is a kind of praise which never made any one better or happier. I do not think there is any confidence to be placed in expectations from his father's family ; they are less wealthy than reported to be. I have seen a person who lived years with the mother, who, she says, is a woman of sense and great fortitude ; that her fortune cannot be immense, as, although a great economist, she was obliged to spend great part of her income.

The princess has a large income from her husband, who was *forced* to make her an allowance much against his inclination.

The King of W. spends everything he can get hold of, and will keep up kingly state until his expended means leave him a beggar. He has never taken the slightest notice of his son, and is said to be as extravagant and thoughtless as he was fifteen years ago. He buys houses and then leaves them, and is less popular than any of his family.

Joseph is said to be the richest, and is a man of sense ; his family are not allowed to inhabit their chateau in Switzerland. I know Bo has written to you for money to buy a horse, which I beg you *not* to send him. He pretends it will be more economical for him to keep a horse than for me to pay nine francs per week for riding lessons ; but I prefer paying twice that sum rather than allow him to ride about the country.

He has been very ingenious in finding reasons of economy for this arrangement, but I have stopped his eloquence by positively assuring him that I would rather pay for a lesson every day, than allow him to ride gratis by the year. Bo has lessons of every kind ; his hours of *recreation* are *filled* by *dancing, fencing* and *riding ;* Sundays are exclusively devoted to exercise. In short, I trust and hope his time is spent profitably. I am not laconic when counsel is wanting, which prevents him from forgetting his English. He speaks French very fluently, as he takes all his lessons in this language, the knowledge of which I always considered highly important in his circumstances.

I expect every day an answer to my letter, sent enclosed to Mr. Astor. I shall not neglect to keep up the correspondence during the summer. It is impossible to travel in that country in the summer season, even if I were well enough to go now, which I am not, having been very unwell for the last two months. I am looking out for some travelling companions for the autumn, as I shall positively go, unless they write me not to come. There is certainly no doubt of the policy of my keeping the child on the best possible terms with them ; one can lose nothing by that. I shall write and act as if I firmly believed there was something to expect, although I confess I am not sanguine on the subject, distrusting all good which I do not find perceptible to the touch.

If I do not take him instantly, it is because I do not think it advisable for him, as my own convenience is not considered, certainly, in such a determination. My acquaintances and intimates here are elderly people, who, altho' they suit me very well, are surprised at the soberness of my taste, and altho' I am really obliged to them for their kindness to me, I can readily imagine that Italy is more agreeable, and should like very well to live there. There is nothing like this town, however, for young men. Instruction of the best kind, good company, economy, and no vice; no idleness among the inhabitants, greater morality than in any other country among the higher classes—the lower interested and disposed to cheat when they meet with good subjects for stripping. I cannot complain of being more duped than other strangers, however.

Education here is by no means gratuitous. I pay 6 louis per month, and all the lessons d'agrément besides, which are 3 frs. per lesson independently of extra sums for which there is no agreement made; in short, the whole amount with his clothes is fully 5000 francs per annum. There is no method of lessening this expense, or I should find it out probably as soon as another. My resolution is to spare no expense on education; it is a bad calculation, because it is the only advantage over which circumstances have no power. The child does not yet know a syllable of my correspondence; it is a pity to give him false hopes on the subject.

I think I must make him, however, write a letter to the old lady, to jog her memory.

There is a son of Sir Robert and Lady Wilmot going out with the British ambassador. I have given him a letter to Robert Gilmor. I know his mother and father, to whom I gave the letter here, not knowing the young man. If you should be giving a family dinner, you might invite him; but I do not advise people to take any trouble about strangers, as they are very ungrateful in general, and their acquaintance of no great advantage unless one has daughters to get rid of.

Adieu, sir,
Yours affectionately.

In the following letter to Mr. Gilmor, of Baltimore, Madame Bonaparte solicits his kind attentions for Mr. Wilmot, to whom allusion has just been made.

MME. BONAPARTE TO ROBERT GILMOR.

GENEVA, 22 April, 1820.

MY DEAR MR. GILMOR,—You will certainly meet Mr. Wilmot, who is one of the British Embassy to America ; but, as I have the advantage of knowing Sir Robert and Lady Wilmot personally, I solicit for this gentleman any services you may have in your power to render him. There is no person in Baltimore to whom I would sooner address a distinguished stranger than to you. If my father should be in town when you receive this letter, I beg you to make him acquainted with Mr. Wilmot. I do not write him by the present occasion, having written a few days since.

I found the Willinks, of Amsterdam, very agreeable and useful acquaintances during my short residence in their country ; I thank you infinitely for your letters to them.

This country me convient assez, bonne société, beaucoup de soirées, et tous les moyens d'une éducation distinguée pour mon fils.[1] I am uncertain whether I shall pass my next winter in Italy. I rather incline towards repose in Geneva, being fatigued with travelling and new societies. I have not had the pleasure of seeing Mr. Wilmot, but I have the advantage of meeting frequently his mother, Lady Wilmot, who is a very charming person, and, like Mrs. Gilmor, a beauty. I find great satisfaction in recalling myself to your recollection and friendship, of which I solicit the continuance. Adieu, sir ; make my compliments agreeable to Mrs. Gilmor, and believe me, with sincerity, your obliged, &c.,

ELIZABETH PATTERSON.

---

[1] [This country suits me well enough ; the society is good, there are any number of soirées, and every means are offered for a finished education for my son.]

CHAPTER V.

Madame Bonaparte's Life in Geneva.—Lady Morgan.—Madame Mère.—
Joseph Bonaparte.—The Princess Borghese and Mr. Astor.—Madame
Bonaparte in Rome.—Kind Reception.—Proposed Marriage of Jerome to
his Cousin Charlotte.—The ex-King of Westphalia.—Pauline Bonaparte.
—1820.

THE greater part of Madame Bonaparte's correspondence during the spring and early summer of 1820 related
to the invitation to Jerome to visit his father's family in
Rome. While she seriously objected to interrupting his
education, she did not wish to lose the opportunity of
his becoming acquainted with his relatives, from whom
she hoped he might gain some pecuniary and social
advantages. Madame Bonaparte limited her expenses
while in Geneva to $3000 a year. She had lodgings in
a boarding-house, and paid $60 per month.

An extract from a letter from Jerome to his grandfather gives us an accurate description of her style of
living at this time. "Mamma lives now in town, in the
cheapest way possible, on account of the troubles in
Baltimore. She has no man-servant, but one single
woman, who does the business of waiter and femme de
chambre; as for the cleaning of the apartment, which
consists of four rooms, a parlour, bedroom for mamma,

another for myself, and a fourth for the maid, that is very trifling. Her meals are furnished by a woman for a certain price per month." Her income did not allow her to keep a carriage at this time. Notwithstanding this plain and economical mode of life, Madame Bonaparte's personal attractions made her courted, and she was invited everywhere.

MME. BONAPARTE TO WM. PATTERSON.

GENEVA, 8th of May, 1820.

DEAR SIR,—I sent copies of my letters to the princess, and Mr. Astor's letters to me, to show you that he coincides in opinion with me that there is nothing to be expected from that family.

Lady Morgan arrived here a few days since. She left Rome the 1st of April; was very intimate with the princess whilst there, who spoke to her of her desire to see us in Rome, but did not mention any intention of either offering her house, or making any provision for Bo. She desired Lady Morgan to write to me to come there, and expressed her interest in us. Lady Morgan describes her extravagance as boundless. She keeps up the state of a queen, and is not at all to be relied on, as she is perfectly capricious, and will spend her whole fortune before a great while, and perhaps much more than her own. Lady M. says I would be mad to take the child there; that his education would be sacrificed: that he would adopt the most absurd ideas of his own greatness, as they all call themselves Majesty and Highness, and expect to return to France as they were formerly; that there is not the least dependence to be placed on her promises, which she makes to get us there, because she hates the Queen of W. and her brother Jerome, who have both behaved very unfeelingly to the family since their dethronement, whom they seem now anxious to cut, and have ceased all correspondence with them. That she perhaps thinks she takes an interest in the child, but that it would be highly imprudent in me to take him to Italy, as their situation there is very insecure; and that *she*, Lady Morgan, believes the child has nothing to rely on but his own merit, and that all hopes of fortune from that family would prove illusory.

She says the old lady has sense and dignity; that, if she had promised, she would place greater confidence, but that she said nothing on the subject, and that it is more than probable she will have very little to leave; and I think it more natural she should leave what little she has to her own children, who are all helpless and expensive, than to grandchildren. Lady Morgan knows the princess perfectly well, as she took a great fancy to her, and invited her on all occasions. She told the princess that Jerome had refused to do anything for his son, even to pay for his education; therefore she knew very well everything on this subject before she had Mr. Astor questioned. She told Lady M. that she had heard that I was like her, and asked her if she saw the resemblance. Lady M. is one of the shrewdest women in Europe, and her opinion is perfectly to be relied on. She knows the value of money as well as any one, and when it is worth while to put oneself in the way of getting it. She thinks the princess would like to have Bo with her, to provoke the Queen of W., but she is firmly of opinion that he would be ruined for every purpose of life if taken to her, and that he should be kept where he is, if it is intended that he should pursue a profession as a maintenance; that there is nothing to expect from the princess or any of them.

I saw a lady who had spent many years in the family. She told me exactly the same thing; her opinion of the princess is exactly like that of Lady Morgan, and both these persons are opposed to the present Royal family of France, and disposed to like the others, so that I think I may rely on their testimony. I have also consulted a gentleman here of the same politics—an old man. He says that unless I have a fortune of my own to give the child it would be madness to interrupt his education, as he does not think any promises of the family to be depended on, even if they have wealth to leave, which is very much doubted. Joseph is the only certain fortune: they all have children except the princess, who has a life income in her husband's estate.

I think what I always thought: that the child's only prospect of fortune is in his own capacity and exertions, and shall keep him closely to his studies as long as I can, so that if he proves an idler it will certainly not be my fault, as all this town will certify.

Yours affectionately.

P.S.—I am very uncertain whether it will be worth while for me to go to Italy next winter.

Lady Morgan, who was the friend and correspondent of Madame Bonaparte for many years, was born in 1783, and commenced her literary career at the age of fourteen, by publishing a volume of poems. Her "Lay of the Irish Harp" attracted much attention, and suggested to Tom Moore his most popular work, the "Irish Melodies."

It may not be generally known that the favourite Irish ballad, "Kate Kearney," was written by Lady Morgan in her childhood. Her novel, "The Wild Irish Girl," published in 1806, established her reputation, and seven editions were called for in two years.

Self-educated as she was, and without any of the fortuitous circumstances that enabled Lady Blessington to acquire an ephemeral literary success, Lady Morgan earned an European reputation by her own unassisted efforts. In the number of her works she has seldom been equalled by any English authoress. In her thirtieth year she married Sir Charles Morgan, with whom she travelled through Europe, residing for several years in Italy, Switzerland, and France. It was in the last country that she met Madame Bonaparte. They were both brave and spirited, with the minds of men and the hearts of women, and this congeniality caused their acquaintance to ripen into a warm and permanent friendship, which continued uninterrupted until the death of Lady Morgan, in the spring of 1859.

Madame Bonaparte met Mr. John Jacob Astor at Geneva, in the autumn of 1819, when he visited that city in order to place his son at school there. The acquaintance thus begun was continued, as we have seen, by correspondence from Rome. Mr. Astor interested himself as a friend in the matter of the invitation of the Princess Borghese to Jerome to visit Rome, and strongly advised Madame Bonaparte against accepting it. Early in the summer of 1820, he returned to Geneva, when he assured Madame Bonaparte "that there was not the least confidence to be placed in the promises of the princess, and that there was not anything to be expected from the family."

MME. BONAPARTE TO WM. PATTERSON.

GENEVA, June 23, 1820.

DEAR SIR,—Mr. Astor is here, after having spent some time in the place with the Princess, having been entertained by her, and questioned minutely about Bo. He says that he thought at first that she intended doing something for the child, but that, upon further investigation of her character, he is of opinion that there is not the least confidence to be placed in her promises, and that he does not believe there is anything to be expected from the family, and advises me not to go to Rome.

This testimony agrees with Lady Morgan's and that of a person here who lived for years with the mother. The old lady has never spoken to any one on the subject ; she is very sensible and very miserly, and probably will leave all she can save to her children, who are all spendthrifts. Lady Morgan and Mr. Astor both advised me to remain where I am, as I should perhaps be obliged to stay there, and the child be a sort of prisoner of state. . . . .

The expense, too, of such a journey is out of the question, and I could not live there for the same sum as I can do here. As to living with her, they say it would be impossible, and she did not tell them she desired it. I have told Bo nothing on the subject, and have taken an apartment for two years, and bought the furniture, with liberty to rent the rooms for three years more if I desire it. Mr. Raoul must either have exceeded his commission, or the lady must have forgotten it.

The Bonapartes are all alike, very affectionate in words, but without the least intention of parting with a farthing. Their fortune is less than is supposed, their expenses very great, and the chance is that they will spend more than they possess. At all events, they have been pretty well probed on my subject, and the result is that if they see their nephew, they will tell him they love him, take great interest in him, and leave me to pay his expenses.

I shall stay where I am, unless I find it my interest to move. The Princess Borghese has not answered my letter. I always was of opinion that she would do nothing, and Mr. Astor has come over to my opinion upon a further acquaintance with the family. He was imposed upon when he wrote me the first letter.

I would have gone there, however, if I had not ascertained that the whole affair was, like their past conduct, a deception.

Lady Morgan, who is very intimate with them, told them everything calculated to get something out of them, but finding there was no reliance whatever to be placed in them, she very cordially advised me neither to go, nor take *Bo*.

Yours affectionately,
E. P.

The Queen of Westphalia is lying-in of another child.[1]

Madame Bonaparte spent the summer of 1820 in Geneva. The town was filled with strangers, and among them there were princes of every nation. The little sum-

---

[1] Prince Napoleon Bonaparte.

mer capital was unusually gay that season ; entertainments of all kinds, public and private, followed each other in quick succession. Jerome speaks of a " superb feast of eight hundred persons, where there were rockets and all kinds of artificial fires." Madame Bonaparte mingled in all these festivities. During this summer, Eliza Bonaparte, the Princess Bacciochi, died and left her children to the guardianship of her brother Jerome. When the news of her death reached Napoleon, at St. Helena, he shut himself up in a room by himself, where he remained for several hours. When his attendants were at length admitted to his presence, he said, "Yes, Eliza has gone—she has shown us the way. I used to think that death had forgotten our family, but now he has begun to strike. He has taken Eliza, and I shall be the first to follow her." He was, for his death happened in less than nine months after.

At a later period, Madame Bonaparte having failed to secure the hand of Joseph's daughter for her son, intimated that the daughter of the Princess Eliza, having a large fortune, might be a most desirable match for him.

In a letter from the boy, dated Nov. 6, 1820, he says in speaking of his mother : " Mamma goes out nearly every night to a party or a ball. She says she looks full ten years younger than she is, and if she had not so large a son she could pass for five-and-twenty years old. She has a dancing-master and takes regularly three lessons a week, and has done so for the last six months ; is every day astonished at the progress she makes, and is fully determined to dance next winter. She con-

86   THE LIFE AND LETTERS OF

stantly regrets that she had not danced at Paris. She
is not fully satisfied with Geneva, for the laws are very
severe. Among others, it is positively forbidden to
dance after midnight, or to go out of town after eleven
o'clock at night without a particular permission from the
chief magistrate."

Jerome did not appreciate European life as highly as
his mother. In one of his letters he says: "Since I
have been in Europe I have dined with princes and
princesses and all the great people in Europe, but I have
not found a dish as much to my taste as the roast beef
and beefsteaks I ate in South Street" (at the house of
his grandfather).

In another letter he says: "I never had any idea of
spending my life on the continent ; on the contrary, as
soon as my education is finished, which will not take me
more than two years longer, I shall hasten over to
America, which I have regretted ever since I left it."

Madame Bonaparte continued to reside in Geneva
during the whole of the year, until late in the autumn of
1821, and in her correspondence at this time are several
letters of interest.

MADAME BONAPARTE TO WILLIAM PATTERSON.

GENEVA, May 22, 1821.
DEAR SIR,—I beg you to do me the favour of sending the enclosed
to the Count de Survilliers.[2] It is an answer to his proposal of my
inhabiting his château in Switzerland. He gives me the choice of

---

[2] Joseph Bonaparte, ex-King of Spain, who assumed this title after the
fall of Napoleon.

three furnished country-houses, and an order to that effect to his agent here. I cannot, however, accept either; for they are too far from town for me, who have no carriage, and I should be melancholy without society. He has been very friendly, and from what Mrs. Toussard writes me, he appears disposed to acknowledge and be fond of Bo. I have not been in Italy, nor do I propose taking the child, having seen at once that it would have been his ruin. I have had a letter from his father, in which he informs me that his fortune is not sufficient to provide for his present family, who will be taken care of by their mother; that I might have known his character too well to suppose he ever thought of laying by a fortune; and that the little he did save he has been cheated out of by the persons he trusted. I believe he is not as bad-hearted as many people think, and that many of his faults and much of his bad conduct proceed from extravagance and folly, which are, indeed, the source of all evil, both to their possessors and to those about them.

I endeavour to impress ideas of economy on the mind of his son; which is an arduous undertaking, young people fancying generally that they have only to dissipate what the frugality of their ancestors accumulated, and that the future will provide for itself.

The count is one of the most esteemed persons of his family, and I feel gratified at the interest he evinces for _Bo;_ all the persons here who know him speak favourably of his character. His property in this country is worth at least one hundred thousand dollars, which brings him in no revenue whatever. Mrs. Toussard writes me that he speaks very affectionately of _Bo_, and I am sure I would like very much to confide him to his protection at some distant period, if he desired it, which can, however, scarcely be calculated upon, or expected, as he has daughters to provide for; and parents seldom find they have enough to satisfy their own posterity, much less to provide for that of their brothers. At all events, his intentions are very friendly.

I am, dear sir,
Yours affectionately,
E. P.

The Prince and Princess of Würtemberg are here, have invited me to see them, and particularly requested Bo should be presented to them. The prince is brother to the late king, and uncle to the ex-Queen of Westphalia. He expressed his surprise at his resemblance to the emperor, which is remarked by every one that sees him.

Bo has a great capacity for mathematics, and in general has made a great progress in his studies. I think he will at least have a good head—at least the persons who teach him mathematics say so—he appears to learn them more easily than the languages.

Miss Spear does not inform me of anything relating to my concerns, her last letter being dated last June.

Bo has grown eight inches since we sailed, and is now five feet seven inches.

P.S. May 23.—I have just received two letters from Miss Spear, one dated October, and the other March, the former enclosed in the latter.

Please have the enclosed letter put in an envelope, and addressed to the count—it not being respectful to send a single sheet of paper to a person of his rank ; and the postage is too dear to allow me to make the package larger for Amsterdam. I should like to know whether you receive this.

The Prince of Würtemberg, alluded to in this letter, was completely fascinated by the beauty and conversation of Madame Bonaparte, and said that Jerome had made a great mistake in deserting so charming a woman. Gortschakoff remarked : " Had she been near the throne, the Allies would have had more difficulty in overthrowing Napoleon." Talleyrand said : " If she were a queen, how gracefully she would reign !"

In her next letter we get a glimpse of how Madame Bonaparte availed herself of every opportunity to increase her income, and with what prudence she managed her business affairs.

MME. BONAPARTE TO WM. PATTERSON.

DEAR SIR,—I have this day received your letter of 24th July. Mr. Dixon writes me he has paid Mr. Vanderhope seven thousand five hundred florins on my account by your late orders. The exchange between Amsterdam and Geneva is always at a loss of four or five per cent. to me. That between London and this place gives a clear gain of ten or twelve per cent. to the English resident here. I had wished to profit by the English means of drawing my money, but find from Mr. Dixon that I should lose as much on the purchase of bills in America on London, as the exchange between England and the Continent would benefit me. Vanderhope allows me four per cent., which is also a consideration in favour of remitting my funds through Holland. For the present I am content to let my business remain in his hands, but I do not wish a further remittance to be made me until I write to you. It is precarious trusting large sums in the hands of individuals. I shall make the three thousand dollars sent by the " William " last a year, and will write to you when I desire more money. I have kept a regular account of *Bo's* expenses ; they amount to a thousand dollars in the last year. People are mistaken in supposing education is cheap here—it may be so to the natives, but everything is dear to strangers, who are cheated by all classes in this country.

I am fully aware of the little reliance to be placed on either promises or expectations from the B—— family. They are prodigal of professions in proportion as they are sparing in actions of generosity. Their habits of expense make it impossible for them to provide for the wants of others ; but, as they say kind things, it is but fair they should be answered in the same way. We reciprocate by all opportunities kind wishes on their part, and grateful expressions of mine—there can be nothing lost by this mutual expenditure of words, because I am too clear-sighted to be the dupe of ill-founded hopes. I have not changed in a single instance my plans. The offer of the house was something like reality of kindness. The count passes in the estimation of the world for being possessed of greater wealth, consistency of character and prudence than the others. The old lady, to do her justice, promises nothing more than she gives. She is said to be avaricious, which, I suppose, means that she does not spend more than her income. Whatever may be her means, she has immediately around her a number of helpless, extravagant relations to consume her fortune whenever she leaves it.

I shall, perhaps, go to Italy in two years, because, although I expect no advantage from such a measure, yet it is a duty to leave nothing undone which offers the most remote chance of benefit. It would be folly to do so, if I made a sacrifice of any kind, which cannot be the case, as, at all events, I shall be improving *Bo's* mind by acquaintance with a country curious in itself, and interesting from its historical recollections.

I am, dear sir, yours truly,
E. P.

After all her hesitation and refusals, Madame Bonaparte finally concluded to spend the winter of 1821-22 in Rome, and to take her son with her; and in a letter to her father gives her reasons for the step.

MADAME BONAPARTE TO WILLIAM PATTERSON.

GENEVA, October 16, 1821.

DEAR SIR,—I have resolved, by the advice of many persons, to spend this winter at Rome, and to take Bo with me. I confess my own opinion is, that this step will avail him nothing, unless it be the conviction that there is nothing to be expected from any one but himself, and that his success in the world must ultimately depend on his own exertions. Nothing, however, can console me for the moment, for the confusion, trouble, and expense this journey gives me, except the consciousness of having done everything in my power for his advantage. I hope his education will not suffer materially from this interruption of his studies, which I intend making him pursue during the few months we shall spend at Rome. He can get lessons there in Latin and Italian. I am perfectly sure we shall be equally desirous to leave Italy in the spring and to return to Geneva.

My desire was to defer this experiment until he was two years older, but as the old lady and the princess may not live so long, it has been urged to me that I was allowing an occasion to escape, which might be irrecoverable hereafter. . . . .

I can only add that I am grateful to the kind Providence which withheld from me the care of a larger family, and amidst all the trials and disappointments which have fallen to my share I take comfort to myself that I have only one child. I do believe that it is impossible to give children sufficient ideas of the necessity of economy and industry when parents are not in absolute want, and that it is only when they are reared in the midst of privation and starvation that they can be made to comprehend the folly of spending time and money on trifles.

I have taken three seats in a carriage which contains six passengers. The terms are fifteen Louis d'or each person hence to Rome, found by the driver for this sum in a seat and two meals per day, bed at night, and fire if wanted. I pay seven Louis d'or only for the maid, who sits on the box with the coachman. We must, however, pay something at the inn to servants, and at least three Louis to the coachman if content with him on our arrival, besides paying for the days we may desire to spend at large towns on the way. This bargain is said to be one of the best that has been made here, but I find it quite dear enough.

It is generally my luck to be cheated in every way, in spite of all my endeavours to avoid imposition. My banker here advises me to take circular notes to save commission to a banker at Rome. I have consulted every one upon the loss I experience of five per cent. in drawing my funds through Amsterdam, whilst the English residents here gain twelve on the exchange between London and Geneva. The result is, that bills bought in Baltimore on London are at a loss of ten per cent. ; therefore, added to the consideration of Vanderhope allowing me four per cent., I have lost less than if I had my money remitted through England. Vanderhope has advised me of the second remittance of three thousand dollars since my arrival in Europe. I do not desire a further remittance until I write to you to that effect, not liking to trust too much in any banker's hands at a time. As my return here in the spring is very certain, being resolved not to remain in Italy longer than the winter months, I desire that you will have the goodness to send my letters through the usual channel.

I remain, dear sir,

Yours affectionately,

E. P.

Bo has grown very tall, and I am persuaded he is quite as industrious and promising as other children of his age, but the solicitude and care of a parent are much greater than any common success can ever repay. His expenses are enormous; the Genevans of all classes cheat strangers ; and education, when I assure you his bills of all kinds amounted to a thousand dollars for the last year, is dearer than in America. The English have doubled the price of everything on the continent.

Madame Bonaparte and Jerome arrived at Rome about the middle of November, 1821, where, as we ascertain from the next letter, they were very kindly received by Madame Mère and by the princess. It was at the very beginning of their acquaintance, as we shall see, that a plan was suggested which became one of Madame Bonaparte's favourite schemes—the project of a marriage between Jerome, now sixteen years of age, and Charlotte, the youngest daughter of Joseph Bonaparte, who was at that time residing in America, under the name of the Count de Survilliers.

Of all Napoleon's brothers, Joseph had been the most devoted to his interests and his ambition. This devotion commenced in their youth, when Napoleon fell in love with Mademoiselle Désirée Clary, sister of Joseph's wife. The lady did not smile on the suit of the young soldier, but married General Bernadotte, and ultimately became Queen of Sweden.

Joseph was his brother's confidant in this unprosperous love affair, as he was in all the most important matters of his life. After Waterloo, he proposed to remain in France, and allow the emperor to escape to America, but the latter declined the generous offer. Joseph embarked, and eluding the British cruisers, arrived safely in the United States, where he remained until 1830.

MADAME BONAPARTE TO WILLIAM PATTERSON.

ROME, November 28, 1821.

DEAR SIR,—We are here since two weeks. The first week I was too unwell to see any one, or to announce my arrival; a cold, caught by crossing a mountain covered with ice at two o'clock in the morning, and from which I am not entirely recovered, obliged me to keep the house.

The Princess B.[3] had heard from Florence that I was on my

---

[3] Pauline Bonaparte (Princess Borghese) was the favourite sister of Napoleon, and the only one of his family who shared with him the exile of Elba, where she surrounded herself with some of the splendour and all of the etiquette of the imperial court. When Napoleon planned his return to France, Pauline acted as his confidante. She sacrificed her jewels in this undertaking, and in order to throw off suspicion gave a large party on the very night of the escape, at which she appeared with all the thoughtless gaiety and lively conversation which had marked her brightest days. When all was finally lost at Waterloo, Pauline established herself at Rome in the Borghese Palace, which became one of the most hospitable houses in the Eternal City. She gave frequent and elegant dinner-parties and weekly soirées, which were attended by the best of Roman society and by the most distinguished foreigners.

At the period of Madame Bonaparte's visit, Pauline, though forty years of age, was still considered one of the most beautiful women in Europe. Like Madame Bonaparte, she was *petite* in figure. One of her chief charms was a way to Rome. She wrote me a note, expressing her desire to see me instantly on my arrival, sent it to all the hotels in Rome, where I was not to be found, having taken rooms in a private house, until an American paying her a morning visit, she discovered my address. I answered her note by asking the hour her Highness would be pleased to receive me. She immediately sent her lady of honour in her carriage to convey me to the palace, since which I have been there every day.

I have waited on Madam [*Mère*], after her expressed desire that I should. They have all been very kind. The princess has presented me with an elegant ball-dress, a pink satin cloak, and a bonnet. She has new dressed Bo even to his flannel jacket, and has promised to allow him two thousand francs, or four hundred dollars annually to dress himself, until he marries, when the pension will cease, and she will give him a capital of forty thousand francs, or eight thousand dollars.

She and Madame wish Joseph to marry him to his youngest daughter, now in America, in which event the princess would leave something to him at her death. She has written this to her brother, and if he likes the match, she wishes me to take the child out, and to return to live in Rome myself for company for her.

Jerome is entirely ruined, his fortune, capital, income, everything spent, and his debts so large that his family can do nothing for him if they were inclined, which they are not. He has two children by his wife, who, I suppose, will be maintained by her family, since they have spent everything they had. The Princess B. says she has just income sufficient to maintain her rank, her husband allowing her fourteen thousand dollars annually. She

---

voice of singular sweetness, and although her conversation was always light and trifling, yet it was easy and graceful.

After repeated requests she obtained permission from the English Government to go to the sick-bed of her brother at St. Helena, but before she had departed the news of Napoleon's death reached Europe in August, 1821. In her appeal to the Earl of Liverpool she said : "The malady by which the emperor is attacked at St. Helena is mortal. I know that the moments of his life are numbered, and I should eternally reproach myself if I did not employ all the means in my power to soften his last hours, and to prove my devotion for him."

lives in great splendour in her husband's palace here during the winter, and at her country-house in summer. She makes many presents to her relations. The family of Louis will have fortunes from their mother. The family of the *ex*-Queen of Naples, Madame Murat, are not rich. Madame lives in a palace in great splendour also. She has a numerous family of grandchildren.

They are all pleased with Bo. I shall be directed by circumstances, which are very mutable in this life. The marriage, I know, was desired by Joseph, who wrote it to the princess. She answered that she desired one between the son of Lucien and Joseph's daughter, now in America. Since our arrival she is still more anxious that my son should be the person chosen instead of Lucien's son, which some time ago she had desired. She has written her preference of my son, but whether Joseph will choose him I know not. Madame, knowing the state of Jerome's finances and the impossibility of his ever doing anything for any one, wishes Joseph to provide for this child by a marriage. I have given my consent and promise that he shall remain with Joseph wherever he may be, but will not incur the expense of a sea-voyage unless Joseph writes me positively his intentions. This I have stated, as well as the impossibility of my giving any money, my income being with great economy barely sufficient for my own maintenance.

Yours truly, dear sir.

Bo feels the propriety of doing what I please on the subject of the marriage, and has no foolish ideas of disposing of himself in the way young people do in America.

I have taken rooms in Rome, where everything is horridly dear, ten guineas per month. I find there is great scarcity of money in all places and all families, and the great expectations and chatterings of travellers are exactly what I always supposed, nothing but smoke. I am very glad I came here. They have received us extremely well, and at all events I have done my duty, which is all we can do in this world, where no one is for his pleasure, and where events baffle all schemes of prudence. No one can command success; wisdom consists in profiting by lucky chances.

If the marriage is offered, I mean to accept it, and as things go in the generalities of families, shall esteem myself fortunate in being able to dispose of my son according to my views, instead of his choosing before his judgment is matured, and probably encumbering himself for life with a poor wife and clamorous offspring. Marriage ought never to be entered into for any other purpose than comfort, and there is none without consequence and fortune ; without these it is more prudent to live single.

Jerome himself writes to his grandfather from Rome, under the date of December 21, 1821 : " I have been received in the kindest manner possible by my grandmother, my uncles, and aunts, and cousins, and all my nearest and most distant relations, who are in Rome. We mean to stay here during the winter. . . . I have been so much occupied in looking for apartments for mamma, making tight bargains, and seeing my relations, that I have not had time to see anything of Rome, except St. Peter's celebrated church, which I have seen but superficially." He makes no allusion to the marriage which his relatives were endeavouring to effect between himself and his cousin.

MADAME BONAPARTE TO WILLIAM PATTERSON.

ROME, Dec. 21, 1821.

DEAR SIR,—Bo has been well received by his family ; his grandmother and his aunt have written to the count their desire to marry him immediately to his daughter now in America, and have asked me to take him in the spring, if the count still perseveres in wishing this connexion, which I know he did some time ago. I have told the P—— that I have no money to give, and as his uncle is so rich I imagine there will be no question of getting anything with the boy. It cannot be expected that I should rob myself, and as it is their wish to keep up the name through him, they will arrange matters to support him. There is one thing, however, which must be insisted upon : in the event of her death before his, part of her fortune must be his. I cannot expose him to the inconvenience of contracting expensive habits, losing his education by marrying at this time, too, without some certain support, if he should be left a widower. This point must be stipulated, and if my health should not allow me to accompany Bo in the spring, I must request you to act in my place. I shall write you particularly to this effect when we receive the count's answer to his mother's and sister's letters. I forwarded him two through France from the princess immediately after my having seen the ladies. . . . . I am rejoiced at having brought him here, although I feared the experiment might prove a dangerous one. At all events, there will be no loss except of a few months from his education. I wait the arrival of the count's letters, but shall not be surprised at a failure of the affair. For this life there is nothing but disappointment. The happiest are those who support misfortune best. I find that travellers exaggerate ; there is scarcity of money in all families, and in all countries people have poor relations to support. The K. W——[4] is ruined, his fortune entirely spent ; his wife has two children. I believe they are always asking money from his mother. She has not enough, had she ten times her fortune, to answer the demands of her family, who all address themselves to her as the fountain-head which is to supply twenty streams. *Bo* takes Latin and Italian lessons, spends every evening with his family, who do not go into any society beyond the family circle. He dines with them almost every day. He is grown handsome and tall ; speaks French quite as well as English. The old lady is a sensible, dignified person, highly respectable, and admired by every one. She promises nothing more than she performs, and raises no false expectations.

I remain, dear sir,
Yours affectionately,
E. P.

---

[4] The King of Westphalia.

CHAPTER VI.

Letters from Rome.—Kind Words but no Money, from the Bonaparte
Family.—The Matrimonial Speculation for Jerome.—The Match is
approved by all of the Family.—Jerome returns to America.—Letter from
William Patterson upon the Subject of the Marriage.—The Caprices of
the Princess Borghese.—Madame Bonaparte's Anxiety about her Son.
She visits Florence.—Last Meeting with her Husband.—Letters from
Paris.—1822.

WHILE in Rome, Madame Bonaparte was so wholly
engrossed with the scheme of marrying Jerome to the
daughter of Joseph, that she never once alluded, in any
of her letters written at this period, to any of the usual
sights of the city.   It has always been the custom of all
travellers who visit Rome, to seek an audience of the
Pope; but Madame Bonaparte makes no mention of
having paid her respects to Pius VII., the pontiff who
had refused to annul her marriage at the request of
Napoleon.   Both her time and Jerome's was otherwise
occupied.

In a letter from Jerome to his grandfather, dated
Rome, January 7, 1822, he says: "I have been now
seven weeks in Rome, and have been received in the
kindest and most hospitable manner possible by all my
relations who are in Rome.   And my father is expected,
but I don't know whether he will come.   My grand-

mother and my aunt and uncle talk of marrying me to my uncle's, the Count of Survilliers' daughter, who is in the United States. I hope it may take place, for then I would return immediately to America to pass the rest of my life among my relations and friends. Mamma is very anxious for the match. My father is also, and all of my father's family, so that I hope that you will also approve of it."

MADAME BONAPARTE TO WILLIAM PATTERSON.

ROME, January 8, 1822.

DEAR SIR,—I have already written you an account of our arrival and reception here. Bo has been received very affectionately by his relations. His aunt allows him a dollar a day to dress himself. I am, as usual, charged with the expense of his board and lessons, which, with the hire of my apartments, servant's wages, carriage hire and dress, eating and washing for him and myself, consume something more than my income. His grandmother and aunt are very anxious to have him married to his cousin in Philadelphia, as a means of getting him provided for, and have written their desire to his uncle.

As I plainly see, it is the only sure way of relieving myself of the expense he occasions me, and which I can ill afford. I have given my consent and now wait the answer from Philadelphia.

I go two or three times in the week to his aunt, who lives in great state; her husband has been compelled to allow her rooms in his palace, and fourteen thousand dollars income of her own fortune.

The grandmother is said to be rich; we may, however, make allowances for an exaggeration of one-half. She lives in great splendour, and with great economy; her principal expense being the interest of her palace and furniture—a palace here is worth about thirty thousand dollars the first purchase. She is very kind to Bo. He goes to see her every day. She gave him forty guineas to buy a horse, but as there was no allowance for his keep, I

persuaded Bo to hire one by the month. The fact is, her own children are always wanting money from her, which perhaps accounts
for her relying on my income to maintain her grandson, which appears to be the intention of all his family also. His father, they
all say, is ruined, therefore it is vain to expect anything from him.
I do, indeed, regret that there is no one of the whole connexion
rich enough to allow me twelve hundred dollars a year for Bo's
maintenance. He dines with them; rides with them, goes to their
boxes at the theatre, and they seem very much pleased with him.
He has resumed his family name, which piece of vanity may give
me some trouble about his passports. I am glad I brought him
because I like to know that nothing has been lost by not coming
after it.

The accounts of Mr. Harper, &c., were rather highly coloured, as
respected money matters and generosity. There is, it is true, every
other kind of attention, and it is certainly a point of some interest,
his being publicly acknowledged and approbated by the family.
From what I have heard and observed of the *old* lady, I could rely
upon any *promise she* would make, which cannot be said of every
one's promises; it does not seem much in her way to promise,
which I prefer to the way I have observed some persons have of
raising expectations which they forget to fulfil. *Bo* has received
your letter of the 1st November. I am very glad Stuart has
given up the picture, and obliged to you for taking the trouble of
getting it from him. It is the only likeness that has ever been
made of me. My other pictures are quite as like any one else as
me.

I am now curious to know Joseph's answer to the ladies' written
desire of a marriage. He told Madame Toussard some months
since that he would like it; he wrote it to his sister here; *she* did
not desire it at the time his letter reached her. Since our arrival
she changed and wrote to urge him to take Bo.

I can only say I have spent my time and money on this boy. I
shall give nothing more until my death. They do not expect me
to do anything, as I have been at the whole expense of his education. I shall not be at all surprised if Joseph has changed his mind
too by this time.

I have not written to Miss Spear since our arrival, on account

of the expense of postage. Have the goodness to tell her so, that
she may not attribute it to any want of regard. When I am near
a seaport I will write her a long account of everything. I should
write Polly and Edward,[5] but really the expense of sending letters
is a consideration. I generally wait for a private opportunity of
writing to my friends from this place, because the letters must be
sent to France—there are few vessels from this country.

I would be very much obliged to you if you could send me some
tobacco either to Dixon or to Leghorn, and write that it must be
kept until I claim it for my son's use.

This climate disagrees very much with me. I have been
plagued by a cough ever since my arrival, which I caught on the
road ; the fact is, *Bo* was so unwell all last winter at Geneva with
a cough, and so bilious all the summer, that it was one of my
reasons for coming here, as, although I did not say it, I was afraid
keeping him shut up at his lessons eleven hours a day might kill
him. He is quite well now.

I am, dear sir, yours affectionately,

E.

They expect the K. W. and his wife here on a visit to his
mother. I fancy he is coming to get money out of her. The
family are all like other families. After all said and done, *Bo*
owes a great deal more to me, because I have tried to give him an
education. I shall not see the K. W., nor would he like it himself, after the unhandsome way in which he has always conducted
himself. I shall hold my tongue, which is all I can possibly do
for him.

In order to further the scheme of the marriage of her
son to Joseph's daughter, Madame Mère, Cardinal
Fesch and Louis Bonaparte advised Madame Bonaparte
to send Jerome at once to America, that he might plead
his own cause with his Uncle Joseph and try the effect
of his handsome person and attractive manners upon the

---

[5] Her brother, and the wife of another brother.

young lady. The next letter is full of this proposed marriage. It will be observed that she is anxious for strong settlements, for, with her own unhappy experience before her, she was not disposed to put any faith in any merely verbal promises. She had set her heart upon this match, and looked upon any one that opposed it as " an idiot and an enemy."

MADAME BONAPARTE TO WILLIAM PATTERSON.

ROME, 29-30 January, 1822.

DEAR SIR,—Jerome sails in the " White Oak," to leave Leghorn the 14th or 20th of February. His grandmother, who has been very kind to him, his Uncle Louis and the Cardinal, all advise me to lose no time in sending him to his Uncle Joseph. The princess, after having been consulted the first person, and having approbated highly the project of embarking him, has since changed her mind now that his passage is engaged, and every preparation made for sending him. If Joseph should continue to desire the marriage it will be one that all the family desire, and the only probable way of ever getting anything like pecuniary aid for the boy from any of the family. Madame is most anxious for the match ; I do not think it absolutely necessary for me to go out, as I should think you might do everything I could do. The principal and only thing is to see that he will not be left without any provision if she dies before him, or that he will not be entirely dependent on her as long as she lives. They tell me here, Joseph means to give a hundred thousand dollars on the marriage. If he does not secure the whole or any part to her, there is nothing to be said, as the money becomes her husband's. But if he means to tie it up, I wish at least fifty thousand to be settled on my son. There is no knowing how marriages may turn out—women may treat husbands ill, leave them, die before them, but if a good provision be made for the husband, there is nothing lost by risking a marriage. I shall, if absolutely necessary, go out, when I receive Joseph's letters, although it will be horridly inconvenient to me ; and if he tells me his project is to give them a hundred thousand dollars without restriction, there is only for you to see it is so.

If he does not now intend the match, it will be well to place *Bo* at the Cambridge College.

If Joseph desires to have him in Philadelphia with him, of course it is better to let him stay with him as much as possible. His daughters are the best matches in Europe—in point of both money and connexion. They will have at least five hundred thousand dollars from him each, and something besides from their mother. They are the nieces of the Queen of Sweden. The family are so anxious for my son's marriage—Madame has refused to acknowledge the marriage of Lucien's daughter[6] with an Irishman on accouut of the inferiority of his birth. She would never forgive my son's marrying any woman but of high rank.

I must, my dear sir, caution you against listening to any advice from ——. She has always been an artful enemy of your family, and on the present occasion will have an interest in keeping my son for some of her granddaughters.

I will never consent to his marrying any one but a person of great wealth. He knows I can only recognize a marriage of ambition and interest, and that his name and rank require it.

Mrs. —— has been an old enemy of your family and of every one else she knows. Miss Spear, whatever her advice may be, cannot, I hope, influence you to the detriment of your family. Every one that attempts to advise you or him against this connexion, the first wish of my heart, is either an idiot or an enemy, and as such will be treated by me. The ——s may also try to be mischievous. I beg you, however, not to mention a word I have said about the interference and advice of anxious people. I desire Bo may be as much as possible, and altogether with his uncle, if he desires it. If the match should fail, he can be put at Cambridge.

---

[6] Letitia Bónaparte, the eldest daughter of Lucien, married the Honourable Thomas Wyse, of Waterford, Ireland, a member of the British Parliament. Their son, Lieut. Lucien Napoleon Bonaparte Wyse, of the French navy. is the leading member of the company formed for the exploration of the Darien Canal.

If Joseph makes the marriage it will be better for me to empower
you to act for me, to lose no time.   You hear first what he says
about the money, and then if you can get nothing else, ask for fifty
thousand.   I beg you neither to tell any of the family, nor aunt, nor
Miss Spear, a word about this marriage.   George and Henry[7] know
too little of the world to understand the propriety of this marriage.
The others, although I am sure they have Bo's interest at heart, as
well as George and Henry, have many prejudices and much folly
about love and idle matches.   The examination at Cambridge
takes place the 26th of August.   The boys are only entered then
or in December.

I refer you to Bo for the history of his aunt, the P——.   She has
treated him exactly as she has done all her other nephews—that is,
promised, and then retracted.   She makes a new will every day,
and has quarrelled with every human being on earth, and will finally
leave her property to strangers.   All that has been said of her is
not half what she deserves—neither hopes of legacies, nor any expectation can make any one support her whims, which are so extraordinary as to make it impossible not to believe her mad.

She chooses a new heir every week.   I can now only say, if my
presence is indispensably necessary, I will go to the United States
for a few months to secure everything about the marriage.

I certainly regret being separated from Bo, but parents must let
their children live where their interest or taste leads them.   All is
sacrifice on their part.   I do not expect my poor child to live where
I do, although his society would be a great comfort to me.   If the
marriage takes place, he must live with his uncle in America.   My
health, and the taste I have for European society, render it quite
impossible for me to live near them, as probably they will continue
in Philadelphia.

I hope and trust, my dear sir, that you will have the goodness to
attend to the security of a maintenance for the boy, either by ascer-
taining that the sum of one hundred thousand dollars, promised as
her marriage portion, is given in common, unfettered by trustees,
or that the sum of fifty thousand be secured to him.   Do not talk
of the fifty until you find how they mean to arrange the hundred

---

[7] Brothers of Madame Bonaparte.

thousand. As to the Princess Borghese, she declares she will give nothing, either during her life or after her death. She has made the same promise to all her other nephews, and revoked it solemnly afterwards. She is quite mad.

In February, while Jerome was at Leghorn waiting to embark, he wrote to his grandfather, saying: "Mamma is still in Rome, and is not decided whether she will embark in the spring for America or not. I should rather think not, as the climate does not suit her, and her health is bad in the United States. I am very glad that I shall soon have the pleasure of seeing you and all my relations, and my country; but, on the other hand, I am going to leave mamma and my relations on my father's side, who have been so very kind to me during my stay in Rome."

Sailing from Leghorn on February 23, Jerome arrived in New York on the 12th of April. He wrote immediately to his grandfather saying that before going to Baltimore he would pass a few days with his Uncle Joseph at Bordentown. "Mamma has written to you the object of my journey. I left her in Rome. She intends to go thence to Geneva, there to remain, her health being too delicate [as she thinks] to support the American climate."

In answer to this letter Mr. Patterson told him the plan he proposed, of stopping a few days with his uncle, was very proper. In his next letter Jerome informs his grandfather that he has seen his uncle, who received him in the kindest manner, but he does not say anything in reference to the special object of his visit.

We have already seen from Madame Bonaparte's letters, that Jerome's relatives residing in Italy were in favour of his marriage ; and it will be seen from the following letter from his Grandfather Patterson that he as well as Count de Survilliers, the young lady's father, also approved of it.

WILLIAM PATTERSON TO MADAME TOUSSARD.

BALTIMORE, 2nd March, 1822.

MY DEAR MADAME TOUSSARD,—When I had last the pleasure of seeing you in Philadelphia, you mentioned that the Count de Survilliers was desirous to marry his youngest daughter, lately arrived in this country, to my grandson, Jerome. I received within a few days a letter from my daughter, dated at Rome, 21st Dec., wherein she says that her son was very kindly received by his grandmother and other relations, and that they had written to the count in this country recommending that the above match should take place. My daughter and Jerome will, in consequence, remain at Rome until the answer from the count is received by his mother and sister.

If you have an opportunity you will oblige me by making yourself acquainted with the count's intentions and everything respecting this business, as far as they can be ascertained with propriety ; also that you will inform me of the age and disposition of the young lady, how she stands in the estimation of those who have visited her, and whether handsome or otherwise. This is an unusual way of making matches in this country, for those who are capable of choosing for themselves ; but, if it should take place, I hope it will be for the best—at any rate, it will keep the family and property better together than by marrying with strangers. Jerome is said to be very handsome, and is certainly very promising for a boy of his age, and you may well suppose it will afford me great pleasure to see him happily settled in life before my own departure.

My daughter was in bad health, from a cold taken on her way from Geneva to Rome, and was fearful she might not get rid of her complaint very speedily. With my best respects to Dr. Gillespie, your sister and family, believe me, with sincere regard, my dear madame,

Your assured friend and servant,
WILLIAM PATTERSON.

A few weeks after Jerome sailed, his father arrived in Rome, as we ascertain from a letter of Madame Bonaparte to her son.

MADAME BONAPARTE TO JEROME NAPOLEON BONAPARTE.

ROME, March 8, 1822.

Your father arrived yesterday. Wrote to your aunt, who replied she would not see him, because he would begin *de lui parler des choses désagréables;* he went, however, and found her in bed. She pretended we came to Rome uninvited by her; that she received us from compassion. He contradicted this, &c. I have not seen or heard from him.

I leave this, the 14th, for Geneva, with the Packards, where I think I shall remain until I hear from you whether I must go to America. Mrs. Weis told me what I have said of your father, last night, at Torlonca's. Your aunt sent to me for the dress she gave me before you went away, saying she would return it in an hour, and kept it. The Princess G. says she served her exactly such a trick about a cap she had given her. I am sorry you did not write to Madame by Tari, whom I have seen since his return.

I have not seen Madame or the C——s since you went away. I met Napoleon the other evening at P. Gabriel's. Be sure to write to all the family, and send by Italy. I have heard of the arrival of your uncle's daughter in Philadelphia, from Mrs. Toussard.

Since writing the above, your aunt has sent back the dress. I suppose she has been made ashamed of her conduct by the family.

Most probably I shall not see your father.   He does not wish it for
many reasons.

Recollect all my advice.   They have sent me a bill for six hundred
cigars you took at Leghorn.

For heaven's sake spend as little money as possible, and recollect the smallness of my income and the many privations it subjects
me to.   If Mrs. Toussard would come out we might live together
in Paris.   I am very lonesome, and foresee nothing but poverty and
solitude.   I shall go to America if you think there is the least
necessity for it.   Let me know everything about my finances.   Do
read as much as you can, and improve in every way.   I ask you to
reward my cares and anxieties about you, by advancing your own
interests and happiness.   I am very uneasy about you, and almost
blame myself for not going with you to take care of you, and shall
never forgive myself if you meet any accident by being alone.   Do
take care of yourself morally and physically.   I have been unwell
with my indigestion again, vomiting in earnest, but not in a gold
basin.   I paid Snell for the cigars for which his correspondent at
Leghorn sent in a bill.

Saturday, March 9th.—Madame and your father have been at
the princess's.   Your father is very intimate with her.   Napoleon[8]
was there last night.   They seem to have all made up for the
moment.

MADAME BONAPARTE TO WILLIAM PATTERSON.

ROME, March 8. 1822.

DEAR SIR,—Bo sailed in the " White Oak " from Leghorn, the
23rd of February, bound to New York, which I hope he will reach the
1st April.   His Uncle Louis sent a confidential person with him to
Leghorn to stay with him until he embarked.   He had the goodness
to recommend him in the most particular manner to the American
Consul there and to Mr. Webb.

His grandmother has been very kind to him, gave him shirts and
many other things for his sea-voyage.   They all approved his being

---

[8] Son of Louis Bonaparte.

sent to his uncle, and all desire the marriage with the young lady lately arrived in Philadelphia, which must at all events take place, as it is the only means of providing for him. His father is now here—arrived yesterday morning. I have not seen him, nor has he expressed any wish to see me, and, as I leave this place on the 14th for Geneva, it is not likely we shall meet. They say he is ruined, and is come here to get money from his mother. I must tell you the P—— of B——[9] is exactly what I had heard—capricious beyond all possibility of expression. She has retracted all her fine promises to my son, the very same promises having been before made to all her other nephews, whom she has quarrelled with and turned out of doors one after the other. She abused every member of the family to me, and hates them all, her husband in the bargain, sees none of them, because it is impossible for them to support her whims, which so nearly resemble lunacy that many persons have been put into the mad-house for much fewer symptoms.

It is my ardent wish to marry *Bo* to his cousin. Let nothing prevent it, as he has no other chance of being provided for. His family have certainly shown him every distinction and mark of affection in their power. He has equal rank with them, and will always be in the first society in every country ; but altho' his birth makes him of high rank, his fortune is not likely to correspond with it. The only way to maintain him in the only position that can be natural to his name, is to connect him with his father's family by this marriage, ardently desired by them *all*.

His grandmother has preserved very justly the dignity of conduct which belongs to greatness when unfortunate. She likes him very much, and has signified very pointedly to her family that she will never countenance improper marriages for them. Her desire is to marry them as much as possible in the family, on account of the name, as well as to preserve the fortune in the connexion. I beg, my dear sir, you will advise Bo in this sense, and discourage all that tendency to romance and absurd falling in love which has been the ruin of your own family, at the same time not allowing your judgment, which is naturally good, to be misled by the deceitful advice of people who will not fail to envy such an advantageous

---

[9] Princess Borghese.

marriage. I am a very fond parent, but no foolish or mistaken affection can ever make me sanction an improper match for my son. He owes a great deal to me, a great deal to his position in society, and we both demand that he should never part with a single particle of his consequence, which might be lost in some boyish connexion begun in folly and to end in children, obscurity, and poverty. I am so much agitated about this child's destiny, so torn by desires and fears, that I have brought on since his departure a complaint which renders me almost incapable of doing anything : it is continual vomiting. Everything that I eat swells me almost to bursting, even my feet, nor can I get relief unless I throw it off my stomach. I think, too, this climate has been of great disadvantage to me, which, with a cold taken on the road and the mental agitation *Bo's* affairs have caused me, have made my feelings intolerable. If I hear of his safe arrival and his marriage, I shall be quite well again. I wish him to be as much as possible with his uncle. I fear a dispensation from the Pope will be necessary, which may occasion some delay—his relations here will get it when necessary. His father, they say, regrets not having seen him before he sailed, and is very confident of the marriage taking place.

I dare not expect anything that would give me so much pleasure, as it would exactly meet my wishes, and they have ever been woefully disappointed.

If, however, there is no chance of the match, the next best thing will be to place him at the Cambridge College, and to see that he does not spend too much money. If his uncle desires he should stay with him until the dispensation from the Pope arrives, he must do it. If you can find out that he means to give one hundred thousand dollars, which they say here, on the marriage, so much the better ; but do not let the match be lost, for really without it he has little prospect of support, and a profession, however desirable for him, is more easily talked about than effected.

Yours, dear sir, very affectionately.

After her son's departure Madame Bonaparte remained in Rome a few weeks, and then visited Florence.

It was at this time that she saw her husband for the first and last time after their separation at Lisbon in 1805. They met in the gallery of the Pitti Palace. On seeing her Jerome started, and whispered to the Princess of Würtemberg, his second wife : " That is my American wife." No words passed between them. Her stay in Florence at this time was a very brief one, for in May she was again in Geneva, and early in the summer of 1822 she returned to Paris, from which city we again have a letter to her father.

To Jerome she wrote, on the 2nd of June, that she was just going to set out for Liverpool to embark for New York ; but she was taken with a bilious rheumatism, which, though she had recovered when she wrote, had hindered her from making the journey, wherefore she determined to embark for Havre, if she did not in the meantime receive a letter from her son telling her it was unnecessary. It will be seen by her letter to Mr. Patterson that she had some doubts of the success of the project about which she had written and talked so constantly during the preceding winter and spring.

MADAME BONAPARTE TO WILLIAM PATTERSON.

PARIS, June 19, 1822.

DEAR SIR,—I received your letter of the 15th April announcing *Bo's* arrival. I have been unwell for a month, but am quite well at present. I had intended going to America, thinking my presence there might have been useful to the child. Perhaps nothing that his grandmother and the family so much desired may take place, and my going could do no good. The best plan is to keep the whole affair secret if it fails, as people get nothing by publishing their disappointments. It was the count's wish two years ago, but I well know there is little reliance to be placed on any of that race. My opinion always was to give the boy a good education, and to place little faith in kind words and fair promises. If he should desire the match, I require very positive assurances, or rather deeds, securing one hundred thousand dollars to my son, as she may die or separate from him. If they give the money in common, without tying it upon her, it will do; but I cannot risk leaving the child to their generosity. It is very probable they may have some other plan for her, in which event it will be proper to put the child at Cambridge; and I beg you to attend to his education, and see that he does not lose his time. I wish him to be an economist in everything but education—on that I never did and never will refuse money. It is all he can securely depend upon, and must not be neglected. I will sail at a week's warning if there be any probability of the marriage; but if there be none, it is as well for me not to risk having my feelings hurt by seeming to run after it. I wish, if it does take place, to be very explicit about securing a maintenance to *Bo;* perhaps giving the money in common would not answer. You would of course consult a clever lawyer on the subject, and have all arranged in such a way that there would be no flaw. If they should *exact* that he should only have the money during *his* life, and that it should revert to his heirs at his death, I do not oppose that; but you need not suggest this to them.

Please send the enclosed letter for *Bo* to some one of your friends with an express order to deliver it to him personally, and not by any chance to send it to the house of any one in Philadelphia where he may be staying.

I remain, dear sir,

Yours affectionately.

Madame Bonaparte said she was willing to return to America, provided her presence there would aid her matrimonial schemes for her son. But, having received letters which informed her that the proposed marriage with Joseph's daughter was not likely to come off, she writes :—

MADAME BONAPARTE TO WILLIAM PATTERSON.

PARIS, July 7th, 1822.

DEAR SIR,—I have received a letter from Bo, dated 22nd May, and one from you previously, dated 15th April. I had come on here with the intention of going to the child, supposing from the communications made to me two years ago through Mrs. Toussard, with others made to his family more recently (a year since), added to the unanimous and strong desire they all expressed to me last winter that such an event should take place—imagining, I say, that it would be improper in me to absent myself at a period so important to his future interests, I had resolved to embark, although suffering under a very severe illness, which kept me in my room six weeks, when I received a letter from *Bo*, by which I plainly saw that I might save myself the trouble.

There is nothing can, or ever will, surprise me in that family. The only way is to act and feel exactly as if they said and promised nothing, to hold when one touches, but not to take a step to catch anything from them. They have been all civility and kindness, and will always be ready to acknowledge him. This I do not doubt, but I very much doubt their desire or intention to part with money when they can help it. Some members of the family have spent all they had ; others, much wiser, hold on to what they have.

The old lady is a person of strong natural sense. She desired, and has said, I believe, all she could to effect the arrangement her son suggested two years since. It would be useless to endeavour to account for his present conduct, silly to appear at all offended by it, and mad ever to calculate on any advantage (pecuniary, I mean) from them. When I undertook the journey last year, I merely meant to fulfil the duty of losing nothing by my own inaction, and I still think it was a prudent measure to show that I never would be an obstacle to the boy's advancement.

H

There is one advantage from the connexion, which is, that he is placed by it in the first circles of Europe, that his acquaintance has been sought by persons of the highest rank, and that, with very little money, he can always live with them. This I consider a great point ; and although I sincerely deplore any circumstance or combination of events which oppose his being rich, I console myself under the present disappointment by the comforting conviction that his name and rank are beyond the influence of any one's caprice.

The only thing left us to do is to try to give him ambition, to prevent him ever making a foolish match, which, by the way, his grandmother gave me to understand would mortally offend her ; to seek the best means of perfecting his education ; one part of good education is the most rigid economy, and I fear the example of commercial cities is less calculated than any other to effect so desirable an object.

If by chance the uncle goes back to his former dispositions, you know that not the most amiable verbal promises must induce him to put himself in dependence, that parchment deeds examined by a skilful lawyer are the best and only guarantee for happiness, and certainly the only assurances I shall ever rely on for him.

The boy must neither seek nor avoid being with his relations. If they invite him, let him go to them ; if they do not, he is not called upon to run after them. He ought to avoid lingering in Philadelphia on his journeys to and from college, to save the awkwardness of not being intimate when in the same place with such near relations, and to save the comments of a gossiping population. His conduct should appear natural, respectful, and as affectionate as nephews generally are to uncles, independently, however, of all obsequiousness or meanness. He is in every respect upon an equality with them, and I think there would have been entire reciprocity of advantages in forming a connexion. Although he has not money, he has other advantages. He has name, rank, good natural capacity, good appearance, and if he does not suit them, there are perhaps many other families that he will suit. Another capital point is that he is not a woman, it being much easier to marry sons than daughters—I mean, to advantage ; for, as to the marriages in America, they are simple acts of youthful folly and

inexperience, and, although they may be liable to fewer inconve-
niencies in a commercial or republican society than they would be
in Europe, are still absurd and improper in many respects. . . .
I have no confidence in the banks, insurance companies, road
stocks, or, in short, in any stock in Baltimore. The people of
business there all live above their means, all speculate to support
the extravagant wants of their families, and from folly are driven to
dishonesty. Their want of moral feeling and scandalous effrontery
when detected in the commission of crimes which conduct to the
pillory in other countries, have entirely destroyed the reputation of
the place, and made me take a resolution to sell out the little property I unwarily confided to Baltimore companies. I shall wait,
however, until people forget the explosion that took place three
years ago ; human credulity is so great that confidence may
perhaps revive and purchasers be found for what I think very
precarious property. I can never again consider any stock but
government at all secure, but my want of reliance on all other
kinds is no reason why others should not be firm believers, and
their faith may serve me effectually by giving me a tolerable price
for my property when I decide upon the time to sell it.

Prince Jerome is entirely ruined. He is soliciting permission
from government to change his residence. He and his wife wish
to live with his mother, who, according to present appearances,
will have them to maintain. She has consented to take them into
her house, and to lend them a country house in summer. I must
say the old lady behaves as well as any one could in her position,
and is much respected by every one. I wish *Bo's* education to be
particularly attended to—on that no money to be spared ; every
other kind of saving is a gain, and no one can be more disposed to
save in everything than I am, but a good education is never too
highly paid. Money spent in that way brings a good interest to
every one. Adieu, my dear sir. I think I shall return to Geneva
in some weeks, this place being much too expensive for me. Do
not make me any remittances until I write to you. Exchange is
much against people getting money either from America in Europe,
or from Amsterdam to Geneva. I can make out some plan not to
draw for money yet, particularly as I get six per cent. for my
money in America. I shall let you know when I want remittances !

Vanderhope allows me four per cent. for the money I have in his hands, which my banker in Geneva will not do.

This letter was quickly followed by the following characteristic one :—

MADAME BONAPARTE TO WILLIAM PATTERSON.

PARIS, July 10, 1822.

DEAR SIR,—I have received a letter from you since Bo's arrival, dated April 15th and May 8th. I am sorry to find there is little chance of what I destined for his advancement, but nothing is surprising on the part of those people. The only thing left is for me to put this by with the rest of my earthly trials, and to console myself by the consciousness of having lost nothing by my own folly. I have consulted one of the professors of the Cambridge College respecting the requisites for admittance there. I fear *Bo's* deficiency in Greek may prove an obstacle on the present occasion. West Point is not by any means a proper place for him, it never having been my intention to give him a military education. I desire more than anything on earth that he may be perfectly well educated—his position in life makes it more important for him than for any one ; and to effect this object has been the endeavour of my whole life. I wish him to be a strict economist, a character much ridiculed by the former great people of Baltimore, whose late misfortunes and errors still more confirm me in my desire that my son should on all occasions attend to frugality. There are some idle boys at Cambridge, whose extravagant habits will not, I hope, be imitated by Bo. Sons of noblemen, heirs to twenty thousand sterling annually, are less expensive than the sons of our merchants, which is the great reason of the constant depredations committed on all moneyed institutions in Baltimore, by directors, whose yearly expenditure in their private establishments exceeds their capital. I hope and trust that the child will have too much good sense to be affected by any of the shameful examples of prodigality or idleness which are to be found in all colleges, and that the confidence I repose in him, by allowing him to reside there without my protection, will not be abused.

Should the count retrograde to his former dispositions, I shall give my consent on proper securities being given of permanent advantages. I hope that *Bo* will never allow the silly fancies and romantic nonsense of American boys to change his natural good judgment. Nothing can equal the absurd folly of parents there, or the whimsical self-willed conduct of the young people, who launch into life with the same confidence in their own opinions that sixty years of experience only give in other countries. I think of returning to Geneva, this place being much too expensive for my habits; Mrs. Galatin has some idea of taking the journey with me, which, independent of the pleasure and comfort of her society, will be a means of reducing the expense of a private conveyance. I generally travel by the diligence, incognito; but my health is not sufficiently established to allow me to drive three nights, which must be done between Paris and Geneva. If commerce between America and France be continued on a favourable footing, Havre is the best way of writing to me, on account of postage, which is a very serious consideration in Europe. I shall write when I want further remittances, which I do not at present.

Yours, dear sir, affectionately.

MADAME BONAPARTE TO WILLIAM PATTERSON.

PARIS, August 3, 1822.

DEAR SIR,—I contemplate leaving this place on the 4th of the month, for Geneva, where I shall pass the winter. Mrs. Galatin is not entirely decided on visiting that place, therefore I shall depart by the first occasion.

I suppose Bo is at college by this time, where I hope he will not lose his time. I regret that his dog could not go with him, which, if I had known, I should have insisted on keeping him with me, as a reward for the poor beast's fidelity and many other good qualities which he possesses, not to mention his great intelligence, which renders him superior to half the persons one meets in the world.

The Galatins have shown me great attention and kindness since my arrival here. I have been asked to dine every day with them, and Mrs. Galatin urged me to reside with them during an illness of some weeks, which, however, I refused to do. Poor Madame Villette is as obliging and good, and fond of dinner company as she ever was.

CHAPTER VII.

WHILE the proposed marriage was pending between Jerome and his cousin, the Princess Charlotte, the King of Westphalia wrote to his brother Joseph that such a union would render him very happy, as well as his wife, who wrote at the same time to express a kind interest in the first born of her husband, and a desire to benefit the young man, of whose birthright she, although innocently, had deprived him. Madame Mère was also strongly in favour of the match, as the following letter shows :—

MADAME MÈRE TO JOSEPH BONAPARTE.

"MON TRÈS-CHER FILS.— . . . Vous aurez avant ce moment-ci embrassé Charlotte ; elle vous sera d'une grande consolation. *Vous aviez raison d'être décidé à la réunir avec le fils de Jérôme. Ce jeune homme est ici depuis deux mois ; j'en suis émerveillée ; il n'est pas possible de trouver son aplomb et son bon sens à son âge, et sans doute Charlotte serait heureuse.* Vous trouverez ci-joint copies des lettres du père et de Catherine, dont je vous ai envoyé les originaux par un autre canal, qui vous marquent le désir de voir effectuer cette union. *Je vous ai écrit ainsi que Pauline, le 5 décembre, qu'elle promettait pour cette union 300,000 fr. à sa mort.* Ainsi, si vous êtes du même avis, *il ne s'agirait que de lui écrire pour se rendre sur-le-champ en Amérique.* . . . Donnez-moi souvent vos nouvelles et celles de *ma chère Charlotte* et soyez convaincu du tendre attachement avec lequel je vous embrasse tous deux.

"Louis et son fils sont ici, et se portent fort bien.

"*Addio, caro figlio, sono la*

"*Signé :* VOSTRA OTTIMA MADRE.

"ROME, 25 janvier, 1822."

TRANSLATION.

MY DEAREST SON,—Before this you will have embraced your Charlotte ; she will be a great comfort to you. You were right to decide to marry her to Jerome's son. The young man has been here two months. I am amazed at him ; it is hardly possible to find so much *aplomb* and good sense in one of his age, and there is no doubt that Charlotte will be happy.

You will find enclosed copies of the letters from his father and Catherine, the originals of which I have sent you by another channel ; they will show you their desire to see this union effected. I have written to you, as Pauline did also, that she has promised, in the event of this marriage, three hundred thousand francs to be paid at her death. If you are of the same opinion, it will only be necessary to write to Jerome to return to America at once. . .

Give me frequent news of yourself, and of my dear Charlotte, and be convinced of the tender love with which I embrace you both. Louis and his son are here, and are very well.

Addio, dear son, I am,

VOSTRA OTTIMA MADRE.

ROME, 25 January, 1822.

Jerome's Uncle Louis also highly approved of the match, and after his departure for America wrote to him that "he loved him tenderly, and regretted his absence, but was consoled with the hope that it was for his good."

Madame Mère, anxious to see the projected marriage actually realized, at the end of April again addressed her son Joseph on the subject, urging it vehemently.

After the visit Jerome paid his Uncle Joseph, upon his first arrival in America, he called upon him a second time, but the Count de Survilliers was absent "on his travels." Jerome then proceeded to Lancaster, Mass., for the purpose of preparing, under a tutor, for entering Harvard College the following winter.

We gather from a letter from Jerome to his grandfather, dated July 28, 1822, that the matrimonial project was already abandoned, in his mind at least. He says: "Mamma's letter is dated Paris, April. She begins thus: 'I am now in Paris looking for an occasion to sail for America, feeling so much anxiety about your concerns there, and fearing you require my presence and advice on many subjects. It puts me to great inconvenience to make the voyage, but I prefer any personal inconvenience to leaving you without advice. I shall try to sail from Havre, but, if I cannot find a good vessel there, I must go to Liverpool. It is my intention and desire to embark before the 1st of July, therefore you may expect me.' But, as this letter is dated April, she cannot have received any from me since my arrival in this country ; and if she waits until she receives one of my letters, I do not think she will embark; but she may have embarked before my letter will have reached her, and if she has, she will probably be here in a very short time. She also mentions in her letter, that she had not received any letters from my uncle (who assured me and even showed me the copy of the letter he had written her), nor from Madame de Toussard in answer to hers from Rome."

Madame Toussard, the intimate friend of Madame Bonaparte, after the marriage scheme was broken off, wrote to Mr. Patterson from Philadelphia: "I meet Joseph Bonaparte and his daughter very frequently in company; she is in size a dwarf and excessively ugly. Jerome is quite too handsome for her; it would be a great sacrifice. The present report is that Achille Murat[1] is coming out to marry her." The young lady finally married Napoleon, the eldest son of Louis Bonaparte, who died during a revolutionary outbreak in Italy, in the spring of 1831, leaving his brother Louis Napoleon the heir of the empire, and head of the Bonaparte family.

About the middle of August, 1822, Madame Bonaparte returned once more to Geneva, where she spent the following autumn and winter. Her letters written at this time are very characteristic.

---

[1] Achille Murat was the oldest son of Joachim Murat, King of Naples, and Caroline Bonaparte, sister of Napoleon. He resided in Florida for many years, and died there in 1847. He married the daughter of Byrd Willis, a grand-niece of Washington.

MADAME BONAPARTE TO WILLIAM PATTERSON.

GENEVA, 15th September, 1822.

DEAR SIR,—I find, with pleasure, that Bo is in a clergyman's house, preparatory to entering college. The information given me last summer at Paris by one of the professors, accidentally there at the same time with myself, made me fear that the child's knowledge of Greek was insufficient to admit his being received. It would in that case have been perhaps necessary to place him at the military school at West Point, which I would have regretted on many accounts, although I am told a pretty good education may be had there.

My letters from America induced me to change my plan of going there, and rather to return to this place, which combines cheapness, or rather comparative cheapness, with great resources of society. I have found my friend, the Princess Potemkin, here. She was always particularly kind to, and fond of my son, which is a great reason for my feeling pleasure in her society, although she has become so excessively bigoted in her religious sentiments, and so determined to convert me, that I feel less comfort than formerly with her. I hope *Bo* will attend to his studies, and avoid bad company and expensive habits. I regret excessively that his dog could not go with him, not only because he would defend him from danger at night, but because he could amuse him during his hours of relaxation, and be a safer companion than many others he will meet. I am anxious to learn whether the examination for Cambridge has proved satisfactory.

I remain, dear sir,

Yours affectionately.

I shall write Miss Spear very soon, having been so continually occupied with visits and parties since my return, that I have not had a moment to myself.

MADAME BONAPARTE TO WILLIAM PATTERSON.

GENEVA, October 15th, 1822.

MY DEAR SIR,—I have no letters from Bo since the 29th June. There is a report that his grandmother is dead, which may be true, but I have no letters from any of the family. I write you this in haste, and beg you to make him acquainted instantly with the report. I hope it is not true. She appeared to me an estimable person in every respect ; showed great fondness for this poor child. I lament his having left her so soon, as, from the sense and penetration which distinguished her, I am convinced she would have taken great interest in him had he been more with her. She appeared to be exempt from the shuffling and double-dealing common to people on the Continent of Europe, which troublesome qualities are as useless to their possessors as wearisome to those on whom they are exercised.

I have established myself for the winter in this place, which agrees very well with my health. I hope *Bo* is comfortably and usefully established, and that his good conduct and attention to his studies will justify the confidence reposed in him by my trusting him without my superintendence, and at too great a distance to profit by my counsels. I beg you, my dear sir, to endeavour to inculcate to him the necessity and propriety of care and frugality in his mode of living, which the young people of the present day are far too neglectful of. I well remember that the examples of extravagance in our family are little calculated to enforce what I so much desire for this child, but I hope the advice I have given him may in some measure counteract the effects of imprudent conduct in those he now lives with.

I shall write the instant I have any confirmation of the death of Madame.

Adieu,
Yours affectionately.

MADAME BONAPARTE TO WILLIAM PATTERSON.

GENEVA, 11th December, 1822.

DEAR SIR,— . . . . I am most happy to learn that Bo is applying himself assiduously to his studies, and that his absence from me has not abated his diligence or ambition.   It is possible that my great and unceasing efforts to stimulate him to farther exertion might have teased him into idleness, as young people are often perverse and self-willed ; not that I, however, can complain of these qualities in him, but have rather cause to rejoice in the goodness of his disposition.   However, after much reflection, I am not now sorry that he is under college discipline.   The report of his grandmother's death has been contradicted in the gazettes, and from some intelligence given me by a lady who has lately visited Italy, I am confirmed in the assurance of her being still alive.   I am very glad of it for many reasons, besides really respecting and admiring the dignity of her character, and the strong natural ability which distinguishes her.   The will published must have been the invention of the editor of the paper who so prematurely announced her decease.   I have not heard from his uncle for a long time, and concur with you in the idea that he is waiting the operations of time and his own expediency.   He is a prudent character. As I have had no little experience of the versatility of the politics of that family, I shall not be surprised if they confine their affection for Bo to kind words, of which, to do them justice, they have been very lavish.

Their reception of Bo was not only affectionate, but highly flattering, which latter was a proof of penetration, for, without partiality, I may say that there is not in the world a boy who combines greater intelligence with more remarkable personal beauty. In his situation a good appearance is important, because, although every one cannot appreciate mental superiority, the most stupid and ignorant are sensible to a handsome exterior, and for one conspicuously placed as he is, it is fortunate that he is not misshapen nor disgraced by vulgar common features.   Mrs. Toussard writes me that Mrs. Sherlock has made a love-match with Mr. Dorsey. As poor Mrs Sherlock never was gifted with much sense, nor tormented by any aspirings after greatness, one cannot be surprised at her marrying her father's secretary. I hope, however, she has taken some care of the interests of her daughter.

I am very much obliged to you for your care of poor Le Loup. The poor animal has been accustomed to much attention, and was considered one of the handsomest dogs in Europe. I hope he has a warm place to sleep in, as the cold would certainly kill him, having been in the habit of sleeping on a mattress with sheets and blankets, with his head on his master's pillow. I fancy the black faces in the kitchen must have frightened him, as he had been used to drawing-rooms and fine ladies here.

I hear Mrs. R. P.[2] is coming out ; she will be the best sailor in the world. Her sisters are not yet married, which, considering their persevering endeavours and invincible courage, rather surprises me.

I remain, very affectionately yours,

E. P.

Miss Spear[3] places every year longer intervals between her letters. If I do not write her more frequently it is because I know nothing here that could interest her, as she is unacquainted with the actors of the theatre upon which I am. She has much information that would interest me, because I know every one she sees. I suppose she spends her winters at Washington, as usual, with the general's family.

MADAME BONAPARTE TO WILLIAM PATTERSON.

GENEVA, 24th December, 1822.

DEAR SIR,—I have been here since the middle of August, and I find my health much improved by my residence in this place, which, indeed, suits me better in every respect than Paris.

---

[2] Mrs. Robert Patterson, a sister-in-law of Madame Bonaparte, and grand-daughter of Charles Carroll, of Carrollton.

[3] Miss Nancy Spear, aunt of Madame Bonaparte, was in the habit of going to Washington every year to attend the sessions of Congress. Her brother-in-law, General Smith, commander of the old Maryland line during the American revolution, resided there, and was a member of Congress. Mr. William Patterson, another brother-in-law, left her a legacy on condition that she gave up attending the sessions of Congress.

There is more society and of the best sort in Europe, to be had on more easy terms than in larger towns. The French language is, however, indispensable, being that alone spoken in company.

There are balls or parties every night, and I have not spent one during five months at home. My intimate friend is a lady of your age, who never passes a day in her own house unless she gives a ball or a card party, which she does every Friday. . . . . I am happy to learn *Bo* is industrious, and that he has a chance of entering college in February. The report of his grandmother's death has been contradicted by those who published it. I am very glad it was untrue. It is perhaps as well that he should be in an American college for two years, although I should not have thought of changing the plan of his education, had not the views presented to me by his family induced me to consent to his departure.

I shall never regret taking Bo to Italy, because, although people cannot command success, they ought to secure to themselves their own approbation, and the conviction of having done all that depends on their own exertions. Bo is neither deficient in capacity nor the knowledge of the demands of his situation in life. I think myself fortunate that he was not born a fool, which two-thirds of the children brought into the world are ; had he been one, it would have embarrassed me exceedingly to know what to do with him. It is only permitted to women to be idiots, or men whose fortunes have been accumulated by their wiser ancestors, and which they may enjoy without trouble. . . . . *Bo's* genius for mathematics is more remarkable than for the acquirement of languages, although he seems not unwilling to submit to the inconvenience and toil of learning Greek.

Dec. 27.—I have kept my letter a day or two, the weather having been too cold for me to go to the post-office, and I never trust a letter to a servant. . . . . In this place people are great economists, although they go out a great deal and enjoy themselves very much. One Baltimore family dinner would feed a family here for at least a fortnight. I hope Bo will not learn to be a spendthrift. I have talked to him enough on the subject, but young people never have profited by the experience of those who have lived longer than they, and I fear he must, like others, purchase experience at his own cost. I laboured unceasingly to impress him with the opinion of all sensible people, the high value of money, and the importance of always increasing one's fortune ; but I fear the examples of thoughtlessness and prodigality, and the improper way in which he will hear prudent people talked of, may counteract my advice.   I recollect that living within one's income used to be considered parsimony, and I have little doubt that I have been considered almost a miser (although I believe I am one of the worst managers possible) because I have not spent everything.   I wish *Bo* to be reminded often of the importance of saving, although I do not desire that he should want the means of living as well as those with whom he associates, and above all I never will withhold any money to procure him the solid or ornamental parts of education.   I consider a good education to a person of sense the best possible investment of money, because it always commands both money and consideration in the world.   It is equally unwise to force learning on children without capacity, because, although study may improve sense, it can never create it.   I think Bo clever enough to conduct himself better than most children of his age, but the unhappy propensity of his father to throwing away money makes me perhaps more fearful on this subject than I need be.   He is entirely ruined by his and his wife's absurd prodigality, added to their confidence in rogues.   Poor man, his faults always proceeded from want of judgment more than badness of heart ; but, when the first is wanting, nothing improper can excite surprise.

I hope poor Le Loup has not suffered from the cold, much more intense than that he has been used to in this country.   He was the admiration of all who saw him here, and every one knew him. When he walked with me, many unknown to me used to call him by his name and bid him good day.   Miss Fabri once wrote him an invitation to a large evening party, which I took him to.   I have constant inquiries after him from every one.   Adieu, my dear sir.   Believe me very affectionately yours.

Please write Bo that his grandmother is *not dead.*   The report was entirely untrue in every respect.

We have seen how anxious Madame Bonaparte was that her son should have a finished education.   In her letters to her father she repeatedly declares that upon the education of her son no money should be spared— she who was saving in everything else was prodigal in this. After studying eight months under a private tutor, Jerome passed a successful examination, and was admitted into Harvard College in February, 1823.

Soon after entering the university a difficulty arose in regard to his attendance at Protestant worship, and he requested his grandfather in Baltimore to write to the President of Harvard College stating that he did not wish Jerome to attend the Protestant Church. Upon this subject Jerome wrote : " I would appear very inconsistent if, after having stayed away from their church for upwards of a year, I were to go there now ; and as I have been brought up a Catholic,⁴ I would not wish to change my religion ; and moreover, my grandmother and several of my father's family being great devotees, they would think it a crime were I to enter an heretical church."

Although Madame Bonaparte disclaimed the idea of being one of the *femmes d'esprit*, still she was on the most intimate terms with M. Denon, Lamartine, Madame Rochefoucauld, Madame de Genlis, and other literary celebrities. Her letters to Lady Morgan are in striking contrast with those to her father in point of affectionate interest. From her earliest years Mr. Patterson seemed

---

⁴ Although Madame Bonaparte was not a Catholic herself, she had a great respect for the Roman Catholic belief as " the religion of princes and kings ;" and as it was the religion of his father's family, she had her son brought up a Catholic, in which faith he lived and died.

to take a singular pleasure in repressing his beautiful and gifted daughter. He showed no sympathy for her sufferings, nor appreciation of her ambition, while her admiration and enjoyment of European society found no response in his stern and simple nature.

She knew how to flatter Lady Morgan most success-fully. She writes: "If I were to write all that your admirers and friends tell me, I should never put my pen down. Your work on *France* is anxiously expected, and if it is what every one supposes it will be, as nothing mediocre can come from you, all those who love you will be highly gratified."

She complained of being very ill and very *triste*—that *tout m'ennuie dans ce monde, et je ne sais pas pourquoi*— unless it were the remembrance of her sufferings.

She thought the best thing she could do would be to return to her dear child in the spring. " I love him so entirely," she says, " that perhaps seeing him may render my feeling less disagreeable. I hate the *séjour* of America, and the climate destroys the little health which has been left me; but any inconveniences are more support-able than being separated from one's children. How much more we love our children than our husbands; the latter are sometimes so selfish and cruel, and children cannot separate their mothers from their affection."

Lady Morgan gave Tom Moore a letter of introduc-tion to Madame Bonaparte, but the sentimental poet failed to attract her—a beautiful woman destitute of all *sentiment*. She ridiculed the idea of love in marriage. She declared " that she married for position, and any-

body was a fool who married for love ;" that all sentiment was a weakness below her strong and determined
nature.

Tom Moore showed Madame Bonaparte an extract
from a letter of Lady Morgan's which mentioned one
of the Duke of Wellington's lady friends, upon which
Madame Bonaparte comments in the following characteristic style :—"You would be surprised if you knew
how great a fool she is, at the power she exercises over
the duke ; but I believe that he has no taste *pour les
femmes d'esprit*, which is, however, no reason for going
into extremes, as in this case. He gave her an introduction to the Prince Regent, and to every one of consequence in London and Paris. She had, however, no
success in France, where her not speaking the language
of the country was a considerable advantage to her,
since it prevented her nonsense from being heard. Do
not tell what I have written to you of this affair, since I
should pass for malicious and unfriendly towards my
compatriots."

Even at this period, when Madame Bonaparte was still
in her prime, she complained of the state of her health.
Her letters to Lady Morgan contain frequent mention
of past or present sickness, of seeking relief by change
of place and scene, &c. She announces the death of
Lady Morgan's old friend, M. Suard, and relates an
anecdote which is exceedingly French. His widow
gave a dinner a week after his death, because she
was afraid of being *triste*, as she said. She received
visits as usual, and took her daily promenade on the

Boulevards, because, as she said, "*mon bon ami m'a dit qu'il fallait vivre.*" Madame Bonaparte said the lady's friends are encouraged to flatter themselves that her great sensibility will not kill her, and at the same time that it induced her to give them parties and attend their reunions.

Madame Bonaparte said she was of the opinion that, in spite of her own unfortunate marriage, the best thing a woman could do was to marry—that even quarrels with one's husband were preferable to the ennui of a solitary existence—that there were many hours besides those appropriated to the world, which one could not get rid of (at least one like herself, who had no useful occupation in life) ; that she had sometimes wished to marry a second time to avoid *ennui* and *tristesse*.

CHAPTER VIII.

MME. BONAPARTE thought that the "rank" of her son, being more "conspicuous" than that of the "middle classes," demanded from him better conduct, better manners, and more elevated sentiments than are required from "many very excellent people" whose position was so different—that it would require every exertion on his part not to appear "unworthy of the distinction which his name gave to all who bore it." Therefore, she constantly urged him not to neglect the opportunity of acquiring a good education.

Even at this early day, when Jerome was only seventeen years old, his mother expressed a fear of his forming an imprudent marriage, and spoke of the folly of marrying "some poor young woman from the caprice of the moment," and being compelled to endure her "insipid society" and the "torment of bringing up a family of children." She urged her father to put such "nonsense" out of her son's head.

MADAME BONAPARTE TO WILLIAM PATTERSON.

GENEVA, 5th February, 1823.

DEAR SIR,—I have received no late letters from you. I wrote you the report of Madame's death was untrue. I wrote you his father was entirely ruined by his extravagance and that of his wife. I hope Bo will apply this unhappy example, and by his prudence and economy show it has not been thrown away upon him. Young people are all foolish and unreflecting ; they live only for the present moment, and it is useless to expect from them the wisdom which only age and experience of the world can give. I have laboured for years to give him a little premature discretion, and I am not entirely without hope that he is rather more reasonable than most children of his age. His position is more difficult than that of any other young person, because it is more conspicuous, and people expect more sense and better conduct from him than are exacted from the middle classes. I should like to know that he is attentive to his studies, and that his patience resists all temptation to idle-ness and frivolous amusements. I do not object to his being amused when it is not at the expense of his serious duties. On the contrary, I have ever encouraged him to take as much pleasure as he could find which was unattended with future inconvenience. I am not sorry he is in America at this time. A war in Europe renders it imprudent to educate him here. We are too near countries about to begin hostilities to allow young men to pursue learning quietly. My desire to secure some provision for *Bo* leads me to exercise great economy. He has rank in Europe which places him in the best and highest society ; this, no caprice or variable dispositions on the part of any one can change ; but he owes much to this very position. It demands from him good edu-cation, prudence, and good manners. It requires every exertion on his part not to appear unworthy of the distinction his name gives to all who bear it. I always acted on this principle in my un-ceasing endeavours to inspire him with elevated ideas and ambition above what might be necessary in the situation of other young people he was called upon to know. It is very possible he would have been more happy with less dignity of rank ; at all events, he

might have been idle with fewer bad consequences had he been born
the heir of some rich American; but true sense consists in making
the most of the destiny which has been given us, and this exacts
industry in learning and sentiments different from those of many
very excellent people, whose lot in life does not oblige them to the
same pursuits that his does. I know the utility of money too well
to spend it foolishly, and I fear a profession will be rather unsuitable
to Bo's circumstances, although I have never told him so. There
is, I hope, no danger of his [Bo's] forming an imprudent matrimonial connexion; if he cannot marry suitably—and in America he
could not (with one exception, and that I fear is out of the question)
—he can live single. Marriage offers no such comforts as to
induce rational beings to give up their independence without some
return of advantage. I am at times not happy on the subject of his
falling in love, recollecting the extreme folly and great simplicity
of the people he sees, who, without giving a single thought to
prudence or the future, marry some poor young woman from the
caprice of the moment, and consign themselves to her insipid
society and the torment of bringing up a family of children. It
may be patriotic to sacrifice one's time in this way, but it is not
charitable to one's self, and charity well understood begins at home.
I hope you, my dear sir, will inculcate to him privately the nonsense and absurdity of such marriages, which are unknown beyond
the New World. In Europe no one marries unless they have the
certain means of supporting their children. . . . .

Adieu, my dear sir. I beg you to advise Bo, and as he has great
respect for your understanding I am sure your advice will not be
thrown away. Boys always fancy mothers expect too much from
them, although I may say poor Bo is reasonable beyond his years.

Yours very affectionately.

I should like to have Bo's likeness taken by Jarvis, the man who
painted him when a child, if it were possible. There is a painter
here of great eminence, who regrets much not having taken a likeness of him. He says he has the finest head and expression he
ever saw. He is undoubtedly the handsomest boy I ever saw,
which in his situation is a great point. I am not sorry he is at

college for a few years ; the attention he excited and the admiration the ladies in Rome who saw him bestowed on his appearance might have had the bad effect of taking him from his lessons.

When Madame Mère was ill in the autumn of 1822, she made her will, in which she left the bulk of her fortune to the son of the Emperor Napoleon. Madame Bonaparte expressed herself very freely about this matter, and blamed the old lady for forgetting Jerome, especially as she had appeared so fond of the boy when he visited her the previous winter. This partiality led Madame Bonaparte to hope that her son would come in for a share of his grandmother's money, which had been accumulated by saving about two-thirds of her allowance of one million francs per annum during the empire.

It required all Madame Bonaparte's philosophy to meet this new disappointment with tranquillity, but she seemed to fear the effect of the announcement upon her son, as he was so devoted to his grandmother.

So much interested was Madame Bonaparte in the contents of Madame Mère's will that she employed a special agent at Rome to ascertain all the particulars.

MADAME BONAPARTE TO WILLIAM PATTERSON.

GENEVA, 14 February, 1823.

My DEAR SIR,— . . . . . I have heard from a person in Rome whom I wrote to, that Madame was given over in September—her complaint, violent inflammation. She then made a will, by which she left her whole fortune to the son of the emperor, with the exception of fifty thousand piastres (dollars) to each of her own sons, and twenty-five thousand dollars to each of Lucien's sons. Her daughters appear to have been entirely overlooked, although one of them has four children unprovided for. I have little doubt that her family are all dreadfully disappointed, and most of all Jerome, who has two children by his wife, and has spent every shilling he had on earth. It is needless for me to give my opinion of this procedure. If anything would surprise me, I might say that she ought to have left as much to *Bo* as to the sons of Lucien ; but the events of this life, whether capricious or unjust, have lost all novelty for me.

I suppose she thought herself in duty bound to leave all to the child whose father was the origin of her fortune, although he is the person who least requires her aid—this was well enough, particularly as her other sons and daughters might have saved millions as she had done ; but she might and ought to have left *Bo* something, and her not having done so has surprised every one except me. I beg you to say nothing to him on this subject, as, after all her professions and apparent affection, he, not knowing human nature, must naturally be shocked at such injustice. I shall write to him myself—at all events, this is no subject to talk about in public, and he must write to her as if he did not know what she had done. She is now quite well. I am not a little surprised at the publicity given to her will, which I suppose, however, got out through the person employed to make it. It could not have been her intention that it should have been known ; the curiosity of her family obtained the secret, if, indeed, she made one of it, and their disappointment has no doubt made a noise. I know their expectations were very different when I saw them. I suppose her knowledge of the emperor having left nothing to his son induced her to make such a will, or perhaps she received some communications from the persons who returned after his death, which compelled her to comply with a desire of his to provide for this boy. I could bear her out so far, because I like justice ; but her leaving twenty-five thousand dollars to Lucien's sons, and cutting off all her other grandchildren, proves that she was under some other influence. I must write this to *Bo*, and most sorry am I to be obliged to announce to him the little reliance there is to be placed on appearances. She took such interest, and appeared so partial to him, that he cannot help feeling his faith in virtue shaken. She ought to have said she meant to leave him nothing.

The letter I have received is from a person whom I charged to find out every particular without mentioning me. He was absent some months after the arrival of my letters. I think I can rely upon him. I am, of course, not to know this, nor is *Bo* to *act as if he did;* in the meantime, I feel sick at the stomach—the way in which unjust proceedings always affect me.

I fancy her family are not much at their ease, such a blow as it is to them ; none of them are rich, but her and Joseph, who calculated upon at least four hundred thousand dollars from her in addition to his present immense fortune. Some of the others, no doubt, were spending all their own money calculating on what she would leave them. Bo will painfully discover that I have some knowledge of life. My advice to him always was : " Take an education, none of them are to be relied upon." Young people cannot be expected to entertain the same distrust that those who have lived longer, if they have any sense, must do. We see older persons go on flattering themselves with expectations which generally end in disappointment. I never knew any one who lived upon the hope of spending an inheritance, who did not inherit disappointment, after spending their means in the interval.

I shall write to Bo in a few days to announce this. I am willing to spare him a little longer the pain of hearing it—at all events, he must write as usual to her.

I shall write Miss Spear in a few days. I beg you not to mention the contents of this letter until I have written to *Bo* myself, as I wish him to hear it from me before you tell it to him. He never can bear to hear anything against his family, and I know he was very fond of his grandmother, and that he is always mortified when anything comes to light against them, and that his feelings will be dreadfully hurt by her conduct.

I remain, my dear sir, yours very affectionately.

Please take care that George and Henry do not know this.

The day after writing the previous letter, Madame Bonaparte again addressed her father upon the subject of Madame Mère's will, and gave him some additional particulars about the same. She also wrote to her son, informing him that any expectations he may have formed from his grandmother's fondness for him should be dispelled. She thought it was her duty not to allow Jerome to encourage hopes which might lead to habits of prodigality. In her opinion, America was not a country where economy was properly understood and practised, it being rather a subject for ridicule than praise.

Madame Bonaparte began her economical habits soon after the annual allowance of twelve thousand dollars was settled upon her by Napoleon.

.The money thus given to her by the emperor was the nucleus of the large fortune which she afterwards accumulated by a long life of saving and shrewdness in making investments.

Again, Madame Bonaparte expresses her dread of her son's making an imprudent match—of all fatal imprudences, that, she said, would be the greatest.

MADAME BONAPARTE TO WILLIAM PATTERSON.

GENEVA, February 15, 1823.

I write to Bo and you to-day, to inform you both of all I have learned respecting Madame. She is now quite well. The report of her death originated from her having been despaired of in September. She then made a will by which she left her whole fortune to the son of the emperor by Marie Louise, excepting only fifty thousand dollars to each of her own sons, and twenty-five thousand dollars to each of Lucien's sons. As her son Jerome is ruined and in debt, and has an expensive wife and her two children to provide for, she being entirely without property herself, fifty thousand dollars are of little use to them. I suppose the emperor wrote to her in his last moments to provide for his son, which he was unable to do himself, having left his whole property to the people who emigrated to St. Helena with him. She owed everything to him ; therefore justice demanded that she should leave the greater part of her savings to his son ; but justice might have induced her to leave something to Bo, and her not having done it does no honour to her reputation. Her fondness of him, and her attentions, must naturally have led the child to suppose she would not have acted in this way ; therefore it was with great reluctance that I wrote him these particulars, but duty required that I should not allow him to encourage hopes which might lead to improvidence or habits of prodigality on his part.

The country he now inhabits offers no examples of proper atten-tion to economy, which is there rather a subject for mirth and ridi-cule than for praise. I am seldom surprised by disappointments, looking for them as naturally as if they made a part of my exis-tence ; but if surprise had any influence over me, Madame's will is calculated to excite this feeling. My only comfort is that *Bo* may make some use of this lesson : it may teach him to distrust appear-ances, and to depend only on his own prudence ; it may teach him, too, the folly of extravagance and spending on the calculation of future means. As she intended leaving him nothing, it is much better he should know it, that his character and habits may be formed accordingly.

It was, however, with great pain that I wrote him all I had learned from a person in Rome whom I had charged to obtain in-formation for me. The absence of my correspondent, who was in Sicily during some months, prevented his making the inquiries sooner, and the mission was too delicate to entrust to another. Of course, it was done secretly, and I was not ostensible.

Disappointments certainly teach prudence, except to fools, who live uncorrected by experience ; but they spoil the character so far as to render people sometimes too desponding, and produce idleness and want of energy. Extremes, either of prosperity or adversity, produce often the same result on the mind. All these inconve-niences I revolved in my mind, but I still feel it my duty to tell *Bo* what he must be surprised at after her reception of him. Her family had little idea, I fancy, of such strict justice, if so she calls it. I had calculated largely on her affection for them predominating. I cannot say that I think her wrong, except in having left nothing to *Bo*.

It now remains for *Bo* to write to her as usual, and to appear as if he did not know all this. He always feels unhappy when his relations are found fault with on any subject ; therefore, I hope no one will mention this before him.

He has more discretion than most young people on all subjects, and I have always the hope of his acquiring habits of study, which will either procure him the possibility of taking a profession to make money—which, to be sure, in his situation is not very agreeable—or, if he cannot get money, a good education will teach him to fill time with comfort to himself and credit to me.

Adieu, my dear sir,

Yours very affectionately.

I hope *Bo* will be prudent enough to write and act as if I had not found out all I have written him. I will be much obliged to you to point out the propriety of keeping on the *best* terms with them. It is very well to know all this, but there would be no sense in showing any disappointment. The dread of *Bo* making some imprudent match is ever on my mind—of all fatal imprudence, that would be the greatest.

It is almost the only misfortune from which a person of sense cannot recover, and in America there is no attention paid by parents to this subject. Here it is the parents who make all matches, and much better it should be, for they always look out for money.

In one of her letters to Lady Morgan, Madame Bonaparte complains that Geneva is " intolerably expensive— quite as much so as Paris ; there exists, too, an *esprit de corps*, or *de coterie*, appalling to strangers—I mean to *woman* strangers, for men are *les bienvenus partout*.

" . . . They have a custom here *parmi les gens du haut, de prendre à un prix très-fort des étrangers en*

pension seulement 'pour leur agrément.' In these gen-
teel boarding-houses there is no feast to be found, unless it be the feast of reason ; the hosts are too *spirituel*
to imagine that their *pensionnaires* possess a vulgar
appetite for meat and vegetables, tarts and custards ; but,
as I cannot subsist altogether on the contemplation of
la belle Nature, I have taken a comfortable apartment
for six months, en ville, where I hope I shall get something to eat. *La belle Nature, Mont Blanc, le Lac de
Genève, le beau coucher du soleil, le lever magnifique de
la lune*, are in the mouth of every one here, and *parois-
sent tenir lieu de toute autre chose.* I am writing you
all this—perhaps my letter will never reach you. Adieu,
my dear friend ; tell Sir Charles everything amiable for
me, and be convinced of the sincerity of my affection for
you both. My health is entirely restored, and I am
much less in the weeping mood than when you saw me
—I was so ill physically that I had not sufficient force
to support *les maux morales*."

In a subsequent letter from Geneva, Madame Bonaparte informs Lady Morgan that she is devoured by
lethargy and *ennui*, and says that another work from
her ladyship's pen alone could rouse her from depression :—

It is only you that have both power and inclination to make me
forget the ennui of existence, and only in your society that I am
not entirely *bête*. What shall I do with the long mornings in
Geneva ? You know you laughed me out of my *maître de littérature*,
which, *par parenthèse*, was very inconsiderate, unless you could
have pointed out some more amusing method of killing time.

Baron Bonstettin came to see me to-day; you were the subject of our conversation: nothing but admiration and regret when we talk of you.

How is dear Sir Charles? He is the only man on earth who knows my value, which has given me the highest opinion of his taste and judgment.

The Marchioness de Villette wishes me to spend a month with her in Paris. I cannot go, although it would be great *soulagement* to converse with a person who loves me—one has always so much *sur le cœur*, and in this country they are so heartless.

I do *dédommager* myself a little by uttering all the ridiculous things which come into my brain, either about others or myself.

Do not let me forget to tell you that Mr. Sismondi has made my acquaintance—he is married too. I wonder that people of genius marry! By the way, I recollect that you are an advocate for *le marriage*. Oh! my dear Lady Morgan, I have been in such a state of melancholy, that I wished myself dead a thousand times— all my philosophy, all my courage, are insufficient sometimes to support the inexpressible *ennui* of existence, and in those moments of wretchedness I have no human being to whom I can complain. What do you think of a person advising me to turn Methodist the other day, when I expressed just the hundredth part of the misery I felt? I find no one can comprehend my feelings. Have you read *Les Méditations Poétiques de Lamartine?* There are some pretty things in them, although he is too *larmoyant*, and of the bad school of politics. Miss Edgeworth is here. I visited her; she came to see me with Professor Pictet, and we have never met.

She has a great deal of good sense, which is just what I particularly object to, unless accompanied by genius, in my companions.

It is only you that combine *tous les genres d'esprit*, and whose society can compensate me for all the losses and the mistakes of my heart; but I shall never see you again; those whom I love and who love me are always distant; I am dragging out life with indifference. They are so reasonable, and so unmoved in this place, their mornings devoted to the exact sciences, the evenings to whist, that in spite of myself I am obliged to read half the day. There have been some English, but I have seen little of them. They would not like me. I am too *natural ou naturelle*. I believe that women are cold, formal, and affected—just my antipodes, therefore we should not be agreeable to each other; besides, they require a year to become acquainted, and I have too little of life left to waste it in formalities.

I have seen a German countess—that means, seen her every day during three months; she is a practical philosopher of the epicurean sect, a person just calculated to make something of life—unlike me as possible—she has a great deal more sagacity; to do her justice, she tried to *débarrasser* me of what she called *mes idées romantiques et mes grandes passions;* but I am incorrigible, and go on tormenting myself about things which I cannot change. She has more coarse common sense, with greater knowledge of the world, than any person I have ever known. I wish I resembled her, because I should be more happy.

Adieu, my dear Lady Morgan. Write me frequently; your friendship is among the few comforts left me.

E. P.

CHAPTER IX.

Mme. Bonaparte, Napoleon, and Byron.—Albert Galatin.—Letters from
Paris.—Extravagance of the Baltimore Merchants.—Robert Morris.—
Mme. Bonaparte makes a Will.—Reports of her second Marriage.—Love
in a Cottage.—She hopes Jerome will escape all Matrimonial Snares.—
He must distinguish himself in Life.—She is pleased with his diligence
at College, but displeased with the Expense of his Education.—Jerome
offers to reduce his Expenses.—Mme. Bonaparte deplores the Solitude
of a Single Life.—John Jacob Astor.—Miss Astor.—Sismondi.—The
Waverley Novels.—1823.

IT was always a matter of regret to Madame Bonaparte
that she never met the two most celebrated men of her
time—Napoleon and Byron. That she did not meet
Napoleon was no fault of hers ; had they met, both of
their destinies might have been changed. It has been
happily said that Elizabeth Patterson would have been
a suitable match for the great Napoleon, instead of the
weak Jerome ; her wit, beauty, and ambition would have
helped him to rise, while her prudence, common sense,
and practical wisdom would have taught him when to
stop in his dazzling career. She would have exercised
that good influence over him which Josephine was too
timid and Marie Louise too silly to attempt.

Byron, who had been charmed by the graceful accomplishments of Lady Blessington, desired to see Madame

Bonaparte, whose beauty and suffering had made her an European celebrity. But it was not to be. In the summer and autumn of 1815, when Madame Bonaparte was at Cheltenham, Lord Byron was in London in the midst of those domestic troubles which were to have so decided an effect upon his life and writings. In the September of the following year, while Madame Bonaparte was enjoying the long anticipated pleasures of Paris, Lord Byron was boating on Lake Geneva with his new friend Shelley; while Madame Bonaparte was living in Geneva, in 1819-20, Byron was in Italy; in the winter of 1821-22, when Madame Bonaparte was in Rome, Byron was in Pisa; in the spring of 1822, when Madame Bonaparte visited Florence for the first time, Byron was at Leghorn; in the summer of 1823, while Madame Bonaparte was enjoying the gaiety of Paris, Byron was preparing for the glorious struggle for Grecian independence; and in the spring of 1824, while Madame Bonaparte was preparing to return to America, Lord Byron died at Missolonghi.

In May, 1823, Madame Bonaparte again visited Paris, where she spent the summer. From that city she wrote the following highly interesting and characteristic letter. The reader is admonished to accept some of her remarks upon certain men and women *cum grano salis*. She seemed to grow in bitterness as she grew in age; in writing of one family in particular, she always manifests the most determined antipathy—her pen becomes a dagger, her ink poison. Her letters to Lady Morgan are entirely different in style and subjects from those written to her father. To Lady Morgan she confesses her *ennui*, her depression of spirits, her disappointment of life's enjoyment. To her father she describes the brilliant scenes in the midst of which her life is passed—parties, festivities, and entertainments of all kinds, her social triumphs are recorded, all the great people she meets are mentioned, and she seems to exist in an atmosphere filled with music, flowers, sunshine, and enchantment.

MADAME BONAPARTE TO WILLIAM PATTERSON.

PARIS, May 6, 1823.

DEAR SIR,—The Galatins leave Paris on the 15th of this month, for Havre, whence they will sail for America. He has obtained from the American Government leave of absence for six months. I presume his return to France will depend upon the state of his affairs at home. They have been excessively kind to me in every way, and have always, when I have been in Paris, asked me to dine every day, if I liked it. Mrs. Galatin desires *Bo* to see her, if he can, in passing through New York. Mr. Galatin[1] is highly respected by every one in Europe, and excessively admired for his talents. I fear it would be difficult to represent the country half as well, if he should decline continuing minister. I think the plan *now* is to marry young Murat to the *rich* young lady.[2] He is gone out—sent probably by his mother, who, I know, wrote when I was in Rome to beg her brother to take him. I am pretty sure the grandmother does not approve of the arrangement ; but, as she leaves her whole fortune to the son of Marie Louise and the emperor, giving to her *own* sons fifty thousand dollars each, and nothing to her daughters, it is probable that they have all resolved

---

[1] Albert Galatin, who was Secretary of the Treasury under Jefferson. At this time he was Minister to France.

[2] Joseph Bonaparte's daughter, the young lady whom Jerome came over to marry.

not to attend to her wishes, which were very decided to make the match for Bo, whose father she likes much more than either of her daughters, whom, I fancy, she does not like at all. I fancy she conceived it her duty to leave her fortune to the son of the emperor, when she found that his father had left him nothing, which none of the family expected. She s not dead ; but during her illness last autumn she made a will in his favour, leaving her own family to the care of Providence. They are so prodigal, that she had, indeed, little prospect of benefiting them by her savings, which would have passed like water through a sieve, if left to them. I wish, however, she had left poor Bo something. I am in hopes he will know the value of money better than his father. I have been pretty regularly paid twelve hundred dollars per annum for the last two years for Bo's expenses : but, as his father is ruined, I have little expectation of this sum being continued, and I spend not a farthing more than I should do if he had not promised it. It is only so much out of the fire ; whilst it is paid I shall take it thankfully, but no one can suppose I should be such a fool as to spend upon an uncertainty. In money affairs, it is ridiculous to speculate upon sums not received. I am uneasy about Bo's getting the ridiculously extravagant habits of the Americans, who always live beyond their means. George and Henry used to have a great contempt for anything like economy, and the whole family, indeed, gave an example of prodigality and thoughtlessness about expense, which I should consider a great misfortune in a child of mine. Bo has rank—his name places him in the first society in Europe ; but if he contracts the idea of indulging every whim and pampering himself in the way the boys in Baltimore do—if he learns to think that idleness and luxurious habits make a man of consequence, his present advantages of situation will be lost. His system ought to be quite different from that thoughtlessly pursued by the sons of men of fortune, whose labours serve to spoil their families ; he must remember that his position requires industry and unremitting care of his money ; and that, although the first people in Europe would like his society, and place him on an equality with themselves, that none of them would either give or lend a farthing. Mrs. Galatin tells me no one ever spoke of him except to praise him. I am delighted to hear this, and I hope and trust he will never be influenced by imprudent young men to lose his time or spend anything beyond what is absolutely necessary. I shall, of course, never object to any expense that regards education, which I consider the best fortune that can be given to any one : it procures the means of living to those who are poor, and it prevents the rich resorting to bad company or frivolous occupations to get through time.

I came here with Miss Allen, the sister-in-law of Sir James McIntosh and Mr. Sismondi, both men of celebrity. She travelled with a large German Bible, prayed regularly, kneeling morning and evening ; in short, I was forced to say nothing whenever she talked of religion, as I found she had taken it into her head to make a Methodist of me during the journey. . . . .

I have heard that Purviance says a divorced woman should use her maiden name in all legal proceedings. Consulted by me formerly on this subject, he assured me the name was immaterial, and I used that of Bonaparte in all purchases of property. . . . .

One of the best mathematicians in Europe gave lessons to Bo in Geneva. He has said that *Bo* may attain any proficiency in mathematics, and that he has a strong head. I hope he will neglect nothing to improve himself.

Bo was very much attended to by all hands in Europe, and admired by every one. Some ladies in Rome ran after him so much that I feared his being spoiled, although he seemed quite unconscious of it, supposing probably that women old enough to be his grandmother could not be foolish enough to fall in love with him. It is certain that his beauty attracted great attention ; a German princess told me that she had followed him once in Geneva, at a ball, from room to room, to look at him, and that he was the handsomest creature she ever saw. He certainly is the handsomest boy I ever saw of his age, and in all respects the finest creature possible. His modesty and good sense alone prevent his being spoiled, for I assure you he received attentions sufficient to have turned much older heads. The Duke of Würtemberg (brother of the late king) advised me to ask for the twelve hundred dollars from Prince Jerome. He censured both Jerome and his wife (she, by the way, is his *own* niece) for their folly, extravagance, and improper conduct in not maintaining *Bo*, and in-

sisted upon my writing to Jerome to make him an allowance. I
found the duke and duchess always very obliging. They assured
me that anything in their power I might always command for *Bo.*
I suppose you know that great people only mean, when they say
"You may command us," that they will invite to their houses, or
recommend to other great people, or speak a good word if one is
looking for a place from government. None of them ever give
money, which, indeed, they seem much more bare of than American
merchants. The duke once asked me what I thought of him
when he arrived at Geneva. I replied, "I was surprised at your
highness asking to know me and my son; his answer was, "The
Emperor of Russia would have done the same." He inquired
particularly into my mode of education for Bo; gave me a great
deal of advice respecting his *morals*—among other things he advised
me not to let him smoke, because he had lost all his own teeth by
the use of his pipe; but, as he is upwards of sixty, it is possible
that time may have aided tobacco. He told me the Emperor
Alexander, his nephew, had promised to allow Jerome and his
wife sixty thousand francs annually; that he thought the money
badly bestowed, because they were *two* spendthrifts who had run
through immense sums. Miss Clagston, now Mrs. Astor, is here,
delighted with matrimony and French funds. I dined with her
yesterday. She tells me that the Duke of Wellington gave ——
a cool reception on her second visit to England. That the duke is
said to be tired of the ——s; but, tired or not, they pursue him.
live on his estate, and until he gets them husbands he will never
get rid of them. She tells me they are considered *mere* adventurers
and swindlers, but that she should not be surprised at their
taking in some men to marry them, because men are seldom
matches for the impudence, perseverance, and artifice of women.
Miss Clagston knows the world, has a good deal of sense and
shrewdness, which all the Scotch have. She found the ——s
out immediately. —— and —— both made their way in Europe
by impudence; two more ignorant, unprincipled asses never left
their own country. People in Europe are beginning to think the
Americans as shrewd as the Genevans and Scotch. The ——s
have been a great disadvantage to the American character by the
fraud they practised to get husbands, in affirming they had forty

thousand pounds fortune, besides great expectations from grand-papa. I shall in future direct Bo's letters in the name of " Edward Percival," to avoid danger at the post-office, or curious people opening my letters to him at sea. I have seen passengers amuse themselves reading the backs of letters. The letter-bag is often turned out when they have nothing better to amuse them, and letters bearing his name would be a resource during the tedious moments of a sea-voyage. It will be proper to tell George and Henry, that they may not mistake letters with this address. Frances Galatin is much admired in Paris. She is a beauty, but the beauty of Venus would never marry any one in France without money. I forgot to mention to Bo that the Count de St. Criq's uncle died a year since, and left him a hundred thousand dollars. I am sure I did not expect the uncle would die so soon. He turns out to be very rich, as, added to the hundred thousand dollars, his father has made a large fortune. Every one gets some luck for their sons except me. My journey to Rome produced compliments, honours, attentions for Bo ; but I always said Bo would be, like myself, an object of admiration, and that plainer people would get more money. His grandmother and the cardinal were very fond of his company, very liberal in expressions of commendation —poor *Bo!* I hear of every one getting a lucky chance except him.

.   .   .   .

The marriage with Murat's son does not surprise me, as the uncle is notorious for want of stability in his plans, and there is no Frenchman whose word is less brittle than pie-crust. The people on the continent of Europe have not the most remote idea of truth or principle in any way, and no one can live long with them and remain ignorant of their being utterly destitute of anything like moral feeling.

The Swiss, reputed honest, are quite as interested and fraudulent as the French ; they have more sense, but are less agreeable than the French. In Geneva they cheat from the highest to the lowest classes, and all aid in plundering the English who go there. They have acknowledged to me that there are different prices for them and for strangers. The English women pay exactly double what I do for sedan chairs, servants' wages, &c. No one in the country ever tells the real price when applied to for information.

I was the first traveller who found out what the Genevans really paid, and it required some address to get at this useful information. They show me great respect for my adroitness, and seem to consider me now worthy of being dealt fairly with in prices. No Jew has ever been able to get a living in Geneva. The French proverb is: "It takes four Jews to make a Genevan." They are the cleverest people in Europe, and the most roguish, not excepting the Italians.

From Paris Madame Bonaparte watched, with her usual intelligence, the war which was then going on between France and Spain. England, she said, crippled by the extraordinary efforts she had made during the Napoleonic wars, found her interest in maintaining a strict neutrality. Even at that early period the sovereigns of Europe were jealously attempting to keep down what Madame Bonaparte calls "liberal ideas." She declares that there is a confederacy of kings banded together against the introduction of free governments into Europe. From the subject of European politics she proceeds to condemn the extravagance of the merchant princes of Baltimore, and alludes to the fatality attending the building of "palaces" there.

MADAME BONAPARTE TO WILLIAM PATTERSON.

PARIS, May 22, 1823.

DEAR SIR,—I have received your letters enclosing those of M. Spear, dated 21st March and 5th April. I have received two from Bo, in the last of which he mentions having had a bad cold and sore eyes.

One of the best oculists in London says, *weak* eyes should be washed with *cold* water; but that inflamed eyes should always be washed with *warm* instead of *cold* water. There is war between

France and Spain. Before it actually was declared, or rather before the *French* army *marched* into Spain, every one predicted great calamities to the French government; since that, we hear nothing more, and people appear quite pleased and tranquil in Paris. England is perfectly resolved to maintain her neutrality, unless *directly* attacked. They have no money, and must let the powers of the Continent do everything, except take their possessions abroad, their ships, or commit some outrage upon them, such as they are now doing on Spain—nothing less than these three things will induce the English ministry to declare war, for two good reasons—want of money, and fear of Jacobinism. The object of all the governments on the Continent is to keep down what are called liberal ideas, and as they have patronage and money, it is not likely the revolutionists will get any advantage over them. There is a confederacy of kings against those who entertain the desire of introducing free governments, and it is natural to suppose that the former, *united* as they are, must be successful.

I think it very wrong of the people in Baltimore to speculate on the possibility of a *general* war; they ought, in common prudence, to avoid risking their capital until they see how things turn out on the Continent. The war between France and Spain, of course, throws more business into their hands; but, to make any speculations to the success of which a general war of the powers of Europe would be necessary, is, I assure you, highly imprudent. What I have mentioned of the determination of the English government to keep England neutral, you may rest assured I have had from good authority; and that the French people will submit to anything and everything, rather than undergo another revolution, is certain. The Holy Alliance are pledged to aid each other on every occasion, which renders revolutions much more difficult than they were formerly. I have had a conversation with an American merchant, who tells me he has no doubt the people in Baltimore will act as if they were sure all Europe was in combustion again, and be ruined again, as they were by former erroneous calculations. I am resolved, when a favourable moment arrives of public confidence being restored in State banks or institutions of any descriptions in Baltimore, to sell out, and place my money in the United States Government stock, which I believe to be the only secure investment in the country. I shall never forget the depredations committed on banks, which brings me to speak of my regret at hearing of the death of poor James Buchanan, whose father has, by this tragical event, been severely punished for the folly which led him to build and furnish with regal magnificence a palace.

I am sorry to express my conviction that General Smith's fine house, and the extravagant mode of living he introduced into Baltimore, caused the ruin of half the people in the place, who, without this example, would have been contented to live in habitations better suited to their fortunes; and certainly they only made themselves ridiculous by aping expenses little suited to a community of people of business.

It is to be hoped that in future there will be no palaces constructed, as there appears to be a fatality attending their owners, beginning with Robert Morris and ending with Lem Taylor. I do not recollect a single instance, except that of Bingham, of any one who built one in America, not dying a bankrupt. . . . .

It would be a great mistake to judge of the people on this continent by what you know of English or Americans, who are much less demoralized, and whose ideas of liberty have no resemblance to the sentiments entertained by people here, who, provided they can get places and pensions, care little for forms of government.

I hear Mme. M.'s [3] son is gone to Philadelphia, and have little doubt he will marry his cousin. I wish them joy of the union, but until they have been at church it is impossible to be quite certain that the family politics may not change. I rather think the grandmother's wishes were not consulted on this occasion, having some reason to believe that she remembers how little her family stand indebted to the folly of the young gentleman's father, which contributed greatly to the misfortunes of the emperor, her son.

I remain, dear sir,

Affectionately yours.

Mr. Galatin wrote to his family in Geneva, recommending me most particularly to their attention, and on all occasions both he

---

[3] Madame Murat, widow of Joachim, King of Naples.

and Mrs. Galatin have shown me kindnesses, and by their treatment proved that they liked me more than any American in Paris.
He was highly respected by the Diplomatic Corps here for his
talents, and is considered a man of great abilities. Miss Galatin
was thought a great beauty in Paris. Mrs. Galatin desires very
much to see Bo.

I beg you, my dear sir, to visit Mr. Galatin if he should pass
through Baltimore, and to ask Mrs. Galatin to dine, if she should
accompany him—a family dinner would do ; they always had a
plate every day at their table for me, whenever I was in Paris, and
as they never did the same for any other American, I feel particularly grateful to them.

This long letter was followed in June by the following
note :—

MADAME BONAPARTE TO WILLIAM PATTERSON.

DEAR SIR,—I have received yours of 21st of March and 5th of
April. Please send the enclosed to *Bo*, and tell him I shall in
future write to Edward Percival,[4] as my letters by the Galatins
will explain. I wrote to you I had been paid fifteen thousand francs
since my arrival in Europe. The person is completely ruined, and
is gone to live in Rome. He had promised me six thousand francs
per annum, but of course he cannot pay them. Pray do not tell
Bo a word about his grandmother's will, as he likes her very much,
and there is no use putting children against their relations. I
I have spent two hundred and twelve francs in finery for M. Spear,
which I have sent to Beaseley. I fancy the Baltimore people will
ruin themselves in speculations upon a general war, which most
probably will not take place. I hope *Bo* is economical. I hear

---

[4] Madame Bonaparte was afraid that her letters could be opened and
read by passengers on the American packets to beguile the tedium of a long
voyage, the letters being very loosely carried in those days ; therefore she
addressed her son as Edward Percival.

from M. Spear, his teachers praised him to Mr. Eustis. I hope and trust he will make use of his time, and take care of his money.

Yours, very truly.

PARIS, June 22, 1823.

I have said nothing about the six thousand francs to my friends, having foreseen they would not be paid for any length of time.

In the next letter Madame Bonaparte continues to " harp on the daughter " of Joseph, and does not seem at all pleased at the idea of young Murat's marrying her.

MADAME BONAPARTE TO WILLIAM PATTERSON.

PARIS, July 12th, 1823.

DEAR SIR,—I enclose a letter for Miss Spear, one from Lord Henry Cholmondeley to Bo, and another from myself to him. My letters by the Galatins have explained the reason of my directing in this name to him [Edward Percival]. Should the count marry his daughter to young Murat, I am convinced it will displease Madame, who hates the M.'s cordially. As to me, I shall act just as if it pleased me highly, and never take the least notice of it in any way. Bo.'s conduct ought to be the most perfect indifference, and if they are civil he should be so too. He ought to keep well with them, if he can do so without meanness. At the moment they were marrying me, in the American papers, I was, by comparing dates since, making my will.

Mr. Sheldon, chargé-d'affaires, has it. I have retained a copy, witnessed duly. I am now inclined to corpulency, and subject to violent diseases, of course. Last summer I nearly went off with an inflammation of the stomach and bowels. Poor Madame Villette's sudden death has taught me the necessity of making a will. I have left Bo my sole heir, and only wish I had millions to leave him. If he dies without legitimate children before the age of twenty-one, you are to inherit his whole fortune ; that is, you are to spend the income, the principal at your death to be equally divided between the rest of the family. I have left no legacies to any of my acquaintances. When Bo comes of age, if I live that long I shall consult and see whether it will be proper to let him dispose of the property in case of his death. The present will is drawn up to prevent his family inheriting if we should die before he is of age.

It is improbable that I shall every marry, but I will marry no one unless *Bo* is made the heir of what I have saved up for him. My first inclination, and my first duty, are to provide for that child, who has the charge of a great name, which shall be supported if economy and pains on my part can do it.

I drew up the will myself. Sheldon says, and Warden, the witnesses, that it is as explicit as possible. I do not wish Miss Spear to know I have left her nothing, as it is probable both she and Mde. Toussard might have expected me to leave them something, to the amount of a hundred dollars, which I have not done. Miss Spear writes me that a small portion of Mary's land is to be divided by law among her husband's heirs. No feelings of romance or false delicacy shall prevent my taking what the law allows me, and I only regret it is not more. It is not on my own account, because I shall never spend a farthing of it, but because I consider the will, which left her mistress to dispose after her death of the whole, as highly unjust. No one should leave their property from their family, whatever cause of complaint they may have against them, for, after all, strangers have less claim on them, and no gratitude.

The next letter, also, is largely occupied with the marriage question.

GENEVA, 9 November, 1823.

DEAR SIR,—I have resolved to pass the winter here instead of going to Mrs. Payne, which last plan would have occasioned me much inconvenience in travelling at this season. I have had no letter from Miss Spear acknowledging a box of finery shipped by Beaseley from Havre, by my direction. I hope she found the articles agreeable to her taste, which I had chosen as judiciously as I knew how. The amount of costs I prefer being paid in America, as the exchange, &c., would give me more calculation than the money is worth, besides not wishing to place money in the hands of European bankers more than I have at present. It is hazardous having deposits with them beyond one's immediate necessities.

I learn from you with great satisfaction that Bo is now profiting by the advice I have never ceased giving him since he came into the world, which was, to distinguish himself. It would have been a sad mistake if he had fancied an ordinary education, or common attainments would have sufficed for him. He is too conspicuously placed to permit himself to rest contented with the exertions made by other people ; and, however agreeable it may be to bear a great name, it is less easy to bear it with propriety than one which attracts less notice.

I have only to hope that he will continue to pursue his studies with his present attention. He is more discreet in his general conduct than most young people, therefore I have little fear of his compromising himself by folly or imprudence. His expenses must unavoidably be greater than those of boys differently circum-stanced. I have only to hope he will circumscribe them as much as he can with decency and comfort. The unfortunate example of his father in this respect will perhaps teach him what is to be avoided. Miss Spear's account of his expenditure has not reached me. I cannot help thinking the Americans, in general, much too luxurious in their habits, and that they confide imprudently in their servants. No one here trusts to anything except weights and measures and strong locks for the preservation of their property in their own houses. I am sorry the Galatins are not likely to re-turn, independently of the pleasure I feel in their society. I know Mrs. Galatin prefers living in Europe. I believe the little prospect they had of marrying their daughter in Paris, which is quite impossible without giving her what they have not to give—a fortune —was the only consideration which reconciled the ladies to going home; and even this weighty calculation could not entirely com-fort Mrs. Galatin under the grief of leaving a society which amused her. Miss Galatin is very pretty, was very much admired, and required only money to have married ; but the truth is, no one will take girls without fortunes—people have too much sense here (I mean people who are worth marrying) to marry only for love, as they do in America. There is now and then, to be sure, a marriage of inclination made by Englishmen of rank, but the Galatins would have been imprudent to calculate upon such rare chances ; besides, it requires uncommon good management to secure luck of this kind. I was in hopes they would have married her to some rich American, and then have come out again. I quite agree with you that it is necessary for *Bo* to keep well with his connexions, whether the match takes place or not, which, indeed, I fear is not likely ; but there is no use fretting about what one cannot help. If he takes a good education, and continues handsome, there is always a probability, with his name, of my marrying him advantageously. But if I cannot, for "the race is not always to the swift, nor the battle to the strong," he has only to live a bachelor, because the next best thing to making a good match is not to make a bad one. If he were a girl it would be much worse, as it would be scarcely possible for me to dispose of her, and would be much more necessary ; as it is, I shall not worry myself any more about marrying him. If they change their minds, it will be time enough for me to think of the subject. I do not believe they know what they want, but at all events it is quite certain he ought to keep well with them, for although they are likely to want and keep all the money they have, they are liberal of attentions, professions, and apparent affection, which have their value coming from people in their situation. Whether sincere or insincere, they are not to be neglected by him, for many reasons, which, of course, I need not enumerate to any one who knows the world. He has considerable discretion, and much more penetration than young people generally possess, who, indeed, one out of a thousand excepted, never see further than their noses ; whatever talents and acquirements they may possess, it is only dear-bought experience, or uncommon ambition that give prudence to make one's way in the world. I hope he will get no romantic fancies or false views of life where he is.

The land of romance is now only to be found on the other side of the Atlantic. People on this side know the exact value of everything, and turn existence to its best account. Love in a cottage is even out of fashion in novels. I should consider an amiable, prolific daughter-in-law, a very poor compensation for all the trouble and anxiety I have had with that boy, and most sincerely hope the amiable, scheming (for even in America the women know their own interest, and look as sharply after matches as they do here) young ladies will select some other unsuspecting dupe.

Women in all countries have wonderful cunning in their intercourse with men ; they succeed better in America because the men there are a century behind them in knowledge of human nature and instinct of their true interest.   I hope Bo will escape all ambitious plans of the women he meets, and make himself worthy in every way of the pains I have unremittingly bestowed on him, and the sacrifice I have made and am still willing to make for him.   I have desired him to take care of his eyes, which are weak, and even to intermit his studies until they are stronger.

Yours, dear sir, affectionately.

There have been persons bitten by mad dogs here this summer. I have felt uneasy about Le Loup, as possibly they may neglect to keep him out of the sun, and to give him plenty of water with a roll of brimstone in it—a precaution taken here by the ladies, who all keep dogs.   Some of them have likenesses taken of their favourite dogs.

Although Madame Bonaparte had repeatedly assured her father that no money should be spared upon Jerome's education, yet she was both astonished and displeased when she learned that two thousand one hundred and fifty dollars had been expended in fifteen months by him.   Jerome was conscious that this was an extravagance that his mother would not allow, and he requested his grandfather not to inform her, until he, Jerome, could find out what was the least he could live on at college. " The expenses of Southern students," he says, "vary from nine hundred dollars to ten hundred and twelve hundred a year, and even more.   I know a student in college at present who spent two thousand three hundred dollars during his freshman year.   Now, I wish to

live genteelly, and to be remarked neither for my close-
ness nor my extravagance. And I hope in future not
to exceed one thousand a year." In order to reduce
his expenses, Jerome proposed taking a room-mate, by
which means he would be able to save half of the cost
of firewood, lights, and rent, but gave as an objection to
this that it would interfere with his studies. His only
indulgence was a ride on horseback twice a week ; this
he offered to give up if his grandfather thought it too
extravagant.

In all his letters to Mr. Patterson he expresses himself willing to follow his advice in everything, and always
signed himself "Your most affectionate and devoted
grandson."

Madame Bonaparte said she was willing to allow her
son eleven hundred dollars a year for his college expenses, which she thought quite sufficent, and if he
could save anything without prejudice to his lessons
out of this sum, he was at liberty to dispose of such
savings as he liked.

GENEVA, December 11, 1823.

DEAR SIR,—Your letter of the 21st of October, enclosing one from
Miss Spear, reached me to-day. I find that Bo's expenses have
amounted to two thousand one hundred and fifty dollars since his
return to America—that is, in about fifteen months. I am perfectly
at a loss to account for such a sum having been spent in such a
space of time, particularly as he writes me that he accepts no
invitations. He mentions his having furnished rooms ; this might
have been avoided if he had boarded in a private house, which I
know is very possible ; at all events, there must have been some
great mismanagement, which I trust will be remedied in the next
year, as neither my means nor any possible contingency can warrant

L

such expenditure. I am disposed to excuse the folly and thought-lessness of youth (wishing it were possible people could come into this world wiser than they do) ; but it is quite impossible for me to authorize such expense in future, and I must beg you to devise some means of restraining him to a more reasonable mode of living in future. He must not exceed eleven hundred dollars a year, which I know to be fully adequate to all proper expenses. Pray do not tell him this, as possibly he may now contrive to live upon even less. I shall write him my opinion on the subject when I recover the first shock Miss Spear's letter has given me. How fortunate it is that I have never repeated the experiment of marriage, which, indeed, the dread of laying up trouble for my old age in a family of children has prevented me from. I perceive content was no end of our being ; if people do not marry they are condemned to soli-tude, and if they do marry they must make up their minds to toils and privations to pay for the indiscretion and extravagance of their posterity. I have met with no one who does not complain of their lot in some way : those who have no children of their own to plague them have those of others, or are tormented in some other way.

I quite agree with you, that abusing the ——s can do me no good, and have resolved not to speak of them again. The prosperity of the wicked is a proof that some other state of being attends us, because it is impossible that the world was made by chance ; and as I feel convinced of this fact, I console myself at the success of iniquity here by the reflection that the time must arrive when justice will be dealt to all. I rather believe, however, that from those to whom little has been given of intelligence little will be ex-pected, which, perhaps, will exculpate that family. At all events, I leave them to their fate here and hereafter, having indeed quite enough occupation with my own temporal affairs, and feeling that immoderate hatred ought to be exchanged for silent contempt towards all my past, present, and future enemies.

Mr. A. and daughter are here. He seems, poor man, afflicted by the possession of a fortune which he had greater pleasure in amass-ing than he can ever find in spending. He is ambitious, too, I fancy, for his daughter, to whom nature has been as penurious as fortune has been the reverse. She may marry by the weight of her person, but any idea of disposing of her except to some pains-taking man of business, or ruined French or Italian nobleman, would be absurd. She is not handsome, and sense cannot be bought; therefore they will wander from place to place a long time before their object is accomplished. The father has no small portion of natural sense, and, could he have commanded the advantages of instruction which he gives his children, he might have made that figure which he desires, but will never attain for his family. Education improves, but can never give capacity—a truth some people never discover. Had Bo been born a fool, I should not have toiled to beat learning into him; as he has natural sense, I thought it my duty to give him an education.

15th December.

Dear Sir,—After reflecting last night upon the two thousand one hundred and fifty dollars, I have come to the resolution of insisting upon Bo's spending eleven hundred dollars annually, and I beg you to write to him, on reception of this letter, that my instructions to that effect have been given to you and Miss Spear. I will not on any pretext allow a farthing more; it is ample, and even more than my fortune authorizes me to allow him. I have economized in every way myself—perhaps more than my position in society allowed, that I might have it in my power to leave him above want; but, although disposed to grant him every reasonable indulgence, after procuring him every advantage, however expensive, of education, I am resolved not to permit him to suppose that I was born only to administer to his extravagant fancies.

I may as well spend my income myself, as see it squandered by him; and there is indeed little encouragement for me to endure privations, if their result is to be—

" This year a reservoir to keep and spare,
The next a fountain spouting through my heir."

The fact is, that, being out of the sphere of my observation, he has profited by the opportunity to spend my money; this experiment shall not, however, be repeated. . . . .

I observe what you say of the proposed departure of the young lady,[b] to whom I wish a pleasant voyage, hoping the family have at length fixed their resolutions respecting her destiny, that no new scheme may compel her to take ship a second time, after matrimony. I have remained here to avoid the expense of moving.

I have conversed with Mr. Steele, a nephew of a Mr. Henry Payson, of Baltimore, on the subject of Harvard, where he was educated; he says he spent eight hundred dollars a year. He spent the evening at Madame Sismondi's with me. He seems intelligent, well educated, and has very good manners. There was a circle of the most learned men in Europe, whose presence might have made a stout heart tremble. To my astonishment, this youth bore his situation like a hero. I am sure they must have admired his composure, perfect ease without impudence, and really wonderfully good manners in so young a person. His self-possession was not the result of folly or ignorance, which always give to their possessor confidence and self-satisfaction. Mr. Sismondi is the author of a voluminous work on the republics of Italy, which I recollect having seen at John Smith's, besides having published other books. They are a very agreeable family. She is the sister-in-law of Sir James McIntosh. It was with her sister, Miss Allen, that I went to Paris last spring. Their society is composed of all the most profound literary characters in Europe: so Mr. Steele has fallen upon company which requires some intrepidity of disposition in those who frequent them. They are all very civil to me; being a woman, of course they only expect me to look pretty.

I am learning to play whist, which amuses me very much. I am sorry to hear Miss Spear's bonnet was damaged, and that she thought herself obliged to part with some of them on account of expense. They were all in the latest fashion. I suppose you have all read Lady Morgan's "Italy." I have only been able to procure it here in English lately.

Walter Scott's novels would amuse you very much. They are read by people of all ages, and are almost all historical. "Nigel" gave me a perfect idea of James the First of England, as did "Quentin Durward" of Louis the Eleventh of France. Bo ought to read them all. Walter Scott has made a large fortune by his novels.

---

[b] Charlotte Bonaparte.

CHAPTER X.

ALTHOUGH Jerome did not meet his father till the
year 1826, still he kept up a correspondence with him
from the time of his first visit to Rome, in 1821-2.
He speaks of having received from him affectionate
letters, expressing a wish to see his son, and assuring
him that he would do so before two years had elapsed,
but did not say how or where. Jerome thought it improbable that his father would visit this country. He
allowed his son a pension of twelve hundred dollars a
year.

We have already seen how displeased Madame Bonaparte was on account of the large amount spent by her
son in the first year of his college life, and her determi-

nation to limit his annual expenses to eleven hundred dollars. Thereupon Jerome reduced his expenses as much as possible, and lived, as he says, "as economically as he could and at the same time maintain the appearance of a gentleman."

In the following letter he defends himself from the charges of extravagance continually alleged against him both by his mother and grandfather.

JEROME NAPOLEON BONAPARTE TO WM. PATTERSON.

CAMBRIDGE, March 3, 1824.

.   .   .   .

Mamma complains of my expenses a great deal in three several letters which I have just received from her, and says that she will allow in future eleven hundred dollars per annum for my expenses. I am perfectly satisfied with that sum, and will not let my expenses exceed it, and do not think that they will have exceeded it for the last year, or, at most, only by the additional expense of going to Baltimore, on which subject I consulted you. However agreeable it may be for me to go home once a year, I should prefer giving it up and not going home again until I graduate ; or, however advantageous I may conceive a college education to be for me, I should prefer giving it up too, rather than to hear these continual and uninterrupted complaints about my expenses, when I am conscious to myself of doing everything in my power to avoid giving dissatisfaction of any kind. When I received a letter from you ten months ago of the same nature as the one I have now before me, though I was much hurt to hear complaints, yet, knowing the cause, and conceiving it very possible to avoid the repetition of complaints by removing the cause, I was in a measure consoled ; but now I cannot find the same consolation when I reflect that I am doing all in my power to give you satisfaction, and that your complaints increase, for during this week I have received four letters, three from mamma and one from you, all teeming with reproaches.

Adieu, dear grandfather. I hope to hear shortly from you again. Give my love to the family, and believe me ever

Your most affectionate and obedient grandson,

JEROME NAPOLEON BONAPARTE.

Mme. Bonaparte remained in Geneva until the 10th of March, 1824, when she left for Paris, intending to spend the spring of that year in the French capital. On the 19th of May, Jerome wrote to his grandfather from Cambridge: "I have received a letter from mamma, dated Paris, March 27th. She does not say anything certain about her return to this country. I have advised her to leave Europe this summer and not to return there. I have received another letter from my Cousin Charlotte: she invites me, in the name of her father, to pass the coming vacation at their country-seat. I have been obliged to decline doing so, because the vacation lasts only two weeks, and I do not wish to go as far as Philadelphia without going to Baltimore, and the vacation is too short to do both; moreover, it would cost a good deal of extra money, which is as well saved."

Finally, on the 15th of July, Mme. Bonaparte sailed from Havre for New York, where she arrived toward the end of August. We have only one letter from her at this period, in which she gives her reason for returning to America, and her plans during her residence here. She also furnishes some interesting facts concerning King Jerome.

Madame Bonaparte was joined by her son immediately upon her arrival in America, and accompanied him to Lancaster, Massachusetts. For a trifling breach of dis-

cipline he had been rusticated for three months, and was
passing the time in this quiet country town.[6]   She

---

[6] The following letter to his grandfather explains the cause of Jerome's
suspension :—

LANCASTER, August 16, 1824.

DEAR GRANDFATHER.—Since my last to you, which as yet is unanswered,
an occurrence has happened which I could neither foresee nor prevent.   I
have been suspended for three months—a circumstance at which I should
rather rejoice than regret, were I not prevented by it from going home. My
not being allowed to go home is doubly unpleasant, as it deprives me of
seeing you for four months, and as I have some business with my uncle, at
Bordentown, which I shall be obliged to transact by means of letter.   I
should otherwise be rather pleased with my suspension, as it gives me an
opportunity of improving myself a great deal, and as the cause of it is such
as neither to injure me in the estimation of the government or any one else.
I suppose the president has written you all about it ; but, as he may have
left out some circumstances, I shall give you a detailed account of it.   There
are several clubs in college authorized by government, which have libraries
annexed to them.   I am a member of one of them, secretary of another.   The
first, of which I am a member, had a meeting on Friday, the 29th of July,
for the purpose of choosing a librarian, and, after the business of the club
was transacted, the members stayed about three-quarters of an hour drinking
some punch, which had been provided for that purpose by the vice-president
of the club. There was no riot nor disturbance. The club has been assembled
regularly two or three times a term for the space of fifty years, and has always
had something to eat and drink after the business of the club had been transacted.   Ever since I have been chosen a member, about fifteen months ago,
I have regularly attended the meetings, and no notice of them had been taken
before by the government.   The meetings of the club are always published
on the college boards, so the government must have known that they had
meetings.   I have been present at twelve of the meetings, which are always
held in one of the college rooms.   No one had ever been punished for them
before, and I assure you I was not a little astonished when the president
told me I was suspended for three months.   He told me at the same time
that he was very sorry ; that the government was much pleased with my
regularity and attention to my studies ; that they blamed me, not for anything I had done, but only for being a member of a club, which, by-the-bye,
they themselves authorized.   I do not know what the president has written
to you, but the facts are as I have stated them.   I am aware that you will
not blame me for suffering an unjust punishment ; but you may think that,
had I been more prudent, I could have avoided it ; such, however, is not the

remained with him until his return to college on the 2nd of November, 1824, after which, as we ascertain from a letter from Jerome to his grandfather, he accompanied her as far as Hartford, where she took the steamboat for New York on her way to Baltimore, where she arrived about the middle of November. In the same letter Jerome says, " I called to see General Lafayette in Boston. I see by the papers that he has paid a visit to my uncle at Bordentown. I am glad you have interested yourself in the preparations being made for his reception." In another letter, dated October 24, 1824, this wise young man says to his grandfather, " I am glad to hear that you have got through with General Lafayette. I fear that you must have been very much fatigued with the noise and disorder which accompany him wherever he goes. I think that the general will find that living on *honours* will not agree with his age and broken constitution. The papers say that he is only sixty-eight years old. I am sure he looks near ninety-eight. He was very civil to mamma when she was in Paris; therefore I called on him while in Boston."

MADAME BONAPARTE TO WILLIAM PATTERSON.

LANCASTER, 23rd September, 1824.

DEAR SIR,—I observe by the contents of your letter of the 14th of this month that you were under the impression that I meant to reside in Baltimore, which is not, however, my intention. I am fully aware of all the inconveniences which you have pointed out, and should be unwilling to expose either others or myself to them for any length of time. I came to this country because it is incum-

---

case, as no prudence can teach a man how to avoid that which has never happened before, and of which he can have no idea until after it takes place.

bent on me to attend to my property ; and more particularly is my
presence necessary at the present moment, that the government is
going to pay off part of their debt, which will compel me to seek
some advantageous mode of reinvesting my money. My funds too,
in the State banks, call for my attention. To keep together my
little property is naturally an object of consideration to me, but I
think I shall be able to make the changes necessary in three or
four months at farthest. Jerome must remain two years longer at
college, and I consider it my duty, after settling my affairs, to be
as near him as possible, for which reason I shall try to establish
myself at Cambridge or in Boston. It is very uncertain what he
may be called upon to do in two years ; if nothing better should
offer in the interval, it will then be time enough for me to form a
permanent establishment for him and myself in Baltimore. I can
be of more use to him at present in New England than I could
possibly be in Baltimore. I found him suspended on my arrival,
which annoyed me excessively ; but as every one who has been
educated at Cambridge has found himself at least once in the same
predicament, I have consoled myself. His professor of metaphysics
tells me he has seen no one with a better capacity for this study,
which is a far greater proof of intellect than the facility of learning
languages. I have allowed Henry to go on without me, because
I desire to remain with Jerome until his suspension is past, and
to avoid the month of October, the bilious season in Baltimore.
Jerome has, as you know, received several letters from his father,
who is gone to Trieste, where his nieces, the Misses Bacciochi,
reside. They were, I believe, left by his sister, the Princess Eliza,
under his guardianship. They have large fortunes, and would be
excellent matches for any young man with a great name and a
slender purse. Prince Jerome's finances are, I fancy, in a very
bad state. The Emperor of Russia allows him twelve thousand
dollars annually. His children by the Princess of Würtemberg
will of course be provided for by her brother the king. I suppose
Madame will leave the fifty thousand dollars she destines for each
of her sons in the hands of trustees, who will pay Prince Jerome
the interest monthly. Without this precaution, his creditors would
seize the whole. I have not received the twelve hundred dollars
from him for the last year ; but as I never spent a farthing extra

whilst it was paid, and as I always calculated upon the *non*-payment, it causes me no pecuniary embarrassment. I have endeavoured through life not to let my yearly expenditure exceed my income, and have thus avoided the contraction of debts.

I remain, dear sir, very truly yours,

E. P.

Will you have the goodness to remember me to Miss Spear, and to say I have been so busy since my arrival that I have written to none of my friends.

During her residence in America, Madame Bonaparte wrote to Lady Morgan a letter, in which she took occasion to assure her that the latter's reputation was as great in the United States as in Europe, and adds :—

I wish I could see and listen to you once more ; but this, like all my desires, must be disappointed, and I am condemned to vegetate for ever in a country where I am not happy. My son is very intelligent, and very good and very handsome—all these advantages add to the regret I experience at the destiny which compels me to lose life in this region of *ennui*. You have a great deal of imagination, but it can give you no idea of the mode of existence inflicted on us. The men are all merchants ; and commerce, although it may fill the purse, clogs the brain. Beyond their counting-houses they possess not a single idea ; they never visit except when they wish to marry. The women are all occupied in *les détails de ménage* and nursing children ; these are useful occupations, but do not render people agreeable to their neighbours.

I am condemned to solitude, which I find less insupportable than the dull réunions which I might sometimes frequent in this city. The men, being all bent on marriage, do not attend to me, because they fancy I am not inclined to change the evils of my condition for those they could find me in another. Sometimes, indeed, I have been thought so *ennuyée* as to be induced to accept *very respectable* offers ; but I prefer remaining as I am to the horror of marrying a person I am indifferent to. You are very happy in every respect— too much so to conceive what I suffer here.

Paris offers too many *agrémens*, too many agreeable recollections —among the latter you are my greatest—and I think with pain that I shall perhaps never see you again. . . . .

I suppose you will return to Paris, where I hope you will be happy and pleased. It is very easy to be pleased and happy in your situation, because every one is pleased with you, and you are loved whenever you choose to be so. The French admire you so much that you ought to live with them. Suppose you were to come to this country ; it is becoming the fashion to travel here, and to know something of us, and I assure you that if you would spend some time here you might find materials for an interesting work—*de toutes les manières*. You would make any country interesting that you wrote about.

I wish I could return to Europe, but it is impossible—a single woman is exposed to so many disagreeable comments in a foreign country ; her life, too, is so solitary except when in public, which is not half the day, that it is more prudent for me to remain here ; besides, I have at present only eleven hundred pounds a year to spend, which you know make only twenty-five thousand francs— not enough to support me out of my own family, where I have nothing to spend in eating, or in carriages, rent, &c. . . . .

I should write you more frequently were there any incidents in this dull place which might interest you, or any anecdotes that could amuse—there are, alas, none. I embroider and read, *pour me défaire de mon temps*—they are the only distractions left me. Do you remember the description Madame de Staël gives of the mode of life Corinna found in England, and the subjects of conversation at Lady Edgerman's table, which were limited to births, marriages, and deaths ? I am so tired of hearing these three important events discussed, and my opinion of them has been so long decided—that it is a misery to be born, and to be married I have painfully experienced without lessening my dread of death. So you may imagine how little relish I have for the conversation on these *triste* topics, and how gladly I seek refuge from listening to it by retiring to my own apartment.

Adieu, my dear Lady Morgan—*il ne faut pas vous ennuyer davantage.* Make my best love acceptable to Sir Charles, and ask him to think sometimes of me. Write to me, I entreat you. J'ai plus que jamais besoin de vos lettres pour me consoler de tout ce que j'ai perdu en vous quittant pour revenir dans mon triste pays. . . . .

I remain most affectionately yours,

ELIZA PATTERSON.

On the 25th of May, 1825, Jerome writes from New York to his grandfather: "I went to Philadelphia to meet mamma, agreeably to her request, and remained there two days, when we left it for this place. We arrived here about two hours ago, and shall remain here until my vacation is over. I had hoped to go to Baltimore to see you during this vacation, but mamma was anxious to come to New York immediately, so that I have not had time and was obliged to defer it. Mamma was very much pleased in Philadelphia, and received a great many attentions from the inhabitants."

MADAME BONAPARTE TO WILLIAM PATTERSON.

NEW YORK, June 4th, 1825.

DEAR SIR,—I have been some days here. I find from Mrs. Greenwood and Mr. Palmer, whom I had commissioned to get lodgings for me in Boston, that there is nothing there which could at all suit me. The professors at Cambridge do not approve of the mothers of the students living at Cambridge. I have been obliged either to determine upon opening my house in Baltimore, or accompanying Mrs. Toussard to Paris, which latter I have preferred, as it will not cost me more, and I can purchase my plate and other furniture there. I shall board with Mrs. Toussard during my absence, which will lighten both her and my expenses. I shall return next July, when Jerome leaves college, as it would be unnecessary for me to open house before ; besides that, I should be too lonesome living alone.

I remain, dear sir, affectionately yours,

E. P.

Should Edward remain a year in Europe I could return with him. If he should not, I shall come in with Madame d'Outil, the daughter-in-law of Col. Toussard, who is going out to spend a year in France, and means to return to this country.

Thus, on the 6th of June, 1825, Madame Bonaparte again sailed for France for a year's visit. It will be seen that this year extended to nine before she again visited her native country. She arrived at Havre on the 4th of July, after a quick and pleasant voyage of twenty-eight days. She remained in that city over four months, and it is difficult to understand why a woman with her fondness for gay society should have stayed so long in a dull little seaport. In the first letter written to her father after her arrival, she gives an account of her voyage and of her friends in France.

MADAME BONAPARTE TO WILLIAM PATTERSON.

HAVRE, 10th of July, 1825.

DEAR SIR,—We arrived here on the 4th of the month, after a very agreeable voyage. We had a widow lady called Mrs. Ferris, of New York, on board, who has joined our party. We have remained a few days at Havre, to amuse ourselves by visiting the towns in the environs, the theatre, &c. Mrs. Ferris is about sixty. She will accompany us to Paris, and thence goes to Switzerland with her son. The English Consul's family at Havre have been very attentive to us. We dine at Mr. Beasley's to-day. There are a great many English ladies here at present. We had no less than five widows in the vessel in which we came out. We played whist every day, and they seemed to enjoy themselves quite as much as if they had been settled at home with husbands. It is said that Gen'l Devereux has been imprisoned by the Emperor of Austria for having talked too freely about politics. I know not whether the report is true, or whether it was in Austria or in the dominions of the emperor in Italy. It is said that the Princess Borghese left her fortune to her two brothers, Louis and Jerome. I do not believe that she has much to leave. The Catons have returned to England. Mr. Reid writes to me that Mr. Brown is still very ill, and that they are going to a watering-place for his health. Mrs. Brown is very dashing, and goes to all parties in Paris. Mrs. Toussard is in great spirits, and seems delighted at getting back to France.

My old maid Estelle has paid me a visit, and is very anxious for me to take her again into my service, which I have refused to do. Mrs. Toussard and myself have agreed to open house together in Paris. Mrs. Payne and her daughters are travelling through Germany, and will, I hope, spend next winter in Paris. I should be much obliged to you to get an act passed next winter to enable Jerome to hold and inherit real property in the State of Maryland. I think, from what I hear of Mr. Brown's health, that he will not be able to continue in France, which will be a sad disappointment to her.

Yours affectionately,
E. Patterson.

The Bonaparte family having failed to marry Jerome to his cousin Charlotte, did not entirely abandon the hope of a favourable marriage for him. In the summer of 1825 his father wrote to him that, since that marriage did not take place, he had been looking out for another match for his son, and asked what his mother could give in case a suitable person should be found. To this suggestion Jerome replied that his mother's fortune was so small that it would be impossible for her to do anything for him. He consults his grandfather as usual in regard to this matter: "I would wish to have your opinion on this subject. For my own part, I do not think that a wife, however rich she might be, would be

at all desirable for me. I am too young, by many
years, to marry, and as long as I can live comfortably
without a wife, I think it more wise not to marry. I am
perfectly happy and contented with my present situation
and prospects ; a wife would be apt to mar the whole,
and as I have been brought up to hold the single
state as preferable to the married state, my plans have
always been formed with a view to remaining unmarried.
If I marry I must change them all. This is my way
of thinking ; but I would submit it all to your better
judgment and experience."

In answer to the above, Mr. Patterson wrote to
Jerome the following excellent advice, although it was
directly opposed to the known views of his mother on
the subject :—

WILLIAM PATTERSON TO JEROME NAPOLEON BONAPARTE.

BALTIMORE, August 14, 1825.

MY DEAR JEROME,—I wrote you a few days since in reply to
your two former letters, since which I have received yours of the
6th instant, and have duly noted and considered its contents. It
appears to me that your father has not reflected sufficiently on
your situation and prospects in this country, to propose looking
out for a wife for you in Europe. Your education and habits will
not be at all suitable for the kind of life you must lead there in
case of marrying and settling in that country, nor would it answer
to bring a wife from thence to this country ; for she would never be
satisfied or reconciled to our manners and customs. Besides, as you
observe yourself, you are much too young to think of marrying at
present. Your father's family cannot get clear of the notion of what
they once were and the brilliant prospects they then had. Their

fortunes cannot now be very considerable ; they are living in idleness on what they have, and when that property they now possess
comes to be divided among their children, it will scarcely keep
them from want, and the next generation will in all probability be
beggars.   What prospect, then, would you have by marrying into
such a family, as I presume your father means that you should be
connected in marriage with some of your own relations ?   I hardly
think you could be reconciled or happy to live in Europe under
any circumstances.   It will be time enough to think of future prospects and arrangements after you have finished your education.
Your mother's fortune will be sufficient for you and her so long as
you can live together, but will not afford a division for two establishments.   Your father's family are all on the decline and going
down hill, will soon be so reduced and scattered that they will be
of no consequence whatever.   Should you remain in this country
and make a good use of your time and talents, you may rise to
consequence ; but in Europe you would be nothing, and must come
to nothing with the other branches of your family.   I have thus
given you my opinion and advice fully and clearly, which I hope
you will consider well before you take any steps that might interfere
with your future happiness.

I am, dear Jerome,

Yours very sincerely,

WILLIAM PATTERSON.

M

CHAPTER XI.

IT was while Madame Bonaparte was at Havre that
Lafayette returned from his visit to the United States.
She had seen him the previous year in Baltimore, and
the day after he arrived in France he called upon her.

Madame Bonaparte attended all the festivities given
at Havre in his honour. In a letter written to her father
at this time she speaks of these, and also alludes to a
report in the newspapers of a legacy of twenty thousand
francs left by the Princess Borghese to Jerome. The
report proved to be correct. The princess died at the
Borghese palace, near Florence, on the 9th of June,
1825. She appointed her brothers Louis and Jerome
the principal heirs, but left to each of the daughters of
her sister Caroline thirty thousand dollars. Madame
Bonaparte rejoiced that her son's name was mentioned
in the princess's will, as it gave him consequence in the
family.

MADAME BONAPARTE TO WILLIAM PATTERSON.

HAVRE, October 6, 1825.

DEAR SIR,—General Lafayette arrived yesterday, landed at one o'clock, and was taken to Mr. La Roche's (his friend) to stay. He came to see me this morning. We then went to a public breakfast at Mr. Beaseley's. At twelve he set out for Paris in his carriage. Madame George Lafayette and her three daughters have been waiting here for ten days to meet him. There were a great many parties given to her by the inhabitants of Havre. I was invited to them all. General Lafayette desired me to write to you by the packet which is to sail on the 15th of this month, to tell you of his safe arrival, and to recall him to your recollection. He is quite delighted with your present to him of cows. He has requested me to write to him when I arrive at Paris, if he should not be there, and has expressed his wish to see me at his house at La Grange. He wants me to see his cows, he says. Beaseley gave a very fine breakfast this morning. His house is so small that he had a tent pitched in his garden, under which was the breakfast-table. Lafayette left us to set out for Paris. He was accompanied part of the way by a number of gentlemen of this place on horseback. The Commodore Morris and Mr. Somerville came to the breakfast. Somerville appears to be in a dying state, and does not know how to take care of himself. He says he will not be able to go to Sweden next winter. I intend trying the south of France. Edward spent ten days with me here. He was quite pleased with France. I advised him to try the waters of Cheltenham, where he now is. I am certain that his malady is bile. He is very much better, and was very much amused at Havre, which he thinks quite as pleasant a place to live in as Baltimore. Mr. and Mrs. Mansfield and Mr. and Mrs. Hughes were here whilst he was. Mrs. Hughes looks as well as she ever did, and Mrs. Mansfield better. Mrs. Hughes appeared to regret Sweden very much. She and Mrs. Mansfield both agreed that neither of them can ever live in America again. Mr. Hughes says that he could live in any place. It does not appear to me that Laura's health was the cause of their leaving

Sweden. They take out a governess for Miss and Master Hughes. Miss Toussard is still travelling with the Countess Hocquard. She is to let me know when they arrive at Paris. I hear that Mary and the Catons have gone to Dublin, and are travelling about Ireland. I hear that Emily Oliver and Mr. Gibbs are married. I think: was very wise in Oliver to make the match. If my son were a daughter, I should not rest until I got her married ; as it is, I hope he will not think of marrying. Mr. Canning, who was in America, is married. I wrote to you, Jerome, and Miss Spear, by Hughes. I told you that Lloyd Rogers and Gen. Devereux had been very much caressed by the King of Westphalia, when they were in Rome. Devereux told Edward that he had been very much attended to by Jerome. One of Lucien Bonaparte's daughters (the Countess de Possé) left her husband, a Swedish nobleman, and claimed Hughes's protection at Stockholm. She says he treated her ill, and in Europe women have fully as much their own way as the men have. I have seen by the papers that the Princess Borghese left my son a legacy of twenty thousand francs—about three thousand five hundred dollars. I wonder if it be true. I very much doubt whether her whole estate will pay off the legacies. Whether I get paid or not, I am very glad that she has mentioned Jerome's name in her will, as it gives him a consequence, and, in my opinion, consequence is not to be disdained. The whole family inquire about my son of all the Americans who go to Rome, and as you know the English and Americans are crazy about that family, it is of great importance that they should speak of him in the way they do. Lloyd Rogers appears to be very reluctant to return home. I am decidedly now of opinion that people who are to live in America should never leave it. Mrs. Mansfield says that she is afraid to educate her children in France, because they would get a distaste for England and never be happy out of France. This is the reason why she and Mansfield have not moved to Paris.

Adieu, my dear sir,

Yours affectionately,

E. PATTERSON.

General Lafayette looks better than he did last year. Every

one in Europe is astonished at the generosity of the American Government to him.[1]

I am very anxious to get an act passed by the Assembly of Maryland to enable Jerome to hold and inherit real property. By the amendment which General Smith showed me before my departure, I found that he would not have the rights of a citizen until two years after he became of age.

In her next letter Madame Bonaparte announces the marriage of her sister-in-law, Mrs. Robert Patterson, to the Marquis of Wellesley. The lady was the granddaughter of Charles Carroll of Carrollton. Her first husband died in November, 1822, after which she went abroad.

It is a singular circumstance that two Baltimore ladies —themselves nearly related by marriage—should become connected—the one with Napoleon, the other with the Duke of Wellington.

MADAME BONAPARTE TO WILLIAM PATTERSON.

HAVRE, November 2, 1825.

DEAR SIR,—I write by this packet to announce to you the marriage of Mrs. Robert Patterson. Mrs. Brown received a letter from Betsy Caton the day on which it was to take place.

She has made the greatest match that any woman ever made, and I suppose now that people will see that Mrs. Caton was right in starving herself to keep her daughters in Europe. The Marquis of Wellesley is Lord Lieutenant of Ireland. He is sixty-five. He married an Italian singer, by whom he had a family of children. She is dead. He has no fortune ; on the contrary, he is over head

---

[1] For the services rendered and sacrifices made in the achievement of American independence, Congress had voted to General Lafayette during this visit, the sum of two hundred thousand dollars, and twenty-four thousand acres of land, to be chosen from the most fertile part of the national domain.

and cars in debt. His salary is thirty thousand pounds per annum
as Lord Lieutenant of Ireland. He will be there eighteen months
longer, and if the king does not give him another place, he is
entitled, as a *poor* nobleman, to at least a thousand pounds a year.
He is the brother of the Duke of Wellington.

The Catons, I suppose, will be enchanted at the match, and
with reason, too, for it gives them a rank in Europe; and with Mr.
Carroll's money to keep it up, they may be considered the most
fortunate in the United States of America. His being without
fortune is of little consequence when his rank is considered.
There is not a woman in Europe who would not prefer a man of
rank, without money, to the richest man in the world who has no
title. To be sure, it would not have done for a poor woman to
marry a poor nobleman; but, of course, old Mr. Carroll will strain
every nerve to maintain his grand-daughters, now that they have,
beyond all probability, connected themselves so highly. Mary's
fortune is reported in Europe to be eight hundred thousand dollars
cash. It has been mentioned in all the papers at that sum.

I shall leave this on the seventh of the month for Paris. I shall
go with Mr. and Mrs. O'Beirne. He is the brother of the late
Bishop of Meath; she is the daughter of an Irish baronet, and the
niece of Lord Castle Coste. Mrs. Toussard is waiting there for
me. She has been travelling all summer with the Countess Hocquard. She writes in great spirits, and I think she will never
turn to America. She is in the best society in France, and if
her money hold out, she will spend the rest of her days there.

The English consul and family at Havre have been very attentive to me. Mr. Brown has recovered his health, I hear. Mrs.
Brown is enchanted with Europe, and spends a great deal of
money.

Mrs. Caton deserves the unexpected good fortune which has now
occurred to her family, by the sacrifices she has made to support
them abroad. I can only say that if Jerome were a girl, and had
made such a match, I am convinced that I should have died with
joy.

Edward spent some days with me at Havre. He writes to me
that he was on the point of embarking for New York. He takes
out a book which I have not been able to obtain at Havre, and

which Sir Frederick Fourke, a Gentleman of the Bedchamber of the King of England, tells me is a perfectly true account of manners and persons. It is the memoirs of Mrs. Harriet Wilson.

The Marquis Lafayette came to see me at Havre, and desired me to write you an account of his arrival, and to remember him most particularly to you. He has invited me to visit him at La Grange. He was very civil to me.

Adieu, my dear sir,

Yours affectionately,

E. PATTERSON.

Mrs. Dallas, widow of the person who wrote Lord Byron's memoirs, lives at Havre. She has lost the use of her limbs and never gets out of her bed.[2] She sent to request me to go to her, which I did, and spent an hour with her.

She is said to be a woman of genius. I hear that William Forman died with a bilious fever. I hope that Providence will let me die before my son. I pity poor Aunt Forman ; it is enough to kill her. I hope she inherits the farm from him.

There is an English society at Havre. Edward can tell you how gaily I spent my time. He was very much pleased in Europe.

Mr. and Mrs. Mansfield were here some days ; he seems out of spirits. I hope Mrs. Hughes has become more reconciled to her return to America than she seemed to be at the prospect of going when here.

The second week in November of this year Madame Bonaparte again visited Paris, where she spent the fol-

---

[2] The Mrs. Dallas here alluded to was the widow of the gentleman who persuaded Byron to publish the first two cantos of *Childe Harold's Pilgrimage*, upon his return from the East, instead of some verses in imitation of Horace, which the poet thought superior.

When *Childe Harold* appeared, and Byron " woke up one morning and found himself famous," refusing to " rack his brains for lucre," as he had accused Scott of doing, he gave the copyright of the work to Mr. Dallas, who had superintended its publication.

lowing winter, and from that city she wrote to Lady
Morgan the following letter, full of gossip :—

MADAME BONAPARTE TO LADY MORGAN.

PARIS, November 28, 1825.

MY DEAR LADY MORGAN,—Mrs. Evans gave me your welcome
letter; I cannot express to you how delighted I was at hearing
that you had not forgotten me. I passed only a few months in
Italy, where I saw the most beautiful woman in the world, who
since died in her *husband's* palace at Florence, surrounded by
friends, and conjugally regretted by Prince Borghese ! He buried
her in the handsomest chapel in Europe. She left a legacy to my
son of twenty thousand francs. *Voilà e peu de mots ce que j'ai à
dire de la Princesse Pauline.* I have been, *pour mes péchés*, a great
deal in Geneva—that centre of prudery, heartlessness, and illiberal
feelings. I left it with pleasure, and hope that I shall never return
to it. I have paid a short visit to America. "Aux cœurs biens
nés la patrie est *chère*," which does not mean that one should not
prefer the *séjour* of Paris to that of the dullest place on earth.

Lafayette was adored, caressed, and substantially rewarded. I
saw him in Baltimore, and talked to him of you, whom he loves
and admires, *malgré le temps et l'absence;* Miss Wright was with
him, or near him, all the time he was in America. She intends
writing *something*, of which he is to be the *hero*. Why did Moore
destroy Lord Byron's memoirs? It was a breach of confidence—
they were intended for publication.

You are very kind in inquiring after my father and my son. The
former is living, the latter has grown up handsome—a classical
profile, and *un esprit juste*. He is in America. My health is, as
sual, neither good nor bad : nerves very tormenting ; mind, as
ormerly, discontented, although I flatter myself that I am growing
more patient of injustice and egotism.

What do you say of De Genlis? . . . . One of her *truisms*
is that Madame de Villette was convinced of the truth of the Christian religion—a conviction that our poor dear friend certainly im-

parted to none of those who lived with her. Genlis has pleased no one by the publication of this work of imagination—the drippings and last squeezings of her brain. . . . .

Poor Denon is dead; Madame D'Houchin is, I hear, dreadfully grieved at her deplorable *veuvage de cœur.* Nothing can, I think, console for the loss of a person whom one has loved and been loved by. Madame Capodoce is here; she looks dreadfully ill. Madame Suard is still living, and as foolish as ever. Do you know a dull writer called Julien, who publishes a periodical paper? I thank Sir Charles for his kisses, which I reciprocate at the same time; but I send my love to him. I hope the gloves fitted—wedding[3] gloves, sent by the Lord-Lieutenant of the Marchioness of Wellesley!!!! Was the Duke, Great Bolingbroke, at the wedding? Do contrive to get a letter to me by *une occasion particulière.* I do not like the idea of the police, your readers, receiving what was intended for me. Pray let me know what you are doing, &c., &c., &c. Be assured I shall not slip through your fingers through my negligence. Adieu.

Believe me,

Ever most affectionately yours,

E. PATTERSON.

P.S.—Warden is as usual; he never leaves the Faubourg St. Germain. I have no doubt he has *un sentiment*—nothing else could keep any one there. What do you think of Miss Harriet Wilson's life, written by herself? Every one reads it. She is living in Paris, which seems to be the favourite residence of all naughty Englishwomen. Miss Harriet is married to a very handsome man, who was willing to make an honest woman of her. I have fifty scandalous things to tell you; but I write in haste that I may send my letter to England by a friend. I have been in Paris only a few days; I have seen no one. All the people whom I know are dead or absent.

---

[3] Madame Bonaparte refers to the marriage of her sister-in-law, noticed above.

It is remarkable how constantly Madame Bonaparte kept in view the interests of her son. She was advised that it would be a great advantage for him at this time to visit his father and the rest of the family in Ialy, hoping that he would make so good an impression upon them that they would mention him in their wills; also that it would be the means of introducing him into the first society of Europe, which might enable him to form an advantageous matrimonial alliance.

Madame Bonaparte gives a lively description of the Marquis of Wellesley—his debts, difficulties, and infirmities; but, notwithstanding these drawbacks, she thinks Mrs. Caton is to be congratulated upon marrying her daughter to a man of his rank.

MADAME BONAPARTE TO WM. PATTERSON.

PARIS, 23 January, 1826.

DEAR SIR,—I have been advised by several persons in Europe to have Bo sent out by way of Leghorn, to visit his father and the rest of the family; but if it is done, it must be kept a secret from all of his father's relations in America, as there is great jealousy about the old lady's money. The cardinal[4] has sold his hotel in Paris for five hundred thousand dollars. The sum is immense, but, as his establishment took up a whole square in one of the best streets in Paris, it has been considered a fair price.

I confess that I am not at all of opinion that expectations of future wealth are worth running after, but it is certain that they have it in their power to leave legacies, and that I shall be much blamed if I do not put the boy in the way of getting mentioned in their wills. It has been stated to me, too, that he ought to be intro-

---

[4] Fesch.

duced by them into the best society in Europe, and that with his appearance there is a chance of his doing something in the way of an establishment. In short, it is the opinion of every one that I should neglect his interest very much if I do not allow him to go to Rome to pass a few months. I should not think of letting him stay longer, and as it would be useless for me to be there now that he is old enough to take care of himself, and as I have no wish to go to Rome again, I would take the opportunity of going with Mrs. Toussard to Florence to pass next winter. We should be only five days' journey from Rome, and I should hear from him every week, I should not like to be farther from him, and Mrs. Toussard says she would be quite delighted to go with me. The fact is, that nothing would be lost by his going to visit his family; if nothing else should be gained, it will give him a consequence to be seen with them, and enable him to make acquaintance with the first people in Europe. I should pass too for a very unfeeling parent if I do not let him see his father. I shall certainly be the loser in point of expense by his going, as I shall have everything to pay ; but, having brought him into the world, it is of course my duty to spend money upon him when his interest requires it, and to try to render his life as agreeable as I can. If he could find a vessel from some port in the United States, for Leghorn, I should like to obtain a letter of credit upon a banker there for twelve hundred dollars, that he may be at no loss for money on his arrival, hoping that he would have sufficient prudence to spend only what would be absolutely necessary for his comfort. I think, too, that it would be a great advantage to his manners if he could spend a few months with his relations, and, at all events, he would form acquaintances who may be useful to him at a future period. The month of May or June would be the best time for him to sail, and I should take him to America the year after. I suppose you have all heard of Mary's great good fortune in marrying the Marquis of Wellesley. He is sixty-six years old—so much in debt that the plate on his table is hired ; had his carriage once seized in the streets of Dublin, and has great part of his salary mortgaged ; but, with all these drawbacks to perfect happiness, he is considered a very great match, because he is a man of rank. She certainly has had great luck, and Mrs. Caton may, with truth, congratulate herself upon the judgment and patience she displayed in sending her daughters to Europe, and in keeping them abroad until something advantageous offered. The marquis is very infirm, but at his death, she will of course obtain a pension as a poor peeress, and her mother can support her if she does not, which of course she will be too happy to do, now that they are connected so highly. I wish something would offer for my son : every one can marry their children greatly except myself.

Mr. Astor has at length succeeded in marrying his daughter very well. She is married to a Mr. Rumph, a German who represents all the free German towns. He has no fortune, but is well con-nected, and has it in his power to introduce her into the best company. Astor is delighted with the match. He and Mr. Reid managed to make it : and Reid tells me he assisted to draw and sign the marriage articles, by which Astor settled three hundred thousand dollars on her for the present. Rumph is a handsome man of thirty-five, and we all think she has been very fortunate in getting him, as she has no beauty. They are to establish themselves in Paris. I should never have believed that Astor had given three hundred thousand dollars to secure the match, if Mr. Reid had not been one of the witnesses.

Yours affectionately,

E. P.

In the next letter Madame Bonaparte again speaks of her son's visit to Italy, before settling down permanently in Baltimore. She seemed to think that association with the Bonapartes would polish his manners and be an advantage in a thousand ways.

MADAME BONAPARTE TO WILLIAM PATTERSON.

PARIS, 21 February, 1826.

.   .   .   .

DEAR SIR,—I think that it is perhaps a duty to let Jerome know his father, that he may never reproach himself at any future period, at all events. I should not like to take upon myself the responsibility of refusing my consent to such a proceeding, being desirous to fulfil to the extent of my power my duties as a parent. He would have an opportunity of seeing the world, of being introduced to the best company, and improving himself in every way, which is desirable before commencing the study of the law. I should think, too, that it would be agreeable for himself to pass a year in Europe under their protection, before settling down in Baltimore. One cannot tell what may be the future career of a young person, and I confess that I should like his manners to receive that polish which can only be acquired by living with strangers and subjecting one's self to the restraints imposed by society and an early intercourse with the world. Having always had his interest and happiness in view, it has been my constant endeavour through life to procure him every possible advantage; and although it costs me much uneasiness in thinking of the risks of a sea-voyage for him, as well as a longer separation from myself, I prefer making this last sacrifice to the prospect of advantage to him. Madame de Toussard is anxious to visit Italy, and the Countess Hocquard wishes also to spend next winter there, which would afford me an occasion of going as far as Florence, to be near my son. I should return with him in the summer of 1827, and then we should fix ourselves in Baltimore. I do not think Mrs. Toussard will ever return to America; her life is passed delightfully here. I beg you to mention this plan for Jerome to no one. If you could give him a letter of credit on a banker in Leghorn for twelve hundred dollars, I should commission Miss Spear to pay you. If there should be a vessel to Gibraltar—there are constant opportunities from that place to Leghorn—it would be preferable to go direct from New York or Boston to Leghorn; however, I do not wish any of the family at Philadelphia to know anything on the subject, as they are anxious to keep every one from their mother to whom she may be likely to leave anything.

I remain, my dear sir,

Very affectionately yours,

E. P.

While Madame Bonaparte was thus representing to her father the many advantages that her son would derive from a visit to Europe, the King of Westphalia, who had heard of the proposed visit, wrote to his son, expressing some apprehension that his presence in Rome might be misunderstood at the courts of Würtemberg and Russia, as it might be construed into invalidating the marriage of their relative, the Princess Catherine. This letter reached Jerome after he had embarked. Had he postponed his voyage until he was made acquainted with the confidences and anxieties of his father, he would probably have abandoned the visit.

PRINCE JEROME TO JEROME NAPOLEON BONAPARTE.

ROME, le 6 Mars, 1826.

MON CHER ENFANT,—J'ai reçu ta lettre du 26 Novembre. *Tu penses bien que depuis longtemps son contenu m'occupe d'une manière sérieuse; mais ma position est tellement compliquée par rapport à la reine et aux princes nos enfants, que je ne sais comment les mettre en équilibre avec ta position particulière,* puisque, quand même ma femme, dont le cœur noble et généreux est si bien connu, consentirait à beaucoup de choses par rapport à toi, *nous trouverions les cours de Wurtemberg et de Russie qui protesteraient contre toute démarche qui aurait l'air d'invalider le mariage de leur princesse.*

À présent, mon cher enfant, tu es un homme ; il faut donc qu'enfin *je tâche de te mettre dans une position naturelle sans préjudicier en rien à l'état de la reine et des princes nos enfants.*

J'approuve et désire que tu fasses tes dispositions pour arriver à Livourne dans le courant du mois d'Octobre : tu trouveras chez le consul américain une lettre pour toi. *Elle te dira si tu dois m'attendre à Livourne ou bien où tu dois venir me trouver.*

Je parle souvent de toi avec ma mère, et c'est après m'être bien consulté avec elle que je te fais cette réponse, qui, comme tu le penses bien, est à la connaissance de mon excellente femme. Tu trouveras ci-joint copie d'une lettre que m'a écrite ta mère, ainsi

que de ma réponse. Cela te mettra au courant de cette affaire :
d'ailleurs, je pense que tu prendras toi-même ton argent ici, si tu
ne l'as déjà reçu de ton oncle.

Ton affectionné et bon père,

Signe : JÉRÔME.

TRANSLATION.

ROME, March 6, 1826.

MY DEAR CHILD,—I have received your letter of Nov. 26. You
are right in thinking its contents have long occupied my serious attention ; but my position is so complicated on account of the queen
and the princes, our children, that I do not know how to reconcile
their rights with your peculiar position ; for, although my wife,
whose noble and generous heart is so well known, would consent
to many things on your account, we might find that the courts
of Würtemberg and Russia would protest against any act which
would have the appearance of invalidating the marriage of their
princess.

My dear child, you are now a man, and I desire to place you in
a natural position, without, however, prejudicing in any way the
condition of the queen and the princes, our children.

I approve and desire that you should make your arrangements
so as to arrive at Leghorn during next October. You will find at
the American consul's a letter, which will inform you whether you
are to wait for me at Leghorn, or where you are to go to find me.

I often speak of you to my mother, and it is after consulting with
her that I have written this letter, which, as you may imagine, is
known also to my excellent wife.

You will find herewith a copy of a letter written to me by your
mother, and also my answer.[5] That will inform you of the state of
affairs. I think you can take your money here, if you have not
already received it of your uncle.

Your affectionate father,

JEROME.

---

[5] These letters are not forthcoming.

When Prince Jerome heard of the expected arrival of his son, he again wrote to him that he did not wish to expose him to being placed in a false position, and told him that he would be at the Chateau of Lanciano, near Camerino, at the end of September, and would expect him there about the 1st of October.

CHAPTER XII.

MADAME BONAPARTE remained in Paris until early
in the summer of 1826, when she paid a visit of several
weeks to Switzerland. Before her departure from Paris
she wrote a brief letter to her father, containing several
interesting items of news. The Mrs. Brown mentioned
was the wife of the American Minister to France, and
Mr. Hughes was the Minister to Sweden. It will be
seen that Madame Bonaparte continues her deep interest
in the matrimonial affairs of Joseph's daughter. The
match alluded to did actually take place within a few
months after this letter was written.

MADAME BONAPARTE TO WILLIAM PATTERSON.

PARIS, 21st of May, 1826.

DEAR SIR,—I write a few lines in haste for the packet of the
25th, having put off my letters until I have not left myself time to
write long letters. I wrote to you that I thought it would be better

N

for Bo to pay his family a visit, as the year after his leaving college could be spent to advantage in Europe, and then I could return with him to America for him to read law. I have been advised by every one to let him do so, and I feel persuaded that it will be an advantage for his grandmother to see him again, as well as a great improvement in every way. Mde. Toussard and myself intend going on to Florence in the autumn. She talks of returning to America with me in the summer of 1827 ; but I do not believe that she will ever leave Europe again. Mrs. Brown is very attentive to us and lives in great style. Mde. Reubel [1] has just been to see me. She has lost her beauty and looks like an old woman. The cows you gave the Marquis Lafayette are very well. He desires to be particularly remembered to you. Only one of the cows died. They get on finely. I hear that Hughes is expected soon. James Donnell seems a prudent, nice young man. I hope that *Bo* will meet with no accident ; but I *do not* wish his uncle in Philadelphia to *know anything* about his departure. The match between his daughter and the young man she was sent to Europe to marry has not taken place, nor do I think it likely that it will. Adieu, my dear sir,

Affectionately yours,

E. P.

In accordance with his mother's wishes, Jerome sailed for Europe in the month of May, 1826, on the ship "William Penn," from Philadelphia, and after a "very mild and favourable passage," arrived at Rotterdam on the 15th of June. The day after landing he wrote to his grandfather, that he had found two letters from his mother awaiting him, telling him to meet her at Lausanne. He also informed Mr. Patterson that his mother had succeeded in securing a legacy of twenty thousand francs, left to him by the Princess Borghese.

---

[1] Formerly Miss Pascault, of Baltimore, who married Gen. Reubel about the same time that Jerome Bonaparte married Miss Patterson.

It appears from this letter, that Gilbert Stuart, who made studies for a portrait of the young bride of Jerome Bonaparte in 1804, which he never finished, had also undertaken to paint the portrait of the young Jerome; but, in his usual fashion, he finished the head and then stopped. The letter says: "I called upon him frequently for six months before I left Boston, to hurry him, but without success. Perhaps now that I am away he may be prevailed upon to finish it at once. When I left Boston I was on excellent terms with Stuart; but he is so capricious that he may possibly be offended at my having left the country without having given him any notice of it."

Toward the end of June, Jerome joined his mother in Switzerland. They remained a week at Lausanne, and then paid a brief visit to Geneva, after which they proceeded to the baths of Aix, near Chambéry in Savoy. From Aix Jerome wrote a letter to his grandfather, describing " the hot mineral springs, which cure the rheumatism and other complaints; the place itself is small, but the environs are pretty. . . . Mr. Brown, the American Minister to France, has been cured of the rheumatism by the waters of Aix."

In this letter Jerome said he had not heard from Rome since his departure from America. He supposed they had not heard there of his arrival in Europe. He says: "I shall write to my father from Florence, where mamma says she will spend the winter, and where I shall spend a fortnight before going to Rome, expecting to arrive there about the beginning of October, and to leave it on the 1st of April, 1827. So that I shall probably return to America about the middle of next summer. . . .

" I have seen a great many things since my departure from home, but the more I see, the more firmly I am persuaded of the superiority of my own country, and the more I desire to return to it and remain in it. This journey was absolutely necessary for me, on many accounts, but when it is over I shall settle myself quietly in America.

" . . . . I hear that Mr. Galatin has accepted the mission to England ; I suppose that he will not remain more than two years there, so that we will have him for a townsman yet, which will be a great thing for the town of Baltimore, as he is undoubtedly a man of very great talent."

Madame Bonaparte wrote to her father from Aix, under the date of June 19th, a letter full of her peculiar worldly wisdom.

MADAME BONAPARTE TO MR. PATTERSON.

Aix in Savoy, 19th July, 1826.

Dear Sir,—Jerome arrived safely at Rotterdam, and thence joined me at Lausanne. We went from that place to Geneva, where we passed a short time and came on to this place, which is on the road to Florence. I got the legacy paid, but had some trouble about it, and then was obliged to pay a tax to the government, &c. I declared that, if it was not at once given to me, I should appear there and claim it legally ; so, after letter upon letter, and consultation upon consultation with bankers, I succeeded and have got it safe, but curtailed and maimed. When there is question of money

I seldom allow myself to be made a dupe of, knowing that when people are poor they have neither friends nor admirers; therefore I am positive in preserving my rights. I know that I am not the best manager in the world, but it is not owing to any negligence or credulity on my part. I have placed the money at four per cent. in the hands of a banker at Paris, until I can make some arrangement, and at all events I can spend it, and account to Jerome for it out of my property in America, which will save the trouble of any remittances from America.

Mr. and Mrs. Brown are here. They have always been very attentive to me. I am sorry that they are about returning to Paris. I shall pass the winter at Florence and let Jerome go on to Rome. I hear that his grandmother is much out of health, so it is very fortunate that he came out. The old lady is not near so rich as people think, and she means, very properly, to leave great part of her fortune to the emperor's son, because she says his father gave her all she has. I believe that she has a great sense of justice. Her favourite child is Prince Jerome; but she knows that he cannot take care of money, and at all events she seems to think that her own children have less right to her money than the little Napoleon whom she scarcely knows. I hope she will leave *Bo* a legacy, because it is always a compliment to be remembered in people's wills, and a legacy here and there adds to one's means. The cardinal is rich, and as he hates most of his nephews and nieces, I hope he will leave Bo a trifle; but he may live a long time, being not above sixty; at all events, there will be no harm done in jogging his memory by the sight of the boy. Above all, it will improve his mind and manners to travel, and I consider that of equal value with legacies—indeed, of much greater. I am happy to find that he seems to know the value of order and economy, and that he keeps a regular account of his expenses, and that he really is much less foolish and giddy than young people generally are. He reads a good deal now, which will keep him out of mischief; and, above all, I hope he will not marry as they do in America, from idleness. The young people there have no idea of the misery they entail on themselves by early and inconsiderate marriages. I think Mr. Oliver ought to be thankful to Providence that Charles contents himself with a single life. I am sure that I would prefer paying

Jerome's expenses in Siberia or Africa rather than have him married
to some idiot and bringing beggars into the world every year, which
is what we see every day.   A man should never marry unless
he can give a fortune to each of his children, unless, indeed, he
is a mechanic, because *then* his posterity are not obliged to be
ladies and gentlemen.   I am in hopes that this trip will confirm
him in the good principles I have always endeavoured to inspire
him with on this subject, and that if he cannot get a wife to
support him, he will at least not get one for me to provide for.

I am glad to hear that Aunt Forman has turned landed pro-
prietor, and that her turn has at last come to play the great person.
I dare say she will now be thought more highly of than formerly.
There is nothing like prosperity to cover faults, and it may be said
that money covers more than charity.

Yours affectionately,

E. P.

Jerome did not neglect to announce to his grandmother
that he should soon have the happiness of thanking her
in person for her affectionate kindness to him ; and to
his letter she sent the following answer :—

" Rome, 26 Septembre, 1826.

"MON CHER FILS,—Je reçois aujourd'hui votre lettre du 24
Septembre. J'ai appris avec plaisir que vous jouissez d'une bonne
santé, et je vous remercie des bonnes nouvelles que vous me donnez
de celle de..Joseph et de sa famille. *Votre père est ici, il doit
sous peu de jours aller à Sienne, où il vous verra ; je vous engage
à suivre ses intentions, elles sont conformes à ma manière de voir
et d'envisager votre position.* Le Cardinal est absent depuis un
mois, je ne manquerai pas de m'acquitter de votre commission
pour lui aussitôt que je le verrai.

" Adieu, *mon cher fils*, je vous embrasse tendrement et vous prie
de croire à *mon constant attachement.*

" Votre bien affectionné grand'mère,

"*Signé :* MADAME."

TRANSLATION.

ROME, 26 September, 1826.

MY DEAR SON,—I received to-day your letter of the 24th of September. I am pleased to hear that you are in good health, and I thank you for the good news which you give me as to that of Joseph and his family. Your father is here, but he will leave in a few days for Sienna, where he will see you. I request you to follow his directions—they agree with my view of your position. The Cardinal has been absent for a month; I will not fail to give him your message as soon as I see him.

Adieu, my dear son. I embrace you tenderly and assure you of my constant attachment.

Your very affectionate grandmother,

MADAME.

In Florence Jerome met his uncle Louis Bonaparte, who was then living in that city; thence he proceeded, on the 25th of September, to join his father at the Chateau of Lanciano.

In her next letter Madame Bonaparte gives her father a short sketch of her movements after leaving Aix; and in announcing the marriage of the Princess Charlotte shows the great disappointment she felt that her own son did not succeed in marrying that young lady.

MADAME BONAPARTE TO WILLIAM PATTERSON.

FLORENCE, October 6, 1826.

DEAR SIR,—We arrived here near three weeks since, after having spent some time at Aix, a watering-place in Savoy. We spent three days at Genoa, where we experienced many attentions from the Marquis di Ferrari, the richest nobleman in the place. I had

been particularly intimate with his daughter, the Marchioness di
Savoli, whom I met at Aix, and had indeed known her father there.
Bo's cousin Charlotte we found married to her other cousin, who,
by all accounts, was forced by her perseverance into the match.
The young man, they say, showed no small reluctance to marry
this hideous little creature, and I find that her marriage portion,
which they promised to be seven hundred thousand dollars, has
not been paid yet; and I think it probable it never will. They
are living with his father near Florence, and she is said to be a
vixen. I had taken the precaution at Aix to charge a friend of
mine, of the house of Rothschild, to inquire most minutely on his
return to Paris into the state of her father's fortune, as I knew that
if she could not get the present husband her intention was to take
Bo; and I was determined that she should not get him without
paying two hundred thousand dollars ready money. Promises and
expectations would not have answered my purposes. I found her
married, however, on my arrival. My friend wrote to me that,
after the most minute and careful inquiry, and that, too, from the
most authentic source, he had discovered that her father's fortune
was much overrated : that he has a country establishment, it is
true, in France, which is worth two millions of francs (near four
hundred thousand dollars), but that to the value of eight hundred
thousand francs of it was mortgaged already to pay the marriage
portion of his eldest girl now in America. He has, besides, an
estate in Switzerland, which is estimated at one hundred thousand
dollars, but no purchaser can be found to take either of them off
his hands. He has nothing in Europe except these two estates.
He is always writing to his wife to sell and remit him money to
live ; and although he has no generosity, he is a bad manager in
every way and squanders immense sums. His wife is an economist, but the woman must live ; and although not extravagant,
she does not spend less than seven thousand dollars annually.
Her daughters are now both married ; the marriage portion of the
eldest was paid into the hands of the husband's father, who had
given them *as security* a mortgage on property which they *since*
find was already mortgaged. He has therefore cheated them out
of every farthing, and will *not* even, or indeed *cannot*, pay even the
interest. Neither the girl nor her husband, therefore, has any way

of living except upon her father. Miss Charlotte has shown no little sense in getting *herself* married, and in marrying, too, a man who will eventually be very well off. She kept *Bo* as a resource if she could not find a richer husband ; but I can tell her she would have found me rather too sharp to have let him run his head into the noose in the way her present spouse has done, without either ready money or security for the payment in any way. The individuals of this singular family are always cheating each other, and do not verify the proverb of setting a rogue to catch a rogue. I am not sorry that she is married at last, as I see her want of fortune would have been an insuperable objection to her marrying Bo. Her husband's father did not want the match, although, like the rest of his family, he had not sufficient judgment to sift out the truth of her not being as rich as was supposed. She has shown cunning and cleverness much beyond her years, and is said to have great talents. *Bo* is now with his father, who has contrived to get out of his aged parent almost all her whole fortune. It is said that he has spent almost everything she had since his residence near her; that she has given him even her jewels, and that, although avaricious to all the rest of her family, she refuses *him* nothing. Her children are all, naturally, quite furious at the injustice she has shown in giving to the most worthless of the race what ought to have been equally divided between them. I could never have believed that a woman of her judgment could have allowed herself to be duped out of her savings by a spendthrift son ; but they tell me that she is now in her dotage, and that she always preferred him (although the very worst) to all her posterity. The others have quarrelled with him on account of this abominable conduct in stripping his mother of what she had saved. Her mind must have failed singularly since I saw her, and she cannot be more than eighty now, if she is that. There is, I fear, little chance of poor *Bo* getting anything, although she evidently liked him better than any of her grandchildren. After *her* being duped out of her money, nothing can ever astonish me.

I remain, dear sir,

Yours affectionately,

E. P.

I hope Mr. Monk looks over Miss Spear's book every three months.

Pray give my love to Miss Spear, and beg her to be cautious how she invests. I will run no risks of any kind, and prefer a moderate interest upon good security, such as hypothecated bank stock of the United States. I have no confidence in road stock, water stock, fire insurance, cotton manufactories, or State banks. The United States Government loans are the only secure investment for money, and it is better to lend upon the security of hypothecated stock (taking care to see that it has not been mortgaged before) than to invest in trumpery concerns such as I have enumerated.

People cannot be too cautious in money transactions, for, when they lose their fortune, they lose their friends and their consideration in the world.

I brought letters of introduction to the *Austrian* ambassadress at Florence, and have been received at the *Swedish* ambassador's.

Jerome's second visit to Italy did not give rise to any of the difficulties which his father had anticipated. At Rome, at Florence, and at Sienna, he found again affection, kindness, and attention from his grandmother, uncles, aunts, and cousins ; and by each of them he was always treated as the eldest son of Prince Jerome. The young children of the Princess Catharine of Würtemberg became acquainted with their brother. He also knew well Louis Napoleon, the son of Queen Hortense.

In a letter dated Florence, November 28, 1826, Madame Bonaparte again takes up the subject of Jerome's marriage, and says he can only marry a woman of fortune ; that she has no idea of burdening herself with a daughter-in-law and grandchildren.

MADAME BONAPARTE TO WILLIAM PATTERSON.

FLORENCE, November 28, 1826.

DEAR SIR,—*Bo* is with his father, where he has been for the last two months. He is going to Rome. His cousin was married before our arrival here. Her fortune has not been paid, and it is likely to be much less than was expected. *Bo* cannot marry unless he meets with a woman of fortune, as my taking a daughter-in-law to live with me is quite out of the question ; my means are much too limited for my own wants already, and of course I am not such a fool as to burden myself with either daughter-in-law or grandchildren. I have done my duty by my own posterity, and have in so doing spared neither my purse nor my pains ; but any inconsiderate match on *Bo's* part can never meet my consent, or in any way enter into my views ; therefore, it is to be hoped he will have sense enough to live single, and thus save himself the embarrassment of a family. He is very much liked and admired here, and people seem to think that my judgment in the way I have brought him up was not in fault. I hope that on his return to America he will not be such a fool as to marry. The legacy left him by his aunt has been paid me, besides six thousand francs paid him this year by his father. The grandmother, it is said, has given up her whole fortune to P. J., who has contrived to ruin her.

I hope Miss Spear is cautious how she invests. I run risks of no sort, not being a fortunate person in any way. I prefer a moderate interest and good security, to great interest and hazard. Mr. Monk can settle my books every three months to prevent confusion. My ideas about money have never changed. They are to look for *security* in all investments, and to live within my income. I am perhaps not the best manager in the world, but I am not the worst either, and I try to give an example of order and economy to my son as far as it lies in my power. It cannot be expected that a single woman like myself can be as little cheated by servants and tradespeople, as women who have husbands to look after their concerns, or that a capital can be improved by a single woman to the same advantage that it might be by men ; but I flatter myself that my affairs, considering everything, have been as well managed as they could have been by any other person in my position.

It now only remains to avoid all risks, which I hope Miss Spear does, as she well knows my cautions, my disposition, and my little confidence in chance. I spend my time here very pleasantly.

I live in the palace of the Count and Countess Arrighetti, from whom I hire my rooms, which are very handsome. I keep a carriage by the month, which has become indispensable to the preservation of my health. The infirmities of age have not spared me, which I find in my inability to walk as I did formerly, or to sit up late, unless I refresh myself during the day by country air and exercise in a carriage. I have invitations for every evening, and my whole time is taken up in returning visits. I have every reason to be satisfied with the reception I have met with in Florence, which, indeed, exceeded by a great deal my expectations. *Bo* too has been very well received by his relations, and I am now very glad that I consented to his coming. His manners will be improved, and he will learn both French and Italian, besides seeing something more of the world, which is of great use to every one. His spending a few months too with his father will be useful and proper in every point of view, and has met with the approbation of every one.

The climate of this place is exactly the reverse of what I had expected. It is one of the worst in the world. It has rained almost every day since my arrival. It is sometimes very cold, always when it does not rain, and in summer the heat is intense. It is quite as bad as that of America, if not worse ; and I question whether people here do not die as early as they do with us. *Bo* has not improved by growing fat, and I hope to hear that he is growing thinner.

I remain, my dear sir,

Affectionately yours,

E. P.

I wrote to you before that Mary had made a great match in point of rank, although her husband has not a farthing, and is over head and ears in debt.

In the two following letters Madame Bonaparte alludes to Jerome's visit to his father in Rome.

Her father having informed her of the marriage of her brother William, she says she is sorry to hear of the irreparable folly he has committed ; that the highest degree of virtue is not to increase the number of unhappy beings in the world ; that she has no desire to see her son married, or to have a family.

MADAME BONAPARTE TO WILLIAM PATTERSON.

FLORENCE, 18 December, 1826.

DEAR SIR,—I send you by this occasion a letter from *Bo*. He is with his father, and has been there for the last three months. They are now at Rome. I think, everything considered, that it will perhaps be better for us to pass another year in Italy. *Bo* would perfect himself in French and Italian, see something more of the world, and form his manners. He is just at the age when people are improved by society, and I want to give him enough of Europe to prevent his desiring to leave me in America and coming off again. I have, however, not made up my mind on the subject yet, but when he returns—and I expect him in the spring—I shall decide upon what we ought to do. I like Florence more than any place I ever saw, and the climate, although as bad as it can be, agrees perfectly with my health. I never felt as well in Paris as I do here.

I have a great deal of anxiety about by property in America, not knowing what can be done with the money the government are about paying, as well as that I lent Colt. I hope Miss Spear is cautious, as I will not risk in any way, being convinced that I am not a fortunate person. Mr. Monk will settle the books for her every three months. I really wish my money could be placed in some safe way to bring me in *five* per cent., but I prefer *four* to running any risks. I have not yet said a word to *Bo* about my wish that we should spend another year in Italy.

I remain, my dear sir,

Affectionately yours,

E. P.

MADAME BONAPARTE TO WILLIAM PATTERSON.

FLORENCE, 20 December, 1826.

DEAR SIR,—I sent you yesterday, by way of Havre, a letter from Bo and one from myself. He has been for some time with his father, and they are now at Rome. I have good reason to believe that his father is ruined, and that his mother has given him nearly all her fortune; at least, I have heard so in Florence. Bo, of course, has written me *nothing* on the subject, and probably knows nothing about it. His cousin was married before our arrival. She will not be as rich as was supposed, and I have heard that her father in America has nearly spent all his fortune. I believe they are all the worst managers in the world. I am very uneasy about my property in America. I see no safe way of investing the money I had lent to Colt, or that which the government has probably paid me by this time. There is nothing safe except government stock. Miss Spear never writes me about my affairs. I should like to spend another year in Italy, both on my own and Bo's account, but as yet I have not made up my mind on the subject, and shall decide when he comes here, which will be in the spring. I have a great many invitations here. I am sorry to hear of the irreparable folly which William has committed. Marrying is almost a crime, in my eyes, because I am persuaded that the highest degree of virtue is to abstain from augmenting the number of unhappy beings. If people reflected, they would never marry, because they entail misery upon themselves when they bring children into the world. I have no desire to see my son married, and I hope he will never have any family. There are few or no Americans here. The climate is detestable, at least it rains every day. My health never was better, however. Mrs. Toussard remains in Paris to look after her indemnity to be paid the former proprietors of St. Domingo. She lives in a gay boarding-house. The Countess Hocquard, her friend, is now here, and will pass the winter in Italy.

I remain, my dear sir,

Affectionately yours,

E. P.

Under the date of Rome, December 11, 1826, Jerome writes to his grandfather: "I have now been for two months with my father in the country, and arrived in Rome yesterday. . . . From my father I have had the most cordial reception, and I am treated with all possible kindness and affection. I have only seen my grandmother since my arrival in Rome. She is but little changed during the five years which have elapsed since I saw her, and treats me with the same affection and kindness as before. I have not seen mamma for two months; she is still at Florence. I do not expect to see her before the spring. For the last two months, which I have passed in the country with my father and his family, I have seen no one whom I had ever seen before, and heard nothing. Indeed, until your letter arrived, I was at a loss to know what had happened in America since I left it. During this winter I shall have but little leisure for serious study, but will make the most of what time I may have."

CHAPTER XIII.

BARON BONSTETTEN said of Madame Bonaparte : "*Si
elle n'est pas reine de Westphalie, elle est au moins reine
des cœurs.*" She was certainly queen of hearts during
her life at Florence, from the autumn of 1826 until the
summer of 1831. She was received everywhere—at
court, at the various ambassadors', at private parties,
and at public entertainments. Her beauty, vivacity, and
elegant manners made her a welcome guest at all
social gatherings. She dressed exquisitely, and her
jewellery was always such as would best set off her
personal charms. She never criticized the people whom
she met, and said, if she saw a woman enter a room on
her head and in the costume of Venus de Medici, she
would make no comment, but suppose there was some
reason for conduct so singular. Her tact and *savoir-
faire* enabled her to mix with all sorts of people. Living

in the midst of the most corrupt European society, she preserved an untarnished reputation.

In associating with the members of the Bonaparte family she never descended from her position of perfect equality. She always preserved towards them the most formal conduct, which made them all respect her. She soon discovered the light and frivolous character of the Princess Borghese, and was equally quick in discerning the superior qualities of Madame Mère. Of her husband, after he basely abandoned her, she always spoke with the utmost contempt ; and when he offered her the title of Princess of Smalcalden, with two hundred thousand francs a year, she declined the offer, but accepted from Napoleon a pension of sixty thousand francs. When Jerome heard of this, he expressed his displeasure that she had, after declining a pension from him, accepted one from his brother. To which Madame Bonaparte replied that she preferred to be sheltered under the wings of an eagle to being suspended from the bill of a goose. In answer to his offer of a residence in West-phalia, she said Westphalia was a large kingdom, but not quite large enough to hold *two queens*. When Napoleon heard of this witticism, he was so pleased that he made known to her his desire to do something for her. She said : " Tell the emperor I am ambitious, and wish to be a duchess." Napoleon, it is said, promised to comply, but never did so.

While his mother was enjoying the gaiety of Florence, Jerome was living with his father in Rome. A letter to his grandfather gives a glimpse of his experiences there.

JEROME NAPOLEON BONAPARTE TO WILLIAM PATTERSON.

ROME, January 7, 1827.

DEAR GRANDFATHER,— . . . . I have now been three months with my father: two in the country, and one month at Rome. He continues always very kind to me; but I see no prospect of his doing anything for me. I have seen most of my relations since I have been here. My grandmother continues the same in mind, but her constitution seems entirely worn out; she has lost her appetite entirely, and is very feeble, almost always in bed; her memory, however, is unimpaired. She is also very kind to me, but I fear will not do anything for me; indeed, I see but little prospect of ever getting anything secured to me from any of my father's family, who all seem disposed to spend, and none, except my grandmother, to save, and her savings cannot suffice for the extravagance of her children. My father is very anxious for me to remain with him altogether, but I cannot think for a moment of settling myself out of America, to whose government, manners, and customs, I am too much attached and accustomed, to find pleasure in those of Europe, which are so different from my early education. It would, however, give me pleasure to remain this year with my father, and be of some advantage to me; but I see too many objections even to this postponement of my return to America, of which one very important objection is, that with my father I am living in a style which I cannot afford, and to which, if I once became accustomed, I should find it very difficult to give up; moreover, I am now of an age in which I must think of doing something for myself, and America is the only country where I can have an opportunity of getting forward.

.   .   .   .

Mamma is still at Florence, where she is very much attended to, and amuses herself.

.   .   .   .

Believe me ever your most affectionate and most obedient grandson,

JEROME NAPOLEON BONAPARTE.

The patriotic sentiments expressed by Jerome are very different from Madame Bonaparte's opinion. She deemed it a great misfortune that she was born beneath the stars and stripes. She did not agree with Pericles, that republics are the nurseries of great men. In fact, she was more French than American—more cosmopolitan than either. In Europe she lived brilliantly; in America she only vegetated.

We have a second letter from Jerome, giving a deplorable description of the lazy life led by the Bonaparte family, and their enormous debts.

JEROME NAPOLEON BONAPARTE TO WILLIAM PATTERSON.

ROME, January 25, 1827.

MY DEAR GRANDFATHER,—I have been here now about six weeks, and have seen nearly all the members of my father's family who are living. My grandmother is as well as can be expected—that is to say, she has no positive illness, but her constitution is entirely worn out, and she begins to sink under the weight of her misfortunes. She has had no appetite for two years, and is very thin and weak—frequently confined to her bed. She is always very kind to me.

I am excessively tired of the way of living at my father's. We breakfast between twelve and one o'clock, dine between six and seven, and take tea between eleven and twelve at night, so that I seldom get to bed before half-past one o'clock in the morning. My father does not see much company at present, but during much the greater part of the twenty-four hours the whole of his family is assembled together in the parlour, principally for the purpose of killing time. No one about the house does anything, and I find it impossible to read or study; although my time is not entirely lost, because I have an opportunity of examining the antiquities of

Rome, and observing the manners and customs of its inhabitants. The expenses of my father are enormous, and so greatly exceed his means that he has not the power, even if he had the inclination, to do anything for me ; indeed, I fear I have very little, if anything, to expect from my father's family. I spend but very little money—as little as I possibly can ; but I feel that I am living in a style to which I am not entitled, and to which, not being able to support it, I do not wish to become accustomed, more especially as it would totally unfit me for living in America.

My cousin Charles is expected here every day. He comes from America for the purpose of settling his pecuniary affairs with his father, whose fortune is pretty much like my father's—that is to say, equal perhaps to one-third of his debts. I shall be very glad to see Charles, as he will be able to give me some news of America. You have no idea how anxious I am to return home. I was always aware that America was the only country for me, but now I am still more firmly persuaded of it than ever.

I will remain in Rome until the month of April, when I shall go to Florence to meet my mother, whom I have not seen since last October. She will remain at Florence until I go there in the spring, when I hope she will make up her mind to accompany me to America. I shall embark from Leghorn if I find a good ship there, otherwise I will return by way of Holland or England.

Good-bye, dear grandfather ; please give my love to the family, and believe me,

Ever your most affectionate and obedient grandson,

JEROME NAPOLEON BONAPARTE.

Madame Bonaparte gives her father an interesting description of the brilliant life she was leading in Florence during the winter of 1827. She was presented at court, and went to the court balls once a week. She takes a particular pleasure in informing her father of the gay scenes in which she was mingling—parties, dinners, receptions, balls every night.

When Madame Bonaparte made her first appearance

at the court of Tuscany, the Grand Duke gave her a special and private presentation, and honoured her above all the other ladies present. She was so much affected by his attention, that she was ready to cry, but remembered that she might spoil her lovely satin gown and make a scene ; this thought restored her serenity and enabled her to go through the ceremony with proper dignity.

Mr. Patterson had expressed his disapprobation of her partiality for Europe over America. Madame Bonaparte's defence of herself is certainly amusing.

MADAME BONAPARTE TO WILLIAM PATTERSON.

FLORENCE, 12th February, 1827.

DEAR SIR,—I have this day received yours of the 19th December. Those you wrote to *Bo* have been duly received. He is still with his father. I hear that he is a great favourite with the wife of the former. I told you that the grandmother had given almost all her fortune to her pet son, who has spent it all, as well as his own property, and that his brothers are furious at their mother allowing herself to be ruined by a spendthrift child. Her partiality for him can only be accounted for by recollecting the eccentricity of human nature, which in most cases leads parents to lavish their money on the least deserving and least creditable of their posterity. No one except him could ever extract a farthing out of her purse. I believe her means are dreadfully reduced at present by her unfortunate preference. I expect Bo in a fortnight. I have been presented at court, and go there once a week. The balls given there are magnificent, and the finest suppers I ever saw. The English Ambassador gives a ball every week, which are also very agreeable. I can give you no idea of the gaiety of this place. The nobility of Florence give, during the winter, a ball a week, which I attend. No one can go to the balls of the nobles except

persons who can be presented at court. There are several English
families in Florence who give dinners and balls, and my time has
been entirely taken up. I was out every night for three months
until two in the morning, until I became so unwell that for the last
two weeks I have had a fever, which forced me to stay at home.
I am now better, and shall commence my amusements by going to
a party this evening. Florence is much more agreeable than Paris,
and indeed I never had as many invitations as I have had here. I
observe what you say of my partiality for Europe, and am only
surprised that you should wonder at my resembling every woman
who has left America. I never heard of one who wanted to return
there, not excepting Mrs. Gallatin ; besides, I think it is quite as
rational to go to balls and dinners as to get children, which people
must do in Baltimore to kill time. I should prefer a child of mine
going to court and dancing every evening in the week in good
company, to his or her marrying beggars and bringing children
into the world to deplore existence. In America there are no
resources except marriage, and as there was no one there for me to
marry, I very naturally sought to quit a place where I was not
pleased.

I am too old to talk about protection, which indeed only silly
widows such as Mrs. Sherlock ever think of, and that only when
they seek to get rid of their single life. I shall return to America
certainly, but it is quite natural that I should prefer Europe, where
I am more in the way of amusing myself, and where I am much
more attended to. I must indeed do the Americans the justice to
say they are very civil and kind to me, but they are not in the habit
of giving parties and living in society, and I cannot expect them
to change their customs for me. I am sorry to hear of poor
Bentalou's death ; he was an excellent person, but he led such a
dull life that his mind was affected by melancholy, and I believe
he was tired of living.

.   .   .   .

Commerce, as you justly think, is too precarious for any pruden.
person to risk their fortune in. It requires great judgment, great
prudence, and great good luck, and the latter cannot be commanded. I hope Miss Spear is cautious. I am too unlucky a
person to tamper with chance. It has always been against me, and

it has required the utmost exertion of the capacity and prudence which God gave me to make anything out of the hard fate which was allotted me. I am one of the few persons in the world who owe their position in society to their own efforts, and, really considering everything, I have some merit in having worked my way to the consideration and respect which are shown me both in America and Europe. I worked against wind and tide. My company is sought everywhere, and I have reason to congratulate myself upon the discretion and prudence which have directed my course through life.

Hugh Thompson's widow can get herself a husband of her own age. I like his generosity in providing for her so liberally, and thus putting it in her power to consult her taste when she marries the *third time*, which we all know she must have been far from doing when she married Thompson. It is a pity, however, that he made himself ridiculous by such a marriage, as he was to live only a fortnight after this amusing folly. I shall expect to hear of Mr. Oliver marrying some girl of eighteen, and nothing but his pride and fear of being made an object of ridicule to the public will prevent it, as I am certain he thinks it possible for some young woman to fall in love with him. He is a shrewd man, but Baltimore is dull, and people naturally slide into absurdities to get rid of their time. I shall find him married on my return—at least it will not surprise me.

I shall write to M. Spear by this occasion. I have received her letter of November 3rd. I have heard nothing new of the Catons. You all know of their great good fortune in fixing Mary in Europe. Her husband is old and poor, but she has been very fortunate in getting a man of rank.

I remain, dear sir,
Affectionately yours.

.   .   .   .

Bo is thought to have very fine manners, and is very much admired by every one.

.   .   .   .

On the 12th of February Jerome wrote to his grand-father from Rome. He refers to his degree from Har-

vard ; and says if Gilbert Stuart has not health enough
to finish his picture, it would be better to take it in its
present condition, as the head is finished, and the body
can be painted by some other artist.   He regrets that
his father's pecuniary affairs are in such a state that
there was not the least hope of any assistance from him ;
that the greater portion of Madame Mère's fortune has
been consumed in supporting her extravagant children,
each of whom was richer than she was in 1814.   Jerome
says his father has a pension from Russia and Würtemberg of from $12,000 to $15,000 a year, but $30,000 a
year would not cover his expenses, and the excess of
his expenses over his income has to be supplied by his
mother, whose fortune has been reduced in five years
from one million to three hundred thousand dollars.

Jerome further says that his father would like him to
marry and settle in Europe, but he himself feels no inclination to one or the other, and thinks the best thing
that he can do would be to return to America.   He
writes : " I am glad I came to Rome to see my family,
but their mode of living and thinking is so entirely
different from my habits of living and thinking, that I do
not enjoy my residence at Rome ; and if I were once to
adapt myself to it, I should be unfit for the station for
which I am intended and have been educated.   I see but
few persons at Rome, out of my immediate connexions.
Mamma is still at Florence, where I shall go to meet her
in the beginning of March ; she amuses herself very
well at Florence, but I hope will return to America
with me in the spring.   My cousin Charles has been

here; he left America in the month of October, and
returns there in the spring. . . . My grandmother's
health is always the same, but her spirits are very bad.
She is always very kind to me."

In his next letter, dated February 20th, he says that
he and his mother will probably sail for America in
May. He gives the following lively description of the
carnival :—

"Rome is excessively gay at present, and remains so until the
end of the carnival, which continues for ten days longer. Every
day at three o'clock the principal street is filled with carriages and
pedestrians, many of them masked; they remain in the street
throwing sugar-plums at each other until five o'clock, when the
cannon is fired, and the street cleared for the race of the horses :
a dozen horses, covered with ornaments, in the inside of which are
small nails which are always pricking them, without riders, are let
loose at one end of the street and run to the other. The distance
is one mile, and at the place where the horses are stopped, the
governor and senators of Rome are placed at a window, and decide
which horse has won the race, and present his owner with a reward.
After the race there are masked balls at the theatres, and at the
houses of different individuals. My father gave a ball last night,
but without masks. The carnival is the only gay season at Rome,
and lasts from six weeks to two months; but the masks are allowed
only during the two last weeks; it is a great disadvantage to the
country, and it occasions a great deal of idleness, but it is very
amusing for a stranger to look at."

The young man arrived in Florence about the first
week in March, and spent there three months with his
mother, whose head seemed turned by the attentions
she had received from the grand duke and the foreign
ambassadors. Jerome writes to his grandfather :
"Mamma's plans are very unsettled, but she has been

so much gratified by the distinguished manner in which she has been received at court and by the diplomatic corps, that I rather think she will remain another year in Europe before returning to America to settle permanently." In still another letter he says that since he has been in Florence he has gone to a ball every night, and ridden one of his cousin's horses every day; that his mother is delighted with the city, and goes out "all day and half the night." Jerome remained at Florence until the 4th of June, 1827, when he left for England *viâ* Rotterdam. On the day of his departure his mother wrote to her father a letter, in which she gives us still other glimpses of some of her distinguished friends, the attentions paid her, and the brilliant life she was leading.

When we remember that she lived fifty years longer, it is strange to find Madame Bonaparte complaining, in this letter that she was no longer as active either in mind or body as she had been, and that she felt the advance of age.

MADAME BONAPARTE TO WILLIAM PATTERSON.

FLORENCE, 4th of June, 1827.

DEAR SIR,—*Bo* left at one this morning for Rotterdam, whence he goes to England, and will embark from Liverpool for New York. He is accompanied by Mr. Lovel, the brother of the Countess Visconti, whom I know very well, and with whom I arranged the journey. Mr. Lovel only goes as far as England with him. His stay in England will be so short that I have not accepted offers of letters of introduction from Lord Burghersh, the English minister at Florence, or those offered me for the Duchess of Rutland by a relation of hers. He has one from the son of Lord Holland to his father, which he will not have time to deliver. If he could have remained a few months in England I should have availed myself of these opportunities of introducing him properly ; but as his stay will only be of a few days, there would be little advantage in taking letters.

He has been three months with me, and during this time I have presented him to the ambassadors and all my other acquaintances. He has been more in society than could have been expected from so limited a residence in a place, but I was indefatigable in my efforts to draw him out. Young people are not sufficiently aware of the importance of visits, and making proper acquaintances, and getting over bashfulness, which is an insuperable obstacle to getting on in the world. I am sure that backwardness has been a great disadvantage to myself, which is one reason why I have always insisted upon *Bo's* frequenting society. It is scarcely possible to get necessary confidence when one passes the early part of life in retirement.

I should have asked the permission of the grand duke to present him at court, if he could have spent next winter here. There are balls and concerts every week there, and I regret very much that the opportunity is lost of his being introduced. I have been as constant in my own attendance every week as the state of my health would allow, and I believe there is not a more agreeable court in Europe, or more amiable sovereigns. *Bo* not being able to pass through France, where I am obliged to go to arrange my pecuniary affairs and to buy my furniture, I concluded that it was better to let him go to England with Mr. Lovel. I shall postpone my own departure a few months, that I may have the society of a widow lady, who intends going to Paris, which will be a double advantage to me, as I shall have her company on the road and we can divide the expense. There are two English widows now at Florence who would either of them join me to return to France ; but we all desire to stay a few months longer here. I left *Bo's* legacy in Paris at four per cent. interest, and have given him an order on Miss Spear for the amount. He will be able to tell you the state of his family affairs, and that his grandmother has given either two or four hundred thousand dollars in the last five years

to her *pet son*, who has spent them, besides other great sums.   The
family are not pleased with her giving all to one worthless spendthrift, and of course they are all on bad terms with him—which I
suppose she must have expected when she gave more to one than
to the rest.   I pity her very much, although I highly reprobate the
injustice of her conduct.   I refer you to *Bo* for all accounts of
them, as well as for a description of this place and of the habits of
the people.   It was quite impossible for *Bo* to pass through
France, which is the only country I can embark from, as my funds
are there.   Mr. Lovel is a very nice young man, and I feel quite
as much confidence in his care of him as if I had gone to take
care of him myself.   Lovel pays *half* the expense—a consideration
I never lose sight of, having found from experience that one's
purse is the only certain friend.   The journey through England is
much longer than that I shall take, and, of course, much more
expensive.   *Bo* will tell you that Mr. Svertzkoff, whom I knew at
Washington, is the Russian minister here, and that his house is
very pleasant.   I pass every Sunday evening there.   I have
written to Miss Spear that in future I shall pay *Bo* fifty dollars
per month out of my own purse.   I suppose people will think me
very stingy and mean, but it is really all that I can afford.   I
should be most happy to make him a larger allowance ; but when
the public consider that I am obliged to live myself, that I am infirm, that I am no longer the active person in either body or mind
that I have been, that age is coming on me, and that I require
more eating and comforts of every kind than formerly, besides
being obliged to pay taxes and to put up with low rents and
tenants going off in debt, they will upon all this calculation see
that I cannot possibly afford to give more than six hundred
dollars a year ; his board, of course, he always will have with me,
and trifling presents.   The six hundred dollars will be for his
clothing and his pocket-money.   It may seem and is a very paltry
sum, but is proportioned to my means, and people cannot expect
me to give more than I can afford.   I should be sorry to pass for
not giving him according to my means, as I wish to perform my
duty and to keep well with the world both.

I remain, dear sir,

Affectionately yours.

Madame Bonaparte had found it impossible to tear herself away from the delights of Florence and accompany Jerome to America. Month after month her departure was postponed, and she still lingered among the gay scenes which she loved so well. In the summer of 1828 she again determined to sail, and again abandoned the idea. She assigned as her reason that the vessel which was to sail at the time she had fixed for her embarkation was the " Don Quixote," "a ship in which nothing could induce her to sail."

MADAME BONAPARTE TO WILLIAM PATTERSON.

FLORENCE, May 30, 1828.

DEAR SIR.—It was my intention to have returned to America this summer, but, after making my arrangements, I found that the "Don Quixote," a vessel in which nothing would induce me to embark, was to sail on the 15th of July, the period which I had destined for my embarkation—being obliged to pass some time in Paris to settle some business respecting money, with which I speculate in that place. I am afraid to sail later than the 15th, not liking to arrive on the coast late in August. It requires a month for me to reach Paris, as I cannot travel post.

We have lost poor Demidoff, who died most unexpectedly. He was a great friend of mine. I spent three evenings in the week at his house, and took every one there that I chose. The death, too, of the Russian minister, whose house was a great resource on Sunday evenings, we have felt very severely. But Demidoff's loss will be felt by every class of persons, as his charity was greater than that of any person living. His fortune was immense.

His will directed it to be equally divided between his children. He left no legacies to any of his friends, which induces people to suppose that he was not aware of his approaching end. My idea, however, is that he thought very justly that none of his friends had a right to inherit from him, and that to have given them dinners and balls as long as he lived was as much as we had a right to expect from a stranger. He was a person of great natural sense, and the most good-natured creature possible.

Charles [1] called to see me on his arrival, and told me that he had seen you all, and that all the family were well, and that *Bo* would not be marked with the small-pox. He says that he is very much obliged to you for the attention you showed him at Baltimore. He seems civil. He is gone to Rome to try to get some money out of his father. Hy opinion is that he might have saved himself the expense of the journey, as I am sure his father has nothing to give him. We have had balls and concerts at court all the winter, and balls at the English ambassador's, and supper parties at the Sardinian minister's, where I am asked once every week. All the ambassadors have advised me to try to get *Bo* made Secretary of legation to England. The, Swedish minister thinks it would be a great advantage, as there might be a chance of his getting afterwards to Sweden, where the king, he thinks, would be kind to him on account of the connexion. I have little hope, however, of anything ever happening that I desire ; but I think if you and Gen. Smith would write to Jackson and ask for the place of secretary of legation to England, it is possible that out of regard to you he might give it. I should in that event be willing to allow him as much as I can afford out of my income to enable him to live comfortably in England ; but it would be quite impossible for me to live there with him, as my means are inadequate to my living in London in the best society ; and of course I should not think of living in any other in any country. It would be a great sacrifice for me to part with an only child, but parents must consider the interests of their children. Mrs. Caton has set me a good example on this subject. She has, however, been more fortunate in fixing her children than I can hope to be. I think they are the most fortunate people I have ever heard or read of. Louisa [2] has made a great match. He is very handsome, not more than twenty-eight, and will be a

---

[1] Son of Lucien Bonaparte.

[2] Louisa Caton, grand-daughter of Charles Carroll. She married the eldest son of the Duke of Leeds.

duke with thirty thousand pounds a year. Mrs. Toussard wrote me some time ago that her mind was not fully made up to leave France this year.

I hear that Mrs. Brown is in a dangerous state of health. I am sorry the Gallatins have been so unfortunate as not to be able to marry their daughter yet. They are very good people, and she is very handsome; but the truth is that some people are born more fortunate than others, which is the only way in which I can account for the poor girl not getting a husband. If you see Miss Spear, will you tell her that the reason why I do not write to her more frequently is because I do not think that it would interest her to hear of people whom she never saw. It would be a great thing if I could get *Bo* made secretary of legation. Hughes has got on famously, merely by persevering impudence, and Laura's match, which was thought so bad at the time, has turned out very well. I hope, however, that *Bo* will never marry. It is a great advantage to get daughters married, but there is by no means the same necessity to marry one's sons. I hope commerce has improved in America, and that there will be some safe way of investing money. If you and Gen. Smith would get Jackson to give the place to *Bo*, I would make every exertion to find the means to enable him to live in the best society, and to defray his expenses there. Since Demidoff's death Florence is no longer the same place, and many people are moving off, particularly single women and young men. At the baths last year he gave us a ball or a play or a concert every night. The Duke of Leeds, they say, is of course very angry at his son's marriage with Louisa. His daughter ran off a few months before with a man who has not a shilling.

Adieu, my dear sir,

Affectionately yours.

I will thank you to tell Miss Spear that if Colt does not keep my money, I should like it to be invested in government bonds at par, which have some length of time to run. My great object is security, and I prefer moderate interest upon good security to great gains where there is any risk. She may rest assured of seeing me before a great while, but in the meantime it is better to get interest upon my little sums, when it can be done without risk.

CHAPTER XIV.

The Announcement of Jerome's Engagement. — Mme. Bonaparte's Oppo-
sition.—Congratulatory Letters from the Bonaparte Family.—Jerome's
Marriage.—Congratulatory Letter from Princess Charlotte Bonaparte.
—Characteristic Letter from Mme. Bonaparte.—The Grave preferable
to Baltimore.—Mme. Bonaparte threatens to spend her Income.—The
Americans in Europe.—Mme. Bonaparte makes her Will.—Jerome's
Allowance is discontinued.—1829-30.

MADAME BONAPARTE was destined to be disappointed
in all her ambitious matrimonial speculations for her
son.   Two years after his return to America her fond
hopes of a brilliant European marriage for Jerome were
ended by the announcement that he was engaged, and
was soon to be married to a young lady of Baltimore.
This news was communicated to her by her father, and
called forth, for a time, her strong opposition, and
threatened to produce a breach between her father and
herself.   Later, however, the violence of her displeasure
at this interruption of her plans abated somewhat, and
though she never, perhaps, entirely recovered from her
disappointment that her son should marry an American, we shall see by her later letters that she did not
permit it to alienate her from him for any length of time.
For a while her correspondence with Mr. Patterson
expressed her feeling in the most violent terms; then
a long interval succeeded in which she wrote but little.

It seems that Jerome consulted his uncle Joseph in reference to his marriage before the engagement was announced to his mother, for we have a letter from the Count de Survilliers, dated April 10, 1829, more than three months previous to the date of Mr. Patterson's letter to Madame Bonaparte, giving her the first intimation of the affair.

JOSEPH BONAPARTE TO JEROME NAPOLEON BONAPARTE.

POINTE-BREEZE, 10 Avril, 1829.

MON CHER NEVEU,— . . . . . Je ne saurais que te conseiller. . . . . . Ton grand-père m'a semblé un homme de grand sens, et il me semble que tu dois beaucoup de considération et de déférence à ce qu'il croira devoir te convenir davantage. Toi-même, à cette heure, tu dois te connaître et savoir où tu as le plus à espérer de succès et de bonheur.

Je t'embrasse et te prie de me rappeler au souvenir de ton grand-père.

Ton affectionné oncle,

JOSEPH.

TRANSLATION.

POINT BREEZE, April 10, 1829.

MY DEAR NEPHEW,—I can only advise you. . . . . . Your grandfather has seemed to me to be a man of great sense, and it appears to me that you owe to him much consideration and deference in a matter which he believes will be for your advantage. You ought yourself, by this time, to know where you may hope for the most success and happiness. . . . . .

I embrace you, and beg to be remembered to your grandfather.

Your affectionate uncle,

JOSEPH.

P

Jerome announced his engagement to his father, his grandmother, and the rest of the family, and received congratulatory letters from them all. His father wrote to him as follows :—

PRINCE JEROME TO JEROME NAPOLEON BONAPARTE.

ROME, Decembre 1, 1829.

MON CHER ENFANT,—Je me hâte de répondre à ta lettre du mois de Septembre, par laquelle tu m'annonces ton mariage. Dès que je n'ai pas été consulté sur un événement aussi important pour toi, je suppose que tu as bien fait toutes tes réflexions, et dès que mon consentement ne t'est pas nécessaire, je me borne à t'envoyer ma bénédiction paternelle et à faire des vœux pour ton bonheur. Ce qui me tranquillise est de savoir que *tu as l'assentiment de mon bien-aimé frère et que cette union est faite par le bon et respectable M. Patterson.* J'apprends avec bonheur ce que *ton grand-père* a fait pour toi et pour assurer ta fortune, ainsi que ta future est riche et douée de toutes les qualités. Ton bonheur, cher enfant, ne dépend donc plus désormais que de toi. Il faut te mettre dans une situation naturelle et positive, car rien dans le monde ne compense d'une fausse position. Ce qu'il y a donc de plus naturel pour toi est de rester franchement, réellement, sans arrière-pensée, citoyen américain. Tu te trouveras certainement par là plus heureux de toutes les manières que tes frères et sœur. Je suis fâché, mon cher enfant, que tu n'aies pas écrit à la reine : ses bontés pour toi méritaient au moins un souvenir dans une pareille occasion, et je désire que tu remplisses ce devoir le plus tôt possible. Écris-moi souvent, cher enfant, et donne-moi de tes nouvelles en détail, en ne doutant jamais de la tendresse paternelle de ton affectionné père.

Signé: JÉRÔME.

P.S.—Tes frères et sœur te font leurs amitiés ; la reine te dit bien des choses.

TRANSLATION.

Dec. 1, 1829.

MY DEAR CHILD,—I hasten to answer your letter of September, announcing your approaching marriage. Although I have not been consulted about so important an event, I suppose that you have carefully considered the matter ; and although my consent is not necessary, I send you my paternal blessing and wishes for your happiness. I am put quite at ease by knowing that you have the assent of my dear brother, and that the marriage has been brought about by the good and worthy Mr. Patterson. I learn with pleasure what your grandfather has done for you in order to assure your fortune, and that your future wife is rich and endowed with all good qualities. Your happiness, my dear child, will nevertheless only depend on yourself. You must be placed in a natural and definite situation, for nothing in the world compensates for a false position. Now, the most natural thing for you to do is to be really, truly, and without reserve, an American citizen. You will certainly find yourself, in that position, happier in every way than your brothers and sister.

I regret, my dear child, that you did not write to the queen ; her kindnesses to you deserved at least that she should be remembered on this occasion, and I desire that you fulfil this duty as soon as possible.

Write to me often, my dear child, and give me all the news of yourself, never doubting the paternal tenderness of your affectionate father.

JEROME.

P.S.—Your brothers and sister send their love ; the queen desires to be affectionately remembered to you.

This letter was sent to Jerome by his uncle, the Count de Survilliers, who at the same time wrote to him the following note :—

POINTE-BREEZE.

MON CHER NEVEU,—Voici une lettre de ton père qui me parvient ouverte. . . . . Je serai charmé de te revoir au printemps, ainsi que ta femme. Je te prie de me rappeler à son souvenir, ainsi qu'à celui de ta belle-mère et ton grand-père. Je pense qu'il sera bien aussi de ta part d'écrire à la reine, comme le désire ton père. Puisqu'il te le mande, c'est qu'il le juge convenable ; et tu ne dois pas lui refuser ce qu'il désire, lorsqu'il ne s'agit que d'un simple compliment. Je t'embrasse.

Ton affectionné oncle,

Signé : JOSEPH.

TRANSLATION.

POINT BREEZE.

MY DEAR NEPHEW,—I enclose a letter from your father, which came to me open. . . . . I shall be charmed to see you and your wife in the spring. I beg you to remember me to her, as well as to your mother-in-law and grandfather. I think that it will be well for you to write to the queen, as your father desires. Since he commands it, he deems it proper ; you ought not to refuse what he asks, when it is merely an act of courtesy. I embrace you.

Your affectionate uncle,

JOSEPH.

Madame Mère also wrote to Jerome that she had heard with pleasure of his intended marriage, since the object of his choice possessed all the qualities which ought to make him happy. She hoped he would enjoy all happiness in his married life ; and if her blessing could contribute to it, it would be complete and unalterable.

Jerome Napoleon Bonaparte and Susan May Williams were married on the 3rd of November, 1829. The wedding took place at the residence of the bride, in North Charles Street, Baltimore. The ceremony was performed by the Most Reverend James Whitfield,

Archbishop of Baltimore. Mr. Bonaparte's groomsmen were Colonel J. Spear Nicholas, Mr. Charles Tiernan, Mr. William Donnell, and Mr. Pierce Butler, the husband of Fanny Kemble. The wedding was attended by the leading people of Baltimore. Among those present was the French Consul at Baltimore. The day after the wedding there was a gentleman's " punch drinking." There was no bridal tour.

Letters of congratulation were sent to Jerome from the different members of the Bonaparte family, including Madame Mère, Louis, Jerome, the Princess Charlotte his cousin, and her mother the Countess Julie.

THE PRINCESS CHARLOTTE BONAPARTE TO JEROME NAPOLEON BONAPARTE.

MON CHER COUSIN,—Maman me permet d'ajouter quelques lignes dans cette lettre, et j'en profite avec plaisir, car il me tardait de vous faire aussi mon compliment et vous assurer des vœux que je forme pour vous deux. J'espère aussi avoir le plaisir de faire connaissance avec *ma nouvelle cousine*, à laquelle je vous prie de dire mille choses tendres. J'espère que vous ne m'avez pas tout à fait oubliée, quoique votre correspondance soit un peu ralenti.

Adieu. Napoleon vous dit mille choses, et je vous assure de nouveau de mon amitié.

CHARLOTTE.

TRANSLATION.

MY DEAR COUSIN,—Mamma has permitted me to add a few lines to her letter, and I avail myself of this with pleasure, as I have delayed in sending my congratulations and assuring you of my good wishes for you both. I hope soon to have the pleasure

of becoming acquainted with my new cousin, to whom I beg you
to give a thousand loving messages. I hope you have not
forgotten me entirely, although your correspondence has been a
little negligent.

Adieu. Napoleon sends you many messages, and I once more
assure you of my own affection.

CHARLOTTE.

When Madame Bonaparte wrote the following letter
she was not aware that her son's wedding had actually
taken place, for she continues her denunciation of an
American marriage, but says, if Jerome can be satisfied
with living in Baltimore, she has nothing more to urge
against it.

MADAME BONAPARTE TO WILLIAM PATTERSON.

FLORENCE, December 4, 1829.

DEAR SIR,—I wrote, in answer to your letters announcing the
proposed marriage for my son, exactly what I felt at the time. I
had endeavoured to instil into him, from the hour of his birth, the
opinion that he was much too high in birth and connexion ever to
marry an American woman. I hated and loathed a residence in
Baltimore so much, that when I thought I was to spend my life
there I tried to screw my courage up to the point of committing
suicide. My cowardice, and *only* my cowardice, prevented my
exchanging Baltimore for the grave. No consideration could have
induced me to marry any one there after having married the brother
of an emperor, and I believe that to this proud feeling I owe much
of the respect and consideration shown me both in America and in
Europe. After having married a person of the high rank I did, it
became impossible for me ever to bend my spirit to marry any
one who had been my equal before my marriage, and it became
impossible for me ever to be contented in a country where there
exists no nobility, and where the society is unsuitable in every

respect to my tastes. The people, I believe, thought with me that neither nature nor circumstances fitted me for residing in Baltimore. At least, I judge so from the profound respect and homage they have ever shown me, and I believe they perfectly agreed with me that both my son and myself would be in our proper sphere in Europe. I tried to give my son all my ideas and tastes, and, in the first weeks after hearing that he meant to marry an American woman, I was in despair. I think that I did my duty in trying to elevate his ideas above marrying in America, and you well know that I left nothing undone to effect this. I have considered now that it is unreasonable to expect him to place his happiness in the only things which can make me happy. (My happiness can never be separated from rank and Europe.) He has neither my pride, my ambition, nor my love of good company; therefore I no longer oppose his marriage. I perhaps may think myself fortunate that he has not married even worse. If he can be satisfied with living in such a place as Baltimore—and he is the best judge of this—I have nothing more to urge against it. I feel that I have no right to make another person adopt my standard of happiness. I would rather die than marry any one in Baltimore, but if my son does not feel as I do upon this subject, of course he is quite at liberty to act as he likes best. As the woman has money . . . . I shall not *forbid* a marriage which I never would have *advised*. The family here have announced it to me. I replied that there was no one in America on an equality with my son; that I had ever tried to prevent his marrying there; but that, as she had some money, I should no longer oppose it. It is perhaps fortunate that he has not married worse, and I shall not oppose it any longer. He was perfectly aware, as well as yourself, when he commenced this business and when you gave your assent and encouragement to it, that I had always advised him not to marry in Baltimore, and that I detested living there; therefore neither of you could be much surprised at my first letters on this subject. If he has married her, I have only to hope that your and his judgment have been better than mine. I hope too that he has not been cheated, which I think very likely, in the settlements. Part of her fortune ought to have been settled on his children in the event of his death before hers. I hope most ardently that she will have no children ; but, as nothing happens which I desire, I do not flatter myself with an accomplishment of my wish on this subject.

I now repeat what I said in my last letters : that I would as soon have gone to Botany Bay to look for a husband as to have married any man in Baltimore ; but that, if my son thinks it possible for him to live there, and does not feel any of my repugnance to such a connexion, that I no longer oppose it. He is the best judge of what he can support and endure, and I have no right to expect him to feel as I do.

Yours affectionately.

They ought to have given him half of her fortune at least, if he outlived her.

Before she wrote again, Madame Bonaparte had been informed that the dreaded event had actually happened. Her whole correspondence at this period indicates that her marriage with " the brother of an emperor" had for the time turned her head. She talks of not having " the meanness of spirit to descend from such an elevation to the deplorable condition of being the wife of an American."

MADAME BONAPARTE TO WILLIAM PATTERSON.

FLORENCE, 21 December, 1829.

DEAR SIR,—I have received yours and Edward's [1] letters—his of 27th October, and yours of 4th November. I have written you several letters, after having consulted with my friends here, to say that I should not take the responsibility of breaking off the match, but I shall never cease to regret that this alliance was ever thought of. I cannot give him my ambition and my pride, and as it is unreasonable to expect him to be made happy by the only things

---

[1] Madame Bonaparte's brother.

which render life at all supportable to me, rank and living in
Europe, I have no right to oppose his living in the way he likes
best. It is possible that your judgment and his are better than
mine. I hope that they are. I tried to give him the ideas suitable
to his rank in life ; having failed in that, there remains only to let
him choose his own course. A parent cannot make a silk purse
of a sow's ear ; and you found that you could never make a sow's
ear of a silk purse. It was impossible to bend my talents and my
ambition to the obscure destiny of a Baltimore housekeeper, and
it was absurd to attempt it after I had married the brother of an
emperor. I had not the meanness of spirit to descend from such
an elevation to the deplorable condition of being the wife of an
American. I often tried to reason myself into the courage necessary
to commit suicide when I contemplated a long life to be passed in
a trading town, where everything was disgusting to my tastes, and
where everything contrasted so strongly with my wishes.

I never could have degraded myself by marriage with people
who, after I had married a prince, became my inferiors.

The Americans themselves had sense and good taste enough to
feel that I had risen above them, and have always treated me with
the respect and deference due to a superior. When I first heard
that my son could condescend to marry any one in Baltimore, I
nearly went mad. Every one told me that it was quite impossible
for me to make him like myself, and that, if he could endure the
mode of life and the people in America, it was better to let him
follow his own course than to break off a marriage where there was
some money to be got, and leave him to marry a person of less
fortune. I have no dislike to the woman he has married.

I shall leave my fortune to my son. This is my duty as well as
my inclination—and to his children after him ; if he dies without
any (I hope that he never will have any), it must revert to my
nearest relations. I have gained my fortune by the strictest
economy—by privations of every kind ; therefore, strangers must
not profit by my sacrifices. It is my duty to leave my savings to my
own blood, if my son dies without children. I repeat, that I would
have starved, died, rather than have married in Baltimore : but
that my son, not having my pride, my ambition, or my utter abhor-
rence to vulgar company, has a right to pursue the course he

prefers, and I sincerely hope that he will never repent having begun this affair without my knowledge, and, as both you and he supposed, so entirely against my approbation, that I nearly died when I first heard of it; but that I have no right to expect my son to place his happiness in the only things which can ever content me (rank and living in Europe), and that, as I cannot help it, I must try and content myself by the reflection that I did all I could to disgust him with America. I have hitherto lived in the meanest, most comfortless manner, as you all know. The miserly way in which I have lived and the beggarly shifts to which I have been obliged to resort to collect my present means, have been a great disadvantage to me in every respect. If I could have made a tolerable appearance, it would nave changed my affairs very materially, not to say how much more agreeable life would have been to me than it has been. I shall in future spend four thousand dollars a year. . . . I am *clean out* of this *scrape.* It now remains for me to say that Miss Spear must pack up my house linen, &c., and the whole must be sent in good trunks to New York to R. White, to be shipped for Leghorn, to the care of Fenzi's house there. My jewels must be sent by private opportunity to the American Minister at Paris. I educated my son with the intention of his living in Europe. I always told him and you that he never should degrade himself by marrying in America. I have no right, after having said and done so much, to insist upon his living according to my ideas ; and I sincerely hope and am willing to believe, that you and he have been right and that I have been wrong.

I hope too that all persons concerned in this match can reconcile it to their conscience. Edward has behaved well to me on this occasion, and always acted well to me through life. You and my son knew that I never wished the latter to marry in Baltimore, and hurried it over to prevent my breaking it off.

To the Americans in Europe . . . . . I have answered as above, that I had always told him never to marry there, but that I have no right to make him think like me, and that, in fact, the whole was done without my knowledge, and that I would no longer oppose what I could not prevent.

Very affectionately yours.

After her son's marriage, Madame Bonaparte determined to abandon the "miserly" way in which she had
been living as disadvantageous and uncomfortable, and
in future to spend her whole income.

MADAME BONAPARTE TO WILLIAM PATTERSON.

FLORENCE, 27 January, 1830.

DEAR SIR,—I have received yours of 26th November. In answer to that part which relates to a reconciliation, I reply that I
consider it my duty to leave my son at my death my property, and
to promote his pecuniary interests as far as I can during my life.
Should he die before me without children, I shall then leave what
I possess to my nearest relations. I wish my son to write me
every three months a statement of my money affairs, and to look
over all accounts which Miss Spear has in charge. He is equally
interested with myself in doing this. I claimed from Rome the
pension of 500 francs for this month of January, 1830. They have
paid it to me as usual. I will not neglect any means of getting it
regularly paid. It is my intention in future to live up to my income, and to make as good an appearance as I can in the world.
The miserly way in which I have hitherto been obliged to live has
been a great disadvantage to me, besides being very uncomfortable. I should like to know how it would be most expedient to
remit my income. I hope to receive my jewels, laces, and black
lace dress through a private conveyance to the American Minister
at Paris, with an inventory of the contents. Harris is probably
coming out, as I am sure that he will not be able to live there
long.

Very affectionately,

Yours.

Madame Bonaparte reiterates her intention to leave
her fortune to her son, believing that no parent has a
right to disinherit a child; that she would have left him

everything had he attempted to cut her throat and failed in the attempt.

MADAME BONAPARTE TO WILLIAM PATTERSON.

FLORENCE, April 26, 1830.

DEAR SIR,—I had written to you for the form of a will. Not having received it, I have made one here, by which I leave to my son my property of every kind, with the exception of the portraits which A. Smith and Joseph have in charge. *These* portraits, he, of course, will not regret. I have expressly, therefore, left all likenesses of myself to persons who are likely to value them. I feel that no parent has a right to disinherit a child, and I should have done exactly the same thing if he had attempted to cut my throat, and had failed in the attempt. The money I shall leave him has been raised on the privation of my comforts—almost on the necessaries of life. Had I possessed the means of living comfortably, I should not have felt so cruelly the curse of existence. My life, from the want of money, has been a disgusting burden. I am ordered to take a long journey, in the hope that change of company and change of air may restore my spirits, which have, as you must have foreseen, been most severely tried by a marriage, begun against my approbation, and conducted in all its stages with the most open and decided contempt of my sentiments of every kind. I am, however, willing to hope that your judgment and my son's are better than mine, although I have been treated as if I had been a maniac or a wretch convicted of some infamous crime. In reply to that part of your letter which talked of reconciliation, I repeat that I still consider it my duty to leave my son the whole of my fortune, and that I will promote his pecuniary interests as far as I can during my life.

.   .   .   .

I shall leave this on the 1st of May, and return here in September. My spirits, never good, are now dreadfully broken, but I shall drag on the load of life many years. My income I shall in future spend. The miserable economy I was obliged to practise has been a great disadvantage to me. I always had in view the duty of providing for my son. I must change my mode of life and make it more expensive. I never can forget the treatment I have been made to experience in the conduct of this marriage. It is a recollection which will haunt me through life, and prevent my ever knowing an hour of happiness.

I hope that your conscience will not reproach you for your conduct, which has been even more unnatural than that of my son. I have not been able to write to the latter about his marriage since it took place. The subject always brings on the most dreadful feelings, and makes me ill for days. His pension has been paid at Rome for January, February, March, and April, of this year, 1830.

I shall, when I recover my strength, send a copy of my will to my son, with my opinion of his conduct to me. . . . . I shall write to Jerome when there is any necessity about money affairs. Miss Spear must not pay him any longer the fifty dollars per month which I allowed him. I gave them out of my own comforts. He has shown me that *good* conduct in parents cannot command affection in children, which I really had supposed that it always did. . . . . . By a codicil to my will I have desired that the trifling things, such as my inkstand and the little ornaments of little value which I have worn, should be distributed to persons who had shown me some kindness ; but all the money, and everything of value above twenty dollars, to be given to my *natural*, or most *unnatural* heir. I believe that I have conscientiously through life done my duty to my son, and in now leaving him the money, which I owe solely to my own economy, I have given the highest proof that neither duplicity, ingratitude, or unnatural conduct can make me swerve from my duty.

Another letter, at the end of this year, continues the same themes.

MADAME BONAPARTE TO WILLIAM PATTERSON.

DEAR SIR—I trouble you with the present to inform you that the five hundred francs per month, paid by the family at Rome, have been continued ever since the very ill-judged marriage made for my son. Miss Spear is authorized to pay him the *above*, including this month of December, 1830. The fifty dollars per month, which I had been enabled by retrenchments on my table, fire, lights, and dress to pay my son, were discontinued when he married, because it would be folly to starve myself any longer for a child whose conduct has convinced both the public and myself of the disregard in which he holds me. I willingly made sacrifices for him, and would have deprived myself of anything to place him in the position which both his name and birth had marked out for him. . . .

Placed by my marriage in a rank of life which I have hitherto resisted every temptation to disgrace, I feel it incumbent to appear with decency in those societies where alone I will appear, and my whole income is too small for this purpose. Had my means been more ample, not even the . . . . conduct adopted toward me during the whole process of this marriage, could have made me stoop to the mean revenge of suppressing a pecuniary allowance to a child; but I believed that every one who has not made hatred and contempt of me a systematic proceeding must confess that the time has now arrived for me to attend more closely to my interest than my relations have done for me.

I think, because I have a high, perhaps an exaggerated, sense of the duties of a parent, that I ought to leave my fortune to my son at my death, and I mean to perform this act of duty. My idea is that neither unjust conduct on your part, nor bad proceedings on his, can authorize me to act differently. It certainly requires a greater effort of virtue to fulfil duties to those who entirely forgot that they had any to perform towards me; but I feel equal to this effort. This marriage must, as you both and every one knew, separate me from my son. It must, as you all foresaw and calculated upon, be to me during life a source of deep affliction and burning shame. Could I even believe what I sincerely desire—that the judgment which planned it will prove superior to mine—no one ever supposed, none who like or respect me can ever wish, me to forget the treatment I have received.

My son knew the miserable shifts which procured me my present independence, and he ought, after all which has occurred, to have refused six hundred dollars a year out of my savings from the necessaries of life. My money has been hardly earned, and shall be spent as best suits my purposes during my life, and at my death he may inherit what I leave. I shall give nothing to his children during his life to encourage them in disobedience to his wishes; but, on the contrary, allow him to educate and marry them, and provide for them according to his own judgment and desires. I think that both you and he will be perfectly satisfied with the fairness and justice of the conduct I mean to pursue. My sentiments were already known to you respecting an American marriage for him. I had always told you, and him, and every one else, that my consent to his marrying any one in Baltimore, either rich or poor, *should* and *could* never be obtained, and that such a connexion would distress and mortify me more than any misfortune which could ever befall me. My feelings and conduct have been *open* on this subject, and I leave them to be approved or disapproved, as the public best like.

It would be fair in my family, and a justice they owe me and my reputation for pride and sense, to say that this marriage was contracted without my knowledge and in the most decided opposition to the opinions and wishes I had ever expressed respecting my son's interests. I think that I would sooner have begged my bread from door to door than have degraded myself by entering into such a connexion. My son by his *birth* was a much greater person than I have become by marriage, therefore had to stoop much lower than I should have done if any sordid consideration could ever have induced me to forget the respect I owed to my place in society. The only consolation I can ever feel upon this subject is that I can never be blamed for the poor miscalculation and miserable sacrifice which has been made of all his prospects, and that I tried to give him an education and feelings equal to what the world thought belonged to his name. I have now only one duty to perform towards him, which is, to let him inherit what may remain of my fortune at my death. I intended to have written this sooner, but the pain everything connected with this subject gives me affects even my health when I am obliged to write or speak on it. Miss Spear will send me my box of jewels, of which my son has the key, with an inventory in the box of every article, as well as inventories by post, by the first safe opportunity to France—to be kept when there by the American minister until I can get them.

CHAPTER XV.

Birth of Jerome Napoleon Bonaparte, Jr.—Congratulations from the Family.—Kind Words.—Mme. Bonaparte and Gortschakoff.—Lamartine.—Her Departure from Florence.—Letter from Geneva.—Financial Affairs.—Princess Galitzin.—Mme. Bonaparte's Jewels.—Dying of Ennui.—"I am tired of Life."—Mme. Bonaparte and Mr. Dundas,—Countess Guiccioli.—Letter from Paris.—Duchess d'Abrantes.—Letter from Mr. Patterson.—At Home again.—1831-33.

ON the 5th of November, 1830, a son was born to Mr. Jerome Bonaparte, of Baltimore, and congratulations were tendered by various members of his family, the first coming from the Count de Survilliers.

A letter from Prince Jerome, dated January, 1831, contained the following passages :—

À mon fils Jérôme Napoléon, à Baltimore.

MON CHER ENFANT,—C'est avec bonheur que j'apprends par la lettre du 8 Novembre que ta femme t'a rendu père le 5 du même mois. J'espère que ce cher enfant grandira à ta satisfaction et te donnera des sujets de consolation. *Je le bénis, ainsi que toi, et aime à penser qu'un jour je pourrai le serrer dans mes bras.* Embrasse-le bien tendrement, ainsi que ta femme. . . . .

Adieu, cher enfant ; la reine te fait ses amitiés et t'écrit par le même courrier. Je te serre sur mon cœur, et suis ton affectionné père.

Signé : JÉRÔME.

Jérôme, Mathilde et Napoléon t'embrassent.

Q

TRANSLATION.

My dear Child,—I have heard with great pleasure, from your letter of the 8th of November, that you had the happiness of becoming a father on the 5th of the same month. I hope the dear child will grow up to your satisfaction and be a source of great comfort to you. I send my blessing to him and also to yourself, and love to think that one day I may be able to fold him in my arms. Greet him and your wife from me.

Adieu, dear child. The queen sends congratulations, and is writing by the same mail. I fold you to my heart, and

Am your affectionate father,

JEROME.

Jerome, Matilda and Napoleon send their love.

As Madame Bonaparte always said of her husband's family, they were lavish of kind words. While the Baltimore Bonapartes remained quietly at home, and when there was nothing to be gained from their European connexions, these relatives were very affectionate ; but, at the restoration of the empire, when they wished to be restored to their rights and to be recognized as a legitimate branch of the family, their kind words changed into unkind actions, as will presently be seen.

After the birth of this child, Madame Mère also sent her felicitations as follows :—

ROME, 8 Janvier, 1831.

Mon cher Fils,—J'ai appris avec un vif plaisir la naissance de votre premier-né. Je fais des vœux pour qu'il vienne bien et pour qu'il soit pour vous un nouveau sujet de bonheur. Recevez ma bénédiction maternelle, et ne doutez jamais du tendre attachement que je vous porte, ainsi qu'à votre fils. Faites mes affectueux compliments à votre femme. Je vous embrasse avec tout l'affection d'une bonne et tendre mère.

MADAME.

TRANSLATION.

ROME, January 8, 1831.

MY DEAR SON,—I have heard with great pleasure of the birth of your first-born. I offer my best wishes that he may continue well and be to you a subject of great happiness.

Receive my maternal benediction, and never doubt the tenderness I feel for you and also for your son. Give my affectionate regards to your wife. I embrace you with all the affection of a good and tender mother.

MADAME.

We have also a letter written by Louis Bonaparte, who assumed the name of the Count de Saint-Leu, after the fall of Napoleon.

LOUIS BONAPARTE TO JEROME NAPOLEON BONAPARTE.

FLORENCE, 4 Janvier, 1831.

MON CHER NEVEU,—Je m'empresse de vous accuser réception de la lettre du 8 Novembre, que vous avez bien voulu m'écrire, et de *vous féliciter sur l'heureuse délivrance de votre femme*, à laquelle je vous prie de faire mes compliments. Quoique je ne doute pas que vous n'ayez exactement des nouvelles *de votre père et de vous autres parents*, je ne veux pas laisser échapper cette occasion de vous en donner. Votre père est toujours à Rome et se porte bien. *Votre grand'maman* n'est pas rétablie de sa chute, parce que cela est presque impossible à son âge ; mais elle supporte très-bien son état, et, à part sa cuisse cassée, sa santé est bonne. *Votre grand-oncle le cardinal Fesch* est toujours bien faible depuis l'hiver passé qu'il a eu une maladie assez grave dont il a peine à se remettre. *Votre tante Julie* a été très-malade et nous a donné des inquiétudes ; mais depuis quelques semaines elle est mieux, quoiqu'elle ne soit pas encore rétablie. Mon fils aîné et sa sœur se portent bien, grâce à Dieu, mais ils n'ont pas suivi votre exemple : ils sont toujours sans enfants. Mon fils

Q 2

Louis est aussi auprès de moi dans ce moment. Quant à moi, *mon cher neveu*, ma santé est toujours la même à peu près, et comme c'est une goutte froide et nerveuse que l'âge augmente, il est impossible que j'en guérisse, et je me résigne. Je vous prie, la première fois que vous m'écrirez, de me donner des détails sur votre intérieur et de ne pas manquer de me parler aussi de *votre oncle Joseph*. Recevez à cette occasion l'assurance de *l'attachement de votre très-affectionné oncle.*

Signé : LOUIS.

TRANSLATION.

FLORENCE, January 4, 1831.

MY DEAR NEPHEW,—I hasten to inform you of the receipt of the letter of the 8th of November, which you were good enough to write me, and to congratulate you on the happy delivery of your wife, to whom I beg you to present my compliments. Although I have no doubt that you have had news of your father and your other relations, I will not allow this occasion to pass without speaking of them.

Your father is still at Rome and well; your grandmother has not recovered from her fall, because it is almost impossible at her great age [81]; but she supports her condition very well, and, except her broken thigh, her health is very good. Your great-uncle, the Cardinal Fesch, has been very feeble since last winter, when he had a serious illness, from which he has scarcely recovered. Your Aunt Julia has been ill, which made us very anxious, but during the past few weeks she is better, although not yet quite well. My eldest son and his sister are well, thanks be to God; but they have not followed your example : they are still without children. My son Louis is also with me. As to me, my dear nephew, my health is almost always the same, and as I have a nervousness which age increases, it is impossible for me to be cured of it, and I resign myself to it. I beg you, the first time that you write to me, to give me detailed news of your home, and not to fail to tell me also of your Uncle Joseph. Be assured of the attachment of your very affectionate uncle.

LOUIS.

No letters appear from Madame Bonaparte at this time, and we do not know whether she sent congratulations; but as she had previously expressed a wish that her son would have no children, we suppose that she did not.

It was during her long residence at Florence that Madame Bonaparte met the future famous Russian chancellor, Gortschakoff, who was at that time (1830) chargé-d'affaires at the court of Tuscany. They became great friends, and corresponded for many years. He was the only man she would condescend to argue with; she considered him a foeman worthy of her steel; upon other men she would not waste words. He said Madame Bonaparte would make an excellent diplomat—she had so much *finesse.* In Florence, also, Madame Bonaparte constantly met Lamartine in society. He was, at that time, an enthusiastic Bourbonist, and represented Charles X. at the grand ducal court. He was far from being then the "poetical republican" that he became in 1848.

Late in the spring of 1831 Madame Bonaparte left Florence in company with the Russian Princess Galitzin, and they took up their residence during the summer at Geneva. The following letter was written during her stay there :—

MADAME BONAPARTE TO WILLIAM PATTERSON.

GENEVA, 24 September, 1831.

DEAR SIR,—I received two days since your letter of the 15th of August. I agree with you in the opinion that my money ought to be placed in the most permanent funds and those which offer the greatest security for the future. If the five per cents. of the city of Baltimore, and the five per cents. of the State of Maryland offer sufficient guarantees for the safety of capital invested, and regular payment of its interest, I can perceive no objection to Miss Spear purchasing for me in them. My opinion founded on your state-ment of the moneyed concerns of Baltimore, is that my floating capital should be divided into *three* parts : *one* to be invested in five per cents. of the city ; one to be invested in five per cents. of the State ; the other *third* to be equally divided—*one-half* in ground rents, and the other half lent out as at present.

The ground rents will, however, require consideration, as there may be some difficulty respecting the regularity of their payments, although I presume there can be none as to the safety or solidity of capital thus invested. The *half* of one *third* of my present floating capital ought to be loaned for a term of one year, eighteen months, or two or three years ; it being well understood and stipulated that property to its amount is pledged by the borrower to secure lender from loss of capital.

It appears to me that these dispositions of my property might combine safety of investment with certainty of a moderate interest. I do not like paying five per cent. above par on the purchases ; but I prefer submission to this necessity to the most remote chance of greater loss which might occur from the manner in which my funds are at present disposed of. My desire to continue to lend, as at present, one-half of a third of my present floating capital, proceeds from the idea that every one should have at their dispo-sition a sum of money with which they may, when occasion offers, buy a bargain of property.

I suppose that the five per cent. of the city and the five per cent. of the State are based on solid security.

My great object has been and is to risk as little as possible in any way. I believe that a great deal might be made by purchasing in the French funds at their present reduced prices. The king may be changed, or the monarchy take the form of a republic, but the national guard, composed of all who have property to defend, affords in my opinion a sufficient barrier against anarchy. There is no danger of Russia, Austria, and Prussia attempting with success anything against France, because the cholera morbus and revolutionary feelings give them sufficient occupation at home. I do not, however, consider myself rich enough to speculate in any way. My endeavour ought to be to secure in every way my present means, which are much too limited to allow me to risk their diminution ; therefore I will not indulge the inclination I have always felt to gamble in French funds.

Many women in Europe enrich themselves in this way. I have been living with Princess Galitzin ever since May, when I left Florence with her. We travelled in the same carriage at our respective expense, and passed the summer together on the same condition.

She has just given forty thousand dollars for an estate near Geneva, which, under her superintendence, will produce a considerable interest, as she perfectly comprehends the direction of property of every kind.

She is a woman of superior capacity, and, with only ten thousand dollars a year, by her cleverness and rigid economy does what I could not do with twenty. The prince, her husband, has just had a watch made, and will go with me to order one at the same price for Mr. White. The watchmaker requires three months to make such a one, and gives a written agreement to restore the money a year after and take back the watch, if it does not answer the purpose for which it was bought. The prince is a perfect judge of the value of money, and I shall be less likely to be cheated when directed by him than if I were to order a watch alone. My jewels will, I hope, arrive safely. I had given Jerome the key of the box before he left Florence, which I suppose that he has lost, as I find from their letters that they broke open the box, and then incurred an expense of two dollars to cover it with leather. I had desired them to specify in the most minute manner every article in the invoice sent to me, and I find on looking over the invoice that they did not take the trouble to count the pieces of cornelian and gold which I intended for a bracelet. The things sent last year to Leghorn were sent in the most careless manner, without any invoice in the trunks ; in consequence of which, and the keys not having been sealed and sent, they were broken open at the health office, where the officers robbed me of six sheets. I find, upon consulting jewellers, that diamonds and other precious stones have considerably sunk in value in Europe. Diamonds, they say, bring a third less than formerly, and other gems half only.

Commerce of every kind in Europe is depressed by the political convulsions which you have heard of. The cholera morbus is extending, gradually and certainly, to increase the confusion by giving pretexts for rebellion. I should suppose that real property must rise in value in America if revolutions here continue. I intend to pass the winter at Paris, and will leave Geneva very soon, because France will before long establish a sanitary cordon on the frontiers to prevent the introduction of the cholera morbus, which is daily expected at Geneva. I have a presentiment that I shall not die with it, and they say that persons who do not fear it have the best chance of escaping the infection ; but I have arranged all my affairs as if I were certain of dying. I hope and trust that there will be some certain mode found to invest my property in America. At present it appears to me that five per cents. of the State and of the city, for the solidity of which there are of course guarantees, will be the best investment. You can read all this to Miss Spear. My health is perfect at present, and if the cholera does not reach me, I have the prospect of a very long life, therefore feel most anxious that my little fortune may be secured. I have written to my banker at Florence my intentions respecting the will I leave in his hands, when he hears of my death.

I am glad to hear that the Bank of Maryland stock has brought more than its value. My twenty shares cost me originally six thousand seven hundred and sixty dollars. I wish that some other fools could be found to buy Caton's road stock.

It would not meet my ideas of prudence to speculate in the French funds, because I never will in any way risk money. I have always preferred moderate and certain gains, but persons who are rich and fortunate might make money by purchasing at the present moment. A government (there is none there at present except the national guard) must arise out of the confusion, and although no one can tell what the government will be, yet the chances are in favour of the preservation of the national debt.

I would not risk ; but I am a great coward, and not rich enough.

Madame Bonaparte, parsimonious in all other matters, was not so in relation to dress and ornaments. A letter from her to a friend in Baltimore has recently been discovered, in which she describes some of her jewels, and affords a glimpse of her inner life, showing that her eager, active, and unceasing pursuit of worldly pleasure had ended in *ennui* and disappointment. Madame Bonaparte was at the time forty-seven years old, and still one of the most beautiful women in Europe. The letter is dated "Geneva, 30th March, 1832," and after speaking of her future plans—Aix for the summer, and Paris the next winter, she says, "I have had all my emeralds and diamonds, with twenty large pearls and three *white* topazes, added to several rings and my garnet cross, made into a magnificent ornament for my head. My solitaire diamond ring and a solitaire which I took out of a pin (once belonging to Princess Borghese) I have added to my ear-rings. My turquoise ring, my diamond garter ring, my emerald ring, my emerald cross, and two pairs of emerald ear-rings, are all in the head ornament. Princess Galitzin says that it is a royal ornament. It is so contrived as to serve for the head, the neck, and the waist—the three *white* topazes are to be *mis*taken for diamonds.

"Can you, for love or money, contrive to send me a string of *white* topazes? I want to wear it as a necklace, and pretend that they are diamonds. I want, too, as many as will make a buckle for my belt—no one has them in Europe, and they are found in the Brazils. Send for them if you cannot find them in Baltimore, and do contrive to forward them to me by some private conveyance, to *save the duties*. Do not put off this commission, for, even if I have too many for myself, I can give what is left to the princess, who is famous for making shifts, and wearing *false precious* stones, and for contrivances of every sort to make an appearance on economical elegance. Do not shillyshally about these *white* topazes. By the way, if I could procure a large yellow topaz, I should not be sorry.

"I am dying with *ennui*, and do not know in what way a person of my age can be amused. I am tired of reading and of all ways of killing time. I hear that Prince Jerome and his wife are living at Florence, which will prevent me from returning there. There are quantities of Russian women in Geneva, because their emperor does not permit them to go to Paris. Princess Basile Galitzin, however, is going for a few weeks to purchase finery.

"I doze away existence; I am too old to coquet, and without this stimulant I die with *ennui*. The princess tries to keep me up to the toil of dressing by telling me that I am a beauty. I am tired of life, and tired of having lived. Do try to get me a string of white topazes. It is a bore to grow old. I live exclusively with the English and Russians. The Genevans are too odious for any decent person to live with them. Lord Normanby is named Governor of Jamaica. What a fall from his theatre at Florence! but he has no money and great debts. I was very intimate with Lady Normanby the last year of her reign at Florence. She is the very quintessence of fashion—the fine flower of *bon ton*. All is vexation and vanity."

Madame Bonaparte's agreeable society made her very popular with her European friends. As the summer of 1832 approached, she had invitations from three Russian princesses to spend the season with them. Her friend, Princess Galitzin's campagne, near Geneva, was a favourite resort. Here Madame Bonaparte passed two days in every week ; a bedroom was always prepared for her, and a carriage to convey her backwards and forwards.

It was at this period that Madame Bonaparte made the retort to the Hon. Mr. Dundas, which was repeated all over Europe. At a dinner-party given by a "rich idiot, whose *menu* and wines were first-rate," it fell to Mr. Dundas to escort Madame Bonaparte. He was not pleased to have her assigned to him, for he had already in the drawing-room suffered from her sarcasm. At dinner he thought he would get even with his opponent. So, when the soup was over, he asked her, with a malicious smile, whether she had read Captain Basil Hall's book on America. Madame Bonaparte said she had.

"Well, madame," said Mr. Dundas, "did you notice that Captain Hall pronounces all Americans vulgarians?"

"Yes," answered Madame Bonaparte, "and I am not surprised at that. Were the Americans the descendants of the Indians and the Esquimaux, I should be astonished ; but, being the direct descendants of the English, it is very natural that they should be vulgarians."

Mr. Dundas said nothing more to Madame Bonaparte

during the dinner, and took an early opportunity to withdraw from her company. Later, however, they became warm friends.

Among the European celebrities known to Madame Bonaparte was the Countess Guiccioli, Byron's friend. She described her as having nothing of the Italian in her appearance ; on the contrary, she was a decided blonde, with a shower of golden hair falling over a fair, lovely face ; her eyes were blue, her hands delicate, and her teeth white and beautiful.

Madame Bonaparte spent the winter of 1832-3 in Paris. She was prevented from returning to Florence because her husband had selected that city for a residence, and she never wished to see him again. She announces to her father her intention to return to America and go to housekeeping in Baltimore. Her allusion to the Duchess d'Abrantes is interesting, and her refusal to tell that *parvenue* gossip anything discreditable about her unworthy husband gives us a new glimpse of her character.

MADAME BONAPARTE TO WILLIAM PATTERSON.

PARIS, 10 October, 1833.

DEAR SIR,—It was my intention to have left Europe last spring, but I was prevented by several circumstances. I have engaged my apartments here until next June, when I shall go to Havre to embark. I am sorry to learn that my house over the bridge cannot be rented. I hope that Jerome aids Miss Spear in the accounts. I hope that no risks are run in investing. I was obliged to leave Florence on account of my health, which is now perfectly restored.

The Princess Galitzin brought me to Geneva, where I lived with her some time. I could not return to Florence because Prince Jerome went there to live, having no desire ever to meet him.

I should like, on my return, to assist Miss Spear in purchasing a small house. Her proposals to me for ten years have been that *she* should pay one half and that I should pay one-half, and that the property after her death should go to me or to my heirs. When I am in Baltimore I will see what could be done ; but of course during my absence nothing respecting purchases of real property would be thought about either by her or me.

General Reubell's daughter is married to an American. They live very handsomely at Paris. General Devereux is ruined. He is gone to Florence. The Livingstons are here. I cannot write more on account of a sore finger.

The Duchess d'Abrantes has published twelve volumes of memoirs, where she relates everything relating to the Bonaparte family. She has mentioned me in the highest terms, and has overrated my beauty and conduct. Since the publication she has made my acquaintance. I have refused to give her any anecdotes, either of Prince Jerome or of myself. She has already said enough of ill of him, and more good of my beauty and talents than they deserve.

Dear sir, truly yours,

E. PATTERSON.

Please not to show this letter to any one except to my son, nor to speak of the contents unless Miss Spear mentions anything to you about her proposals on the subject of my paying half, on the conditions above mentioned. I cannot enter into arrangements of this description until my return. I will not delay my departure after June, and I may, perhaps, sail in May. The French funds have fallen in the last two days. There is apprehension of war in Spain.

To the above letter Mr. Patterson sent the following answer :—

WILLIAM PATTERSON TO MADAME BONAPARTE.

BALTIMORE, 10 March, 1834.

DEAR BETSY,—I some time since received under cover from Mr. L. Harris your letter of 10th October, which is the only one that has come to hand from you for several years. How could you have neglected the duty of writing for so long a time. But still it affords me pleasure to have heard from you at length, and to find that you have concluded to return to your native country. Time brings about what we little have expected, and sweet home and the natural intercourse and connexion with our family is, after all, the only chance for happiness in this world. We are in great confusion and distress in this country, on account of President Jackson's arbitrary conduct in respect to the Bank of the United States. There is no saying how it may end, or that it may not ultimately bring about a revolution. Your presence here is absolutely necessary to look after your affairs and property, and the sooner the better. We will all endeavour to make your situation as comfortable as we can.

I am, dear Betsy, yours very sincerely,

W. P.

CHAPTER XVI.

Madame Bonaparte's Return to America.—Foreign Finery.—Her Mature
Beauty.—Death of William Patterson.—His Singular Will.—His
Costume and Literary Taste.—Madame Bonaparte revisits Europe.—
Letter to Lady Morgan.—Solitary Life in Paris.—Death of Cardinal
Fesch, also of the Princess Charlotte and the Duchess d'Abrantes.—
Count Demidoff and the Princess Mathilde.—Madame Bonaparte at the
Springs.—Her Brilliant Conversation.—1834-48.

EARLY in the summer of 1834 Madame Bonaparte
returned to America and took up her residence in Baltimore. Nine years had passed since her departure.

Her dislike of everything American extended even to
the fashions, and before leaving Europe she laid in a
supply of finery sufficient to last for many years, some of
which she continued to wear up to the time of her death.
Among other things, she brought with her twelve bon-
nets, which she said "were to last her as long as she
lived." The famous black velvet bonnet with orange-
coloured feather, which is identified with her latter years,
was not, however, one of these twelve.

Another article, which she always carried with her in
the street for upwards of forty years, was a *red* umbrella ;
either open or shut, she was never without it.

The beauty of Madame Bonaparte cannot be exaggerated ; it was not of that perishable kind peculiar to
America, which scarcely survives the teens. She was

now in the fiftieth year of her age, and still so beautiful that one who had received nothing but unkindness from her, and who saw her now for the first time, declared her to be the most lovely creature she had ever beheld. Hers was not the ordinary type of American beauty. She possessed the pure Grecian contour, her head was exquisitely formed, her forehead fair and shapely, her eyes large and dark, with an expression of tenderness which did not belong to her character; and the delicate loveliness of her mouth and chin, the soft bloom of her complexion, together with the beautifully rounded shoulders and tapering arms, combined to form one of the loveliest of women.

She had never had many friends in her native city, and she found most of them either dead, removed, or estranged when she returned. Occasionally she might be seen at the opera or at an evening party, when her beauty and wit always made her the most conspicuous object. Her toilet on such occasions was a black velvet dress with low neck and short sleeves, a superb necklace of diamonds, besides other costly ornaments.

In the winter of 1835 Mr. Patterson died, leaving the longest and most remarkable will that has ever been filed in the Orphans' Court of Baltimore City. Although his fortune was very large, he left his daughter only a few small houses, and the following bitter words :—

"The conduct of my daughter Betsey has through life been so disobedient that in no instance has she ever consulted my opinions or feelings; indeed, she has caused me more anxiety and trouble than all my other children put together, and her folly and mis-

conduct have occasioned me a train of expense that first and last
has cost me much money. Under such circumstances it would not
be reasonable, just, or proper that she should inherit and participate
in an equal proportion with my other children in an equal division
of my estate ; considering, however, the weakness of human nature,
and that she is still my daughter, it is my will and pleasure to provide for her as follows, viz. :—I give and devise to my said daughter
Betsey, first, the house and lot on the east side of South Street,
where she was born, and which is now occupied by Mr. Duncan, the
shoemaker. Secondly, the houses and lots on the corner of Market
Street bridge, now occupied by Mr. Tulley, the chairmaker, and
Mr. Priestly, the cabinet-maker. Thirdly, the three new adjoining
brick houses and the one on the corner of Market and Frederick
Streets. Fourthly, two new brick houses and lots on Gay Street,
near Griffith's bridge ; for and during the term of the natural life
of my said daughter Betsey ; and after her death I give, devise and
bequeath the same to my grandson, Jerome Napoleon Bonaparte."

This discrimination against her in her father's will was
another disappointment added to those already experienced by his daughter. Although the actual injustice
done her did not prove to be great, owing to the ultimate
value of the property she received, and although the will
also contained considerable bequests to her son, she felt
the matter keenly.

Mr. Patterson was the last gentleman in Baltimore
who wore small-clothes and a cue. His portraits represent a man of firm, determined character, with high,
patrician features, which would seem to confirm Madame
Bonaparte's assertion that her father came of an ancient,
but reduced family. He believed and practised the
maxim that " money and merit are the only sure and
certain roads to respectability and consequence." He

R

early learned to love books, and declared that, had
he possessed a fortune of two thousand dollars a year
when a young man, he would have devoted himself to
philosophical pursuits.

In the summer of 1839 Madame Bonaparte again
visited Europe and took up her residence in Paris. She
was accompanied by her son, who visited Italy to look
after a legacy of fifty thousand francs which his great-
uncle, Cardinal Fesch, had recently left him.

In a letter written to Lady Morgan during this visit
we find some reflections on her experiences at home.

MADAME BONAPARTE TO LADY MORGAN.

PARIS, RUE D'ALGERS, No. 4, September 22, 1839.

DEAR LADY MORGAN,—You will be less surprised to know of my
arrival in Europe than I am to find myself here. I never supposed
that I had preserved sufficient energy or moral courage to put into
effect my inclination to absent myself from the *République par
excellence*. A residence for a few months in the États Unis would
cure the most ferocious republican of the mania of republics.

We have security neither for our lives nor our persons in America.
I have been two months in France, a period of time which has
passed very dully. I have found few of those persons whom
I knew and saw habitually five years ago. Death, time, and
absence have left me scarcely an acquaintance at Paris. If our
friends do not die, their sentiments change towards us so much
that really I know not which is most distressing, to hear that they
are gone to the other world, or that they have forgotten us in this
vale of tears and have become strangers to us.

I have met few persons who possess the stability of friendship
that I find in yourself. You are, in this particular as in most

others, *une personne distinguée*. My son is gone from Geneva to
Italy, to visit his relatives and to see after a legacy which the late
Cardinal Fesch, his grand-uncle, had the goodness to leave to him.
He wanted me to go to Geneva to see him, but I could not attain
the courage to extend my long journey farther than Paris. Here
I am in solitary existence. In one of his letters he remarked
that it had been your intention to write to me; if you have had
that goodness, your letter must have reached Baltimore after my
departure. I regret this circumstance very much. I have seen
Mr. Warder; his regard for me has held out against time and
circumstances; he is unchanged in kind feeling; but, poor man,
time has dealt hard with his exterior—he looks as if he had begun
to exist a century ago.

Madame Benjamin de Constant is an agreeable person; has had
the goodness to recollect me. I dined yesterday at her house *en
petit comité*. I have myself grown fat, old, and dull—all good
reasons for people not to think me an intelligent hearer or listener.
They mistake, however; I have exactly the talent to appreciate the
high powers of all others, without being able to contribute much
to the liveliness of conversation myself.

Have you no agreeable work to promise us?

The poor Duchess d'Abrantes, Madame Junot, made a sad end
—the natural consequence of her prodigal expenditure. Her pecuniary difficulties, it is said, caused her death. I liked her very much,
and I always felt pained at the misery which her want of judgment
in the direction of her affairs had brought on her. I believe that
her heart and feelings were warm and generous.

I wonder that you did not select Paris in preference to London
for a permanent *séjour*. I should much prefer living at Florence,
but there lives there one individual whom I wish not to meet again.
Whether persons have been the voluntary or the unreflecting
cause of having spoiled a destiny, I would sooner avoid their
presence. I know not whether the Princess Charlotte, the late
daughter of Joseph Bonaparte, was fortunate enough to be personally of your acquaintance.

I did not myself know her, but I have heard from those who did,
that she possessed some mental superiority and a great many noble
qualities.

I hope that Sir Charles Morgan still recollects me and preserves for myself the friendship he formerly entertained for me.

Adieu, my dear Lady Morgan.

Believe me ever your sincere and affectionate friend,

E. PATTERSON.

This visit to Europe was, on the whole, uneventful, and in July, 1840, Madame Bonaparte returned once more to America. We have a letter from her soon after she arrived in New York, which shows how carefully she had watched her business affairs during her absence. The letter is written to her agent at Baltimore ; it is as precise and clear in its language as a legal document. We give it as a specimen of her business correspondence.

NEW YORK, July 13, 1840.

SIR,—I have received your letter of the 9th of this month. I remark therein two payments of $33.34 made by F——. There existed an individual of a similar name, a vendor of artificial flowers, inhabiting part of the house occupied by P——. I refused the said F—— for my tenant, having understood that payments due to his landlord could not be expected of him. Mr. P., a punctual and highly responsible person, hired the house near Frederick Street from me in *his own* name ; therefore I had no possible objection to his placing trust in Mr. F——. I did not receive, sir, your letter for the month of May last, having left Paris, bound for New York in the same month. Therefore I am ignorant whether Mr. R—— has vacated one of the granite-front houses, and whether Mr. F—— has succeeded him in the occupancy of said house. I hope that J. P. has not substituted him for such a good tenant as I have ever found the former to be. Please have the goodness to inform me of all these circumstances, and at the same time state to me the dates of the days on which, subsequent to my departure from Baltimore, the new tenants had entered my houses. I cannot at the moment designate with any certainty the

period when I may arrive at Baltimore. I have at New York some
business which it is important that I should terminate previously
to my departure. You will perceive that the statement made by
me and left with yourself, respecting the amount of money due from
Mrs. W—— for rent, was entirely accurate ; therefore she is expected to pay in conformity with that.

Your obliged,
E. PATTERSON.

When a marriage was arranged between Count Anatole
Demidoff and Princess Mathilde, the half-sister of Mr.
Bonaparte of Baltimore, Jerome communicated the fact
to the latter ; at the same time the Princess Mathilde
wrote him a most affectionate letter, saying that the new
duties she was about to assume would not lessen her
affection for her brother. The Count Demidoff was a
man of cultivated taste, and spent liberally out of his
princely income, encouraging scientific and literary enter-
prises. They were married at Florence in 1840, and in
a letter written on November 27th, the same year, the
young bride assured her half-brother that her new state
realized all her fondest anticipations. Yet in less than five
years after this the pair were separated. The Emperor
Nicholas compelled Count Demidoff to allow his wife a
pension of two hundred thousand francs a year. The
Princess Mathilde has considerable literary and artistic
talents, and has always been devoted to the society of
literary men. Sainte-Beuve and Théophile Gautier were
among her friends.

After her return to America in 1840, Madame Bonaparte was in the habit of spending her summers at Rock-
away Beach, and sometimes, but rarely, the Virginia

Springs.   Although she did not participate in the gaiety
of the ball-room, she always gathered a crowd around
her by her sharp wit and clever satire.   It is universally
admitted that her conversational powers were of the
highest order, that her great fluency of language and her
large fund of anecdotes made her a most entertaining
companion.   Persons who knew little of her personally,
visited her merely to hear her talk.   She delighted to
speak of her early life, her romantic marriage, her European experience—of her distinguished friends, Gortschakoff, Demidoff, the Duke of Tuscany, Princess Galitzin,
Lady Morgan, the Countess of Donegal, the Earl of
Normanby, and the rest.

During these visits to the Springs she was never
known to enter the pool, thinking that where so many
persons bathed together the water might have become
unhealthful.

CHAPTER XVII.

THE French Revolution of 1848 found Madame Bonaparte buried in that Baltimore obscurity which she so
much deplored ; but the election of Louis Napoleon to
the Presidency of the French Republic seemed again to
open the way to a distinguished European career to her
and her family.

Mr. Jerome Bonaparte had maintained very cordial
relations with Prince Louis Napoleon ever since their first
meeting at Rome, in 1826 ; and when Louis Napoleon
visited the United States in 1837, Mr. Bonaparte invited
him to take up his residence at his country-seat, near
Baltimore.

To this invitation the prince replied that in a month he would commence his travels in the interior, and the first thing he should do would be to visit his cousin. He recalled with pleasure the time they had passed together at Rome and at Forence.

In the spring of 1849, Madame Bonaparte wrote to Lady Morgan that she intended to visit Europe during the next July. Although she was now in her sixty-fifth year, she seemed to anticipate with pleasure what she called an emancipation from her dull native country and her long vegetation. She says that, although the emperor drove her back to what she most hated, a residence in Baltimore, she had ever been an imperial Bonapartist, and she was enchanted that six millions of voices had elected an imperial president. She shows not a little political foresight in anticipating the *coup d'état* of 1851.

MADAME BONAPARTE TO LADY MORGAN.

BALTIMORE, March 14, 1849.

MY DEAR LADY MORGAN,—I was most agreeably surprised by your letter of the 17th of February. I had heard and believed that you were living in Dublin. You may be quite convinced that I consider it a *bonne fortune pour moi* that you inhabi London. To enjoy again your agreeable society will be my tardy compensation for the long, weary, unintellectual years inflicted on me in this my dull native country, to which I have never owed advantages, pleasures, or happiness. I owe nothing to my country ; no one expects me to be grateful for the evil chance of having been born here. I shall emancipate myself, *par la grace de Dieu*, about the middle of July next ; and I will either write to you before I leave New York, or immediately after my arrival at Liverpool.

I had given up all correspondence with my friends in Europe during my vegetation in this Baltimore. What could I write about except the fluctuations in the security and consequent prices of American stocks. There is nothing here worth attention or interest save the money market. Society, conversation, friendship, belong to older countries, and are not yet cultivated in any part of the United States which I have visited. You ought to thank your stars for your European birth; you may believe me when I assure you that it is only distance from republics which lends enchantment to the view of them. I hope that about the middle of next July I shall begin to put the Atlantic between the advantages and honours of democracy and myself. France, *je l'espère dans son intérêt* is in a state of transition, and will not let her brilliant society be put under an extinguisher *nommée la République.*

The emperor hurled me back on what I most hated on earth—my Baltimore obscurity; even that shock could not divest me of the admiration I felt for his genius and glory. I have ever been an imperial Bonapartiste *quand même*, and I do feel enchanted at the homage paid by six millions of voices to his memory, in voting an imperial president; *le prestige du nom* has, therefore, elected the prince, who has my best wishes, my most ardent hopes for an empire. I never could endure universal suffrage until it elected the nephew of an emperor for the chief of a republic; and I shall be charmed with universal suffrage *once* more if it insists upon their president of France becoming a monarch. I am disinterested personally. It is not my desire ever to return to France.

My dear Lady Morgan, do you know that, having been cheated out of the fortune which I ought to have inherited from my late rich and unjust parent, I have only ten thousand dollars, or two thousand pounds English, which conveniently I can disburse annually. You talk of my "*princely* income," which convinces me that you are ignorant of the paucity of my means. I have all my life had poverty to contend with, pecuniary difficulties to torture and mortify me; and but for my industry and energy, and my determination to conquer at least a decent sufficiency to live on in Europe, I might have remained as poor as you saw me in the year 1816.

I shall have much to tell you. Lamartine and Chateaubriand

are giving their memoirs to the public. The first *de son vivant*.
I am now reading *Les Mémoires d'outre-tombe*. I have no doubt
that your memoirs would be infinitely better, more piquant and
more natural. When I knew Lamartine he was chargé-d'affaires
from Charles X. Florence was then a charming place ; I met
him every night at parties. How little did I foresee that he was
to become a poetical republican, and that dear Florence was to be
travestie en république ! ni l'un ni l'autre ne gagnera par le troc.
Hoping that England may remain steady and faithful to monarchical
principles, that at least some refined society may be left in the
world, I shall, *Dieu permettant*, have the satisfaction of seeing you
in the course of next summer.

I am, as ever,

My dear Lady Morgan,

Your affectionate and obliged friend,

E. PATTERSON.

Upon the re-establishment of the empire under Napoleon III., Mr. Bonaparte of Baltimore addressed a letter
to his cousin, congratulating him upon his accession to
the imperial throne of France. He had hoped, he said,
to express these sentiments in person, but had been
compelled to postpone his promised visit to Europe.

The emperor answered him as follows :—

NAPOLEON III. TO JEROME NAPOLEON BONAPARTE.

MON COUSIN.—Malgré votre éloignement et une bien longue
séparation, je n'ai jamais douté de l'intérêt de cœur avec lequel
vous suiviez toutes les chances de ma destinée. Aussi ai-je reçu
avec un grand plaisir la lettre qui m'apporte vos félicitations et
vos vœux. Je vous en remercie. Les nouvelles que vous me
donnez de la vocation de votre fils pour la carrière militaire et de
son entrée dans un régiment de carabiniers ne m'ont pas été moins
agréables.

Quand les circonstances le permettront, je serai, croyez-le bien, fort heureux de vous revoir. Sur ce, mon cousin, je prie Dieu qu'il vous ait en sa sainte garde.

Écrit au palais des Tuileries, le 9 février, 1853.

Signé : NAPOLÉON.

TRANSLATION.

MY COUSIN,—Notwithstanding distance and a very long separation, I have never doubted the affectionate interest with which you have followed all the chances of my destiny. Therefore, I have received with great pleasure the letter which conveys to me your congratulations and good wishes. I thank you for it. The news which you give me of your son's vocation for a military career, and of his admission into a regiment of mounted rifles, has not been less agreeable.

When circumstances permit, believe me, I shall be very happy to see you again. I pray God that He will have you in His holy keeping.

Written at the palace of the Tuileries, 9th February, 1853.

NAPOLEON.

Mr. Bonaparte visited Paris in June, 1854, and immediately upon his arrival was invited to dine at St. Cloud by the emperor. When he entered the palace, Mr. Bonaparte received from the hands of the emperor a paper containing the deliberate opinion of the Minister of Justice, President of the Senate, and the President of the Council of State, upon the subject of the marriage of Prince Jerome with Miss Elizabeth Patterson, to the effect that Jerome Bonaparte ought to be considered a legitimate child of France—that he was French by birth, and if he has lost that title, a decree could restore it to him, under the terms of Article 18 of the Civil Code.

Mr. Bonaparte expressed the most profound gratitude to the emperor, and asked to be restored to the position of a French citizen. In a few days he received the following letter :—

NAPOLEON III. TO JEROME NAPOLEON BONAPARTE.

25 Juillet, 1854.

MON CHER COUSIN,—J'ai reçu vos deux lettres, j'en avais déjà reçu une de mon oncle Jérôme, qui me disait qu'il ne consentirait jamais à ce que vous restiez en France, &c. *Je lui ai répondu que, les lois françaises vous reconnaissant comme fils légitime,* je ne pouvais faire autrement que de vous reconnaître comme parent, et que si votre position à Paris était embarrassante, c'était à vous seul à en juger ; *que Napoléon, s'il se conduisait bien, n'avait rien à craindre des rivalités de famille, &c.* Il faut, sans irriter votre père, continuer de suivre la marche que vous vous êtes proposée. J'écrirai demain à Fould pour les arrangements dont nous sommes convenus.

Bien des choses à Jérôme, et croyez à ma sincère amitié.

Signé : NAPOLÉON.

TRANSLATION.

July 25th, 1854.

MY DEAR COUSIN,—I have received your two letters, and I had already received one from my uncle Jerome, who informs me that he will never consent to your living in France.

I have answered him that, if the laws of France recognize you as a legitimate son, I cannot do otherwise than recognize you as a kinsman, and that if your residence in Paris was embarrassing, you alone were to be the judge of that; that Napoleon, if he behaved himself well, had nothing to fear from family rivalries, &c. You must, without irritating your father, continue to pursue the

way that you intended.   I will write to-morrow to Fould as to the
plan we have agreed upon.

　With kind regards to Jerome,

Believe me,

Yours sincerely,

NAPOLEON.

On the 30th of August, 1854, a decree was inserted in
the "Bulletin des lois," declaring that *M. Jérome Bonaparte est réintégré dans la qualité de Français.*

On the 17th of August, 1855, the emperor signified
to Mr. Bonaparte his intention of creating him Duke of
Sartène ; but, as the object of this was to induce Mr.
Bonaparte to give up the name of his family and his
rights as the eldest son of his father, he declined the
proffered title.

In 1856 the King of Würtemberg arrived at Paris,
and Prince Napoleon, the son of Jerome and the Princess
of Würtemberg, made this a pretext for a more direct
attack against the legitimate rights of his half-brother,
and appealed to an imperial family council to forbid
Jerome Patterson from assuming the name of Bonaparte
"which does not legally belong to him."   On the 4th
of July, 1856, after the family council had heard M.
Allon, who appeared as the advocate of the prince, and
M. Berryer, who represented the Baltimore Bonapartes,
it was decided that the descendants of Madame Elizabeth Patterson were entitled to the name of Bonaparte,
but without the advantages conferred by the 201st and
202nd Articles of the Code of Napoleon.   Napoleon III.
sanctioned the judgment of the council ; but added with

his own hand, "His Majesty the Emperor by his conduct towards the descendants of Madame Patterson, since the judgment was determined, has thought it right to prove that he did not consider them as belonging to his *famille civile*."

Mr. Bonaparte felt the great injustice done to him by this decision, and wrote to the emperor: "As I was born legitimate, as I have always been recognized as such by my family, by the laws of every country and by the entire world, it would be the height of cowardice and dishonour to accept a brevet of bastardy. I have not raised the question—I no longer have any fear of it; and if the family council has rendered an illegal and unjust decision, at least it has been stopped by the impossibility of depriving a man of the name which he has borne from his birth to the age of fifty years without its ever being contested.

"Being the victim of calumnies, intrigues, and lies, it only remains for me, sire, to repeat the desire which I have made known to your majesty in my letter of the 20th of March—*to go with my son into exile, and await the justice which I am convinced heaven will render to me sooner or later.*"

Prince Jerome died on the 24th of June, 1860. He left an autograph will dated the 6th of July, 1852, by which he appointed his son the Prince Napoleon, born of his second marriage, sole legatee of all the disposable share in his succession; he confirms at the same time the marriage portion of his daughter the Princess Mathilde; but he says not a word of his first marriage

—not a word of the engagements assumed by an
authentic contract with his first wife. The prince, at
the moment he thought he was about to die, forgot that
he left in the world a first-born son—a son the heir of
his name—a son to whom he had constantly expressed
the most profound paternal affection—a son to whom
the law assigned inviolable rights in the inheritance of
his father.

After the death of the ex-King of Westphalia, Madame
Bonaparte made a direct appeal through her son, to the
French court, for a share in his estate. The eloquent
Berryer again represented the Baltimore Bonapartes,
and their cause could not have been in better hands ;
all that profound learning, persuasive rhetoric, and
gifted speech could do, was done. He told the story
of the romantic marriage of the beautiful Baltimore
girl to the brother of Napoleon : Miss Patterson was
young ; she was in the enjoyment of every advantage,
when, under the guidance of her father and in the ful-
filment of every legal requirement of her country, she
bound her life to that of the brother of the First Consul.
A little time passed and Miss Patterson found herself
abandoned and repudiated. The hand which her husband had solemnly pledged to her was to be given to
another. That husband was now dead. For fifty-five
years she had been sustained by her brave maternal
love and the noble pride of a life without a stain.
" She comes," said Berryer, " from her distant home
beyond the Atlantic ; she appears before this august
court asking for the declaration of her rights, and

demands the vindication of her honour and the establishment of her child in the position due to his birth." The orator then tells who the Pattersons were ; under what influences his client had been brought up ; how the "great Jefferson" had spoken of her father's house as one of the most honourable and opulent in America. But, notwithstanding the eloquence of her advocate— notwithstanding the justice of her cause, Madame Bonaparte lost her case ; but she won the sympathy of Europe.

The admission of the rights of the Baltimore Bonapartes to membership of the imperial family would have complicated the rights of succession ; hence, while they were admitted to be legitimate, they were denied all claims to imperial rank.

CHAPTER XVIII.

Madame's Bonaparte's last days in Baltimore.—European Reminiscences.
—Her Fortune and how it was accumulated.—Her Business Habits.—
Her Parsimony.—Generosity to Relatives.—Her Regular Life.—Her
Beauty and Vanity.—Anecdotes at the Springs.—Her Religious Views.
—Her Carpet-bag.—Her Trunks of Ancient Finery.—Her Interest in
European Politics.—Marshal Bertrand.—Napoleon regrets the Shadow
he casts upon Madame Bonaparte.—Her last Illness and Death.—Her
Funeral.—Her Will.—1861—1879.

AFTER this last attempt to obtain justice from the
French courts, Madame Bonaparte returned again to her
Baltimore obscurity.

The last eighteen years of her life were spent in retirement. She lived in a quiet boarding-house. Her time
was employed in recalling the brilliant events of her
European career, and in obtaining safe investments for
the savings of her large income. Her fortune amounted
to one million five hundred thousand dollars, which
yield.d her an income of nearly one hundred thousand
dollars per annum, out of which she spent something
like two thousand a year.

The greater part of her money she accumulated during
the last thirty years of her life by saving; for, as we
have seen from her letter to Lady Morgan, written in
1849, she possessed at that time only an income of ten
thousand dollars a year. In her old age she often said,

S

"Once I had everything but money; now I have nothing but money."

Even when she had reached the advanced age of ninety, Madame Bonaparte was in the habit of visiting the business parts of the city, collecting her dividends, making close bargains with brokers, and managing all her affairs with great shrewdness. She invested her money in various ways, because as she said, " It was not wise to put all your eggs in one basket."

Parsimonious to all others, she was very liberal to her grandsons. During the time that her grandson Jerome was in the French army, she gave him very large sums, saying " she wished him to appear in a manner befitting his birth, as the grandson of a king." On the 17th of June, 1870, her son died, leaving his country-seat to his two sons jointly. She bought out Jerome's share and presented it to his younger brother. In the last few years of her life she was accustomed to give at Christmas a present of one hundred dollars each to two or three favourite relatives.

She was very regular in her habits of life, retiring at ten and rising promptly at six, during her residence in Baltimore. Of course, while living in Europe, attending nightly balls and parties, she was compelled to keep late hours, but she never lost sleep at night without making it up during the day.

Contemporary testimony to her beauty is unanimous. As some one said of her, " She charms by her eyes and slays with her tongue." But if her witticisms inspired fear, her gay manner and childlike laughter took away their sting. She was very vain of her personal charms, and once asked a lady, who had recently returned from Europe, if "she had not heard of her beauty on the continent?" She was in the habit of standing before her portrait, and viewing with complacency the wondrous beauty which had led captive the heart of Jerome Bonaparte.

Madame Bonaparte was morbidly sensitive about her age. One summer, at the White Sulphur Springs, she enjoyed the society of a Baltimore gentleman very much, complimenting his manners, conversation, &c., until one day he committed the fatal mistake of asking Madame's age. She never spoke to him again. Another summer, at the York Springs, Pennsylvania, she was annoyed by the familiarity of a Mrs. ——, of Baltimore. One day, while seated at dinner, next to Madame Bonaparte, she remarked: "Madame, I am very glad to meet you. I hear you were once very beautiful. How old are you now?" To which Madame Bonaparte curtly replied, "Nine hundred and ninety years, ninety-nine days, and nine minutes."

Notwithstanding the quiet life she led in Baltimore, Madame Bonaparte continued to enjoy the visits of her friends up to the very last. She conversed freely, often with vivacity, and frequently with bitterness. She had very little confidence in men, but did not withhold her admiration from her own sex, if she met one who came up to her standard, which was very seldom.

In a conversation on the subject of religion with the late Mrs. John Eager Howard, of Baltimore, Madame

Bonaparte said if she adopted any religion it would be the Catholic, because at least "that was a religion of kings—a royal religion." Her niece, who was present, exclaimed, "Oh! aunt, how can you say such a thing? you would not give up Presbyterianism?" To which Madame Bonaparte responded, "The only reason I would not is, that I should not like to give up the stool my ancestors had sat upon."

A carpet-bag containing valuables was Madame Bonaparte's constant companion. If she was called to the parlour to see a visitor, she took it with her and hung it on the back of her chair. In every expedition this carpet-bag was taken, and, on more occasions than one, young gentlemen who wished to show some attention to Madame have been annoyed and embarrassed by being obliged to carry this thoroughly old-fashioned companion. In one of her earlier trips to Europe she carried in her own hands a small trunk containing her jewels. During the journey to Philadelphia she was introduced to a young gentleman of Baltimore, and, upon arriving at the above city, she handed him the trunk, saying, "Young man, take this; it contains my jewels," and taking his arm, she said, "I will hold on to you," which she did until safely settled in a carriage with her treasures. Her room was piled with trunks, and up to the time of her last illness she was in the habit of looking over her ancient finery. Each article had its history; this was her husband's wedding coat; this dress was given her by the Princess Borghese; this one had been worn at the court of Tuscany; this one she wore at the Pitti Palace on the day she met her husband; this she wore when presented to Madame Mère, &c.

To the last she manifested the liveliest interest in European politics, but never cared anything for American affairs. She considered it a misfortune to have been born beneath the "stars and stripes," but said that the fact of being born there did not reconcile her to living there. When negroes were admitted to Congress, she caustically remarked that "baboons were in the senate, and monkeys in the house, which was carrying republican principles out to their legitimate ends."

When Marshal Bertrand visited the United States thirty-five years ago, he requested an interview with Madame Bonaparte. He assured her that the emperor at St. Helena had often spoken with admiration of her talents, and regretted the shadow he had cast upon her life. He had been told of the high opinion she had of his genius, and one day he said to Bertrand, "Those whom I have wronged have forgiven me; those I loaded with kindness have forsaken me."

During the last two years of Madame Bonaparte's life her digestive powers failed, and she lived almost exclusively upon brandy and milk. She went down stairs for the last time on Christmas Day, 1878, but was taken ill five days afterwards. Her physician knew this would be her last illness, for she did not manifest any desire to leave her bed, as she had always done in previous indispositions. She said that she had a disease which medicine could not cure—old age; and on some one's remarking in her presence that nothing was so certain as death, she laconically replied, " Except taxes."

Her remarkable vitality continued to the last ; for sixty hours she was dying, or as her physician said, " For two days and a half her life was entirely automatic." Her perfectly unemotional nature was one of the causes of her prolonged existence.   She was free from all those corroding passions which consume human life.   Her beauty in one form or other never forsook her.   The fulness of figure which generally disappears with advancing age she still retained, and the palms of her hands were as rosy as an infant's.   Her forehead was still fair, and her dark eyes never lost their brightness until quenched by death.   She died about mid-day on the 4th of April, 1879, having completed her ninety-fourth year in the February previous.   Her funeral took place from the residence of her daughter-in-law, and was attended only by her immediate family and a few friends. She was buried at Greenmount Cemetery, where seven years before she had purchased the small lot for herself. As she had been solitary in life, she wished to be alone in death.

Madame Bonaparte belongs to history as well as to romance : she had known princes and philosophers queens and poets, men of science and men of letters. There was about her the brilliancy of courts and palaces, the enchantment of a love-story, the suffering of a victim of despotic power.   Her husband was a king, but she, wore no crown ; her brother-in-law was an emperor, but she was excluded from all the honours of royalty. Yet her name will always be found in history. The story of the most remarkable man of modern times cannot be written without mentioning her ill-starred marriage. By the laws of justice and of the Church she was a queen, although she was never allowed to reign. Born while the Bourbons were on the throne of France, her childhood witnessed its institutions swept away by a deluge of blood. As she grew to womanhood she saw the star of Napoleon begin to rise ; she saw also its decline ; the restoration of the Bourbons and their second exile ; the elevation of Louis Philippe ; the French revolution of 1848 ; the return of the Bonapartes to power in the person of Louis Napoleon as President of the French Republic ; the establishment of the Second Empire and its end. She died while France was trying the experiment of a Third Republic, and declared in her last hours that the people of Europe were tired of kings and empires ; that before the dawn of the twentieth century the celebrated prophecy of Napoleon would be fulfilled—that Europe would become Republican.

The will of Madame Bonaparte was opened two days after her funeral. True to her often expressed intentions, it left her property to her family, dividing it between her grandsons, Mr. Jerome Napoleon Bonaparte and Mr. Charles Joseph Bonaparte, in nearly equal portions. To Mr. Charles Joseph Bonaparte it left the " portraits of King Jerome, his grandfather, and that of myself—the three heads on one piece of canvas painted by Stuart ; a cabinet portrait of myself painted at Geneva, by Massot, and also the portrait made of me by Kinson." Also . . . . " all histories of my life written by myself, my diaries, dialogues of the dead, letters received by me from various correspondents, and all manuscripts whatever belonging to me."

GILBERT AND RIVINGTON, PRINTERS, ST. JOHN'S SQUARE, LONDON.